HIGHLANDER'S PROTECTOR

Called by a Highlander Book Eight

MARIAH STONE

Stone
Publishing

Cover design by Qamber Designs and Media

Editing by Laura Barth and Beth Atwood

Proofreading by Laura La Tulipa

GET A FREE MARIAH STONE
BOOK!

Join Mariah's mailing list to be the first to know of new releases, free books, special prices, and other author giveaways.

freehistoricalromancebooks.com

ALSO BY MARIAH STONE

MARIAH'S TIME TRAVEL ROMANCE SERIES

- CALLED BY A HIGHLANDER
- CALLED BY A VIKING
- CALLED BY A PIRATE
- FATED

MARIAH'S REGENCY ROMANCE SERIES

- DUKES AND SECRETS

VIEW ALL OF MARIAH'S BOOKS IN READING ORDER

Scan the QR code for the complete list of Mariah's ebooks, paperbacks, and audiobooks in reading order.

"Though she be but little, she is fierce."
    —William Shakespeare

PROLOGUE

Islay, September 1306

THE WAVE ROSE OVER ANNA MACDONALD LIKE A SEA MONSTER
and lunged at her. She took the largest gulp of air of her twelve
years, inhaling till her lungs hurt. Then a force hit her like a wall,
and the gray-green Irish Sea sealed over her like a tomb.

Her lungs bursting, she worked her arms up and kicked her
legs, fighting the sea god that kept dragging her forward and
down with no mercy. Cold and unforgiving, uncaring and unkind,
just like the father she'd never met. Wet darkness blocking her
ears, she kept stubbornly swimming up, fighting the power of
the current.

But everything churned around her, pushing her to the
bottom.

To her death.

The sea did not care if she survived this, if she was a good
swimmer.

Nor did people on the gravel beach by Lagavulin Bay, a
quarter of a mile away. Aunt Leitis didn't cry for her to stop and
come back to the shore, nor did her cousin Laoghaire. No one

chastised her and told her to behave like the future lady of a noble house.

Because no one cared.

Why would they? The unacknowledged, unwanted, ignored daughter of one of the most important Scottish nobles, Robert the Bruce, she had been born out of wedlock by Julianna MacDonald, the sister of the laird, who had died shortly after her birth.

Anna thrust her arms up and out, up and out, propelling herself towards the dancing flashes of the cerulean sky glinting through the water.

So close but so far away.

The pressure in her ears left her reeling. Her lungs felt like a fish's swim bladder, so full and tight they were about to burst. The strands of her hair were like seaweed, clogging her eyes and mouth. Her undertunic tangled in her legs like a fish net, dragging her down.

Here, in the world of floating sunlight, fish, and algae, there was no worrying about Laoghaire's jeering. About Anna's failing to be groomed as a noble lady. About Aunt Leitis's tired sighs as Anna once again stitched a tear with the wrong type of seam because she just wanted to be done with it and go outside.

But she couldn't die like this. Not like this, please, Lord. Please, there must be more to life than this.

And then, as though her prayer had been answered, the grip of the sea eased. Her lungs felt singed as she emerged into the world of wind and gawking seagulls, blue sky and green rocks. The sun warmed Anna's wet head. Her nostrils burned from the salt as she gasped desperate, painful breaths into her burning lungs.

After she could breathe again, she realized something felt different. There had been a shift in the air, as though a minstrel had put a different twist on a familiar story. On the shore, Laoghaire wasn't practicing archery but staring straight at her, and Aunt Leitis waved in large arm sweeps for her to come back on the shore. Behind them, Islay was a giant, rocky cliff covered with green, yellow, and dark-red moss. The small gravel beach on which they stood was tucked behind the cliff that held Dunyvaig Castle like a candleholder.

Dunyvaig Castle was a fortress guarding Lagavulin Bay, the MacDonald naval base and trading port, with dozens of ships anchored and docked. The pride and the power of Lord of Islay Aulay MacDonald, and the whole clan, were birlinns, West Highland galleys. They were the legacy of the clan's Viking ancestor, Somerled the Great. Fast and easy to steer, they meant the MacDonalds held power over the Irish Sea and were a threat to their antagonistic neighbors—Ireland and England. Dunyvaig Castle loomed over the bay and the crashing waves, a silent guardian that had defended the clan countless times against naval attacks from any fools who dared.

Anna wanted to get out of the water. Fear tightened the pit of her stomach as she worked her way through the waves. What if she got caught in another current? What if she was dragged down once again? She might not have enough fight left in her to escape that death. Her shoulders and back ached and burned with exhaustion, and only when she stepped onto sharp rocks and pebbles could she finally breathe freely. The linen under-tunic she always swam in clung to her body, sticking to her legs, and wind hit her like a wall of ice.

But she was alive, and even that pain meant she was walking and breathing and living. And she wanted to get away from that sea as fast as she could. She never wanted to set foot in there again.

Leitis spread her arms holding a dry linen blanket, ready to wrap it around Anna. "Why were ye in there so long, sweet?"

"Sorry, Aunt..." Anna murmured as she stopped in front of her and turned to the sea, letting Leitis close the edges of the blanket over her chest.

And then she saw it.

A ship on the horizon. The MacDonald sail was tight and

full, almost as full as Aunt Leitis's pregnant belly. On the yellowish sail, the MacDonald crest reddened: a hand in armor holding a cross. Hope and joy fluttered in Anna's belly.

In the absence of her true father, her uncle Aulay was like a da to her. And Aunt Leitis like a mother.

Laoghaire scoffed, her translucent gray eyes on the birlinn. "The laird is finally back, and ye wilna even be able to greet him properly with yer wet hair and yer wet smock."

Anna gathered her hair and twisted it, pressing seawater out. Laoghaire's jeering always hurt her like beestings, even though she'd never show it. "Mayhap. But I'm of nae consequence. And I spend my days being happy while all ye do is stitching, weaving, counting loafs of bread, and yelling at ale women."

Aunt Leitis rubbed Anna's shoulders with her weak hands. Anna looked back at her. She was pale, with dark circles under her eyes. Normally sky blue and bright, her eyes were now faded.

"Are ye all right, Aunt?" asked Anna as she took the blanket and wrapped herself tighter.

Her aunt's seventh pregnancy was difficult. Previous ones had ended in miscarriages and stillbirths. This time around, Leitis bled often and felt weak, had frequent headaches and no appetite. She was too old to bear a child, and everyone in the clan was worried.

"The laird doesna ken I am with bairn," she said, staring at the ship as if looking into empty space.

"But Uncle Aulay wilna be cross with ye, surely," Anna said. "Will ye hold this, please, Laoghaire? I will change into my dress."

Laoghaire rolled her eyes, put her bow on the rocks, and took the edges of the blanket, holding it around Anna. As Anna peeled the wet undertunic from her body and, shivering, put on the dry clothes, her eyes never left the ship.

"They were away for seven moons," said Anna, pushing her leg through one woolen stocking. Unlike Laoghaire's, her stockings had moth holes, seams, and patches. "Do ye think they bring news of...*him*?"

"They" were Uncle Aulay, Uncle Èoin—who was Laoghaire's father—and his two sons, Colum and Seoras. With a band of the best MacDonald warriors, they'd left for mainland Scotland on some political business concerning her father in February. Since then, rumors had come with travelers about battles with England and some of the other clans.

Leitis didn't reply, just laid her hand on her swollen belly, rubbing it thoughtfully. Maybe she already knew something and didn't want to tell it to a twelve-year-old girl.

Anna put on the shoes she'd inherited from her mother. She was buzzing with joy to see her uncles and cousins. A small flutter of hope tingled her. Would they bring news of her father? He knew of her existence; would he finally want her to join him in Carrick? Secretly, painfully, she wished he'd call upon her and have her live at his home, together with his real family.

Once Anna had her shoes on, Laoghaire tied the strings on the back of her blue woolen dress.

"Mayhap Da brings a marriage proposal for me." Laoghaire yanked the strings and the fabric tore loudly. "It wilna be for ye."

Leitis shook her head. "Lasses, 'tisna time to quarrel. 'Tis a good time to practice the manners ye've been learning to greet important guests."

"Ye mean, the manners *I* have been learning." Laoghaire straightened her back, her neck slightly bowed demonstrating womanly grace and compliance. Her hair was as dark as Anna's— the MacDonald legacy—but she had the most beautiful, piercing gray eyes. The high cheekbones and perfect bone structure under her smooth skin made her look almost ethereal. A picture of a young noble lady ready to be portrayed in monks' manuscripts as the ideal of beauty. "Anna has been doing nothing but swimming and running around with the farmers and the shepherds."

"'Tis enough," said Leitis. "Let us go to the port."

Anna was only too glad to comply. The sea was no longer a friend she came to spend fun summer hours with. It was an unpredictable enemy, like a snake, able to kill her whenever it pleased.

In the port, they stood on a wooden jetty and watched the ship move between the two strips of lands that guarded Lagavulin Bay—the cliff bearing Dunyvaig Castle on the left and rocks sticking out of the water on the right. It was a dangerous passage for those who didn't know the shore well, but the MacDonald navigators knew it like the backs of their hands. Once it was in, it passed smoothly between the anchored ships and boats. The curved bow of *Tagradh*, which meant "claim," cut through the water easily as it approached. The sail was furled, and the men rowed the birlinn, oars rising and falling, water splashing. Behind Anna, Laoghaire, and Leitis, MacDonald clansmen gathered and watched the approach of their beloved laird, talking and pointing. Anticipation was as palpable in the air as the scent of fish and algae that always hung in the port from the fishing boats.

Leitis grasped Anna's hand and squeezed it. Anna felt the quick beating of her pulse against her fingers. Her wet head was cold, but her skin was warm, her stomach twisting in nervous spasms. There he was, Uncle Aulay, standing at the bow, hugging the tall, curved figurehead of a sea monster. He was giant, as broad-shouldered as a mythical Highland hero, his graying hair had grown longer and was tied behind his back. He wore a *leine croich*, the quilted coat armor cut and patched, and a chain coif. His claymore, as always, hung in a sheath on his belt. Her uncle Èoin stood next to him, his shoulder patched, and Seoras, Laoghaire's younger brother. Anna couldn't see Colum, but perhaps he was rowing or on the other side of the birlinn.

Anna waved enthusiastically to the men, while her aunt and Laoghaire stood proud and solemn and ceremonial like true noble ladies. Seoras waved back at her, and Uncle Aulay raised his arm in greeting.

The ship docked, ramparts were put, and the men were descending. Throwing all ceremony to hell, Aulay covered the jetty in four giant steps and scooped Leitis into his arms, burying his face in her hair. Something ached sweetly in Anna's chest at the sight of them. She always thought she'd never have as great a love as Aulay and Leitis shared.

Then greetings were exchanged between her uncle Èoin, Laoghaire, and Seoras. She watched the closest people welcome one another as she stood alone, like a single tree swept by the wind.

And then another nobleman slowly walked down the jetty towards her. He looked a little lost, and there was something achingly familiar about him.

He was tall and mighty, and as dark-haired as she. Scratches marked his face, and his *leine croich* was as torn and bloodied as Aulay's. The sword on his belt had gold and silver cords twisted around the grip.

While the clan gathered around Aulay, she distantly wondered why she didn't see Colum among those descending from the ship. Her eyes were still on the man while the crowd of clansmen gathering around Aulay, Èoin, and Seoras pushed her to the side of the jetty. She couldn't take her eyes off the approaching man. He was in his midthirties, she thought. His dark shoulder-length hair with a few silver strands was a little disheveled. His gaze, dark and piercing, looked over the crowd and landed on her. Whether it was because she stood apart from the cheerful clan or because she still had wet hair and didn't look like a proper noble lady, she wasn't sure.

Like her, the man seemed to not quite know what to do as the rest of the people hugged and clapped shoulders and talked joyfully together.

And then, an elbow from the crowd pushed her and she lost her balance and flew... Only, strong hands caught her by the shoulders, and the man steadied her on the jetty.

"Careful, lass," he said in a soft, Lowland accent.

"Thank ye, Lord," she said.

She should have remembered how a noble lady greeted a guest...

"Did ye have a long voyage, Lord?" she asked.

He stood by her side and then glanced at her, sadness in his dark eyes. "Quite long. Quite hard, too."

"Oh?"

He swallowed, his gaze wandering to the horizon. Seagulls cried above them, soaring on the wind. The wind threw a salty, fishy gust into her face.

"I'm the king of a kingdom nae bigger than one island. A king who lost everything."

Something in her stomach lurched, and she fought back the urge to touch the man to see if he was even real. "Who are ye, Lord?"

He gave her a sad smile. "Robert the Bruce. King of Scots."

The wooden jetty careened under her feet. The voices of the crowd faded into the distance. The world darkened, and only this man stood in the light before her.

"King? My father is king?"

He frowned and looked her over slowly. "Are ye Julianna's daughter?" he asked. "Alice?"

He didn't even remember her name.

"Anna," she croaked out.

He blinked, his features softening. "*Anna*. Julianna always liked the name."

Her chest was bursting with tension, heat, pressure. Her cheeks burned as though scalded. Her hands shook. She felt as if she were in a bag and someone was violently shaking it.

Her father, whom she dreamed of, whom she yearned for, whom she despised and adored...was finally before her.

And he wasn't just Earl of Carrick anymore. He was king now.

She was the daughter of a king.

Oh, Judas, she should have learned all those manners with Laoghaire.

She had an odd sensation of floating up above her body, soaring in the air. "M-may I call ye Father?" she asked, and only knew what she said after she blurted the words out of her mouth.

To her surprise, he grinned and squeezed her shoulder. The touch was like bliss, and she wanted to dive into his arms and let him hug her, inhale the scent of a father who she'd never known.

"Ye may call me Father. My wife, Elizabeth, and my daughter Marjorie are far away. 'Tis good to have family here. Are ye nae afraid to have a fugitive for a father?"

Anna shook her head vigorously. "I'd take ye even if ye were a leper beggar."

She had almost died in the sea and when she came back to the land, she had a father. He was like a vision, a being from a faerie land, a thing of legends. She was afraid to breathe and spook him away like smoke.

And yet doubt ate at her joy like corrosion. "Why didna ye come to see me all these years?" she asked.

He sank to a crouch before her and was now lower than her. His eyes were dark and glistening like wet blueberries. "I am sorry, lass. Yer mother was my betrothed and we...loved each other before we were wed. I had to leave Islay to serve England, and I got entangled in the war...and then she died before I could marry her. I didna ken of yer existence for a while. Once I found out, I set a dowry aside for ye in Carrick. I dinna have much to offer ye now. My lands in Carrick were seized by Edward I, and I have nae a dime to my name."

He cupped her face, and she held her breath at the warmth of the touch of her real father on her skin. How many times had she imagined this happening? How many times had she dreamed of him coming back to her? And now he was right here, talking to her. Not a vision or a ghost or her own imagination.

What could she do so that he would stay or accept her as his own flesh and blood and acknowledge her and love her? Her palm hurt and she realized her fingernails were cutting into her skin.

"But I will tell ye this," he said. "I may be dead tomorrow. But if I am alive and hold a peaceful kingdom one day, I will call upon ye. Ye will live with me and my family at my court. Ye will have yer dowry and ye will have a father. I will arrange a great marriage for ye."

Fire burned in her chest. She'd die for this man if he needed her to.

He nodded. "Make me proud, Anna. Ye may be a bastart, but ye're the daughter of a king now. I will need ye one day. Will ye be ready?"

Good gracious, she'd need to be a noble lady now. She'd need to be better than Laoghaire. Her days of freedom were over. But she would stitch every embroidery in Scotland if it pleased him.

"Aye, Father, I will."

CHAPTER 1

Dunadd Fort, Argyll and Bute, May 1313

"A footprint." David Wakeley shook his head and stabbed his index finger at a carving in the stone he was standing on. It was in the form of a foot, or an ancient axe head, depending on how you looked at it. "I can't believe this is what two years of searching has led to."

Dùghlas Ruaidhrí furrowed his blond eyebrows and crossed his huge arms over his chest, muscles bulging. A tall, broad Highlander with a claymore in the sheath at his back, he stood several steps away from David. They were on top of the Dunadd hillfort, surrounded by the moss-covered remnants of the ancient stronghold and blown by strong winds from all sides. But despite the cold, Dùghlas wore a pale blue linen tunic with his braies, or medieval breeches, because it was May, and May was warm for Highlanders.

Cool gusts coming from the sea in the west made David shiver in his *leine croich*. He hadn't grown up in an icy medieval castle. He'd grown up in Chicago, and though the winters there were freezing, they'd had down jackets, scarves, and hats to keep them warm. And he'd never take central heating, hot water, and warm cars for granted again.

"Um," Dùghlas said, "are ye surprised, man? 'Tis where ye asked me to take ye."

David went into a pocket at the side of his tunic and retrieved a rolled piece of vellum with a hand-drawn map of Scotland showing ten crosses around it. It was soft and smooth, and it was the most precious possession he owned. His way to freedom.

"I did." He looked up at the horizon to the west, where the coast of Loch Crinan silvered between dark hills and mountains. A cloud hung above it, spreading rain like fog.

River Add snaked around Dunadd hill, cutting through green, rusty, and yellowish fields. The country spread all around them in brown, green, and gray valleys, hills, and mountains. The bogs of Moine Mhor extended in a rust and ochre carpet to the west. Black sheep, their fleece still short after the spring shearing, grazed peacefully on the slope. Seagulls squawked above them. Gusts coming from the sea brought the scent of rain and salt and trouble. The wind caught the birds and shut them up, and they soared, fighting against the invisible force, hanging in the air as though someone had put them on pause.

David bit his lower lip. He brought his pointy-shoed foot closer to the carved footprint, attentive to any feeling of strangeness in the air—a buzzing, sucking sensation, the scent of lavender and fresh grass that had accompanied Sìneag, the faerie who had sent his sister, Rogene, through time. And because he had foolishly not believed Rogene and grabbed her arm to stop her, he had traveled in time, too.

And he'd been hunting for that scent for two years.

But the scent of moss, wet earth, and stone, accompanied by a whiff of sea and sheep dung, was undisturbed. Sìneag was nowhere around.

David's stomach flipped, churning and twisting. He had been hoping one of the rocks he had visited over the past two years would glow and buzz and open for him, let him return to the twenty-first century.

Back to the life unlived.

Back to fulfilling his full potential.

Back to the football scholarship that would allow him to go to college and get a degree and make something of himself.

That would allow him to prove to himself—and to everyone —that he wasn't just a dumb fuck with a reading disability born into a family of geniuses. The scholarship was being held for up to three years and would expire in July.

He was only twenty-one; he had his whole life ahead of him. But he was wasting it among fourteenth-century warlords, medieval knights, and warriors.

He had his sister here, but nothing else that held him. He was stuck in this medieval prison the goddamn faerie had put him into without his consent.

Three years. Two of them spent searching. Nine stones he had slammed his hand onto.

Zero faeries found.

Zero tunnels through time open.

Zero chances to go back.

"I just didn't think it would be this, Dùghlas," he said. "This nothing. You told me this place is supposed to be swarming with faeries and spirits or whatever. You told me faeries leave glass beads here and carve things in stone, and people goddamn *disappear*."

Dùghlas's silvery eyes were like a sharpshooter's rifle scope on him. "Aye, 'tis what folk *say*. Did ye really expect to see a faerie?"

Yes, he had. But he couldn't say it out loud. When Rogene had told him a faerie had sent her through time to 1310, he'd laughed at her. Dùghlas would think he'd lost it.

"This was my biggest hope," David murmured. "My sister told me something about this place, but I didn't listen very well. It's a place of power, apparently. The inauguration stone, right?"

Yes, Rogene, a historian in 2021, and wife to Laird Angus Mackenzie in 1310, had told him many things about Scottish history. Only, he'd been too drunk—or too tired of being lectured—to pay attention.

Now, it wasn't like he could pick up a phone to ask her. And Eilean Donan was about a week away on horseback in good weather.

The inauguration stone was different from the time-travel stones, of course, but the principle was the same. Carved symbols in stone had power. There were some carvings next to the footprint that David couldn't quite decipher. They could be connected to the time traveling rocks for all he knew. Maybe they would even work when the time travel stones wouldn't.

Your time will come after you meet the woman you're destined for. That was what James—one of the other time travelers and the husband of Angus's sister, Catrìona Mackenzie—had told him the day David set off on his travels. Sìneag had apparently told James about this when he'd tried to take David back to the twenty-first century with him.

David didn't want to believe it. He was afraid of being stuck here forever if he fell in love like his sister had with Angus, like James had with Catrìona... Others, too.

He stubbornly believed he could find a way through the rocks without Sìneag's unwelcome condition.

But, proving James's words, none of the time travel stones worked for him—the ones with a handprint, with the river of time, and the tunnel carved on them. So, he'd considered Albert Einstein's quote "The definition of insanity is doing the same thing over and over again and expecting different results" and decided to try something new.

This rock.

Holding his breath, he stepped into the footprint.

Nothing happened. He didn't travel in time. He was just standing there, inhaling the wind, and trying to fit his large foot into the small footprint.

"Ye're now King of Dál Riata," Dùghlas proclaimed. "Congratulations."

David cursed under his breath and stepped back, disappointment dripping from him like sweat. Dùghlas went to a bowl carved in a stone five steps away from the inauguration stone, sank to his knees, and gathered rainwater from the bowl in both hands. Then, still on his knees, he stretched his arms to David.

"Would Yer Grace allow Taranis, the feared god of thunder and rain, to bless yer reign for years to come?"

David gritted his teeth. "Only if Taranis sends a lightning bolt up your ass."

The anger, the constant sense of helplessness, of being locked down against his will, was a sickening, corroding storm in his guts. He needed the only thing that helped him to forget.

Uisge.

With a sigh, he sat down on the rock, still warm from a few hours in the morning sun, and took out his flask—a horn with a cork—filled with uisge. He tucked his map under one foot so that the wind wouldn't carry his most precious possession away, pulled the cork, and took three long, satisfying gulps. The fiery liquid burned his mouth and his throat as it descended into his stomach. It was pretty much pure alcohol, bitter but oaky and smoky, and there was the beginning of real scotch somewhere in there. Though whisky wouldn't be invented until the fifteenth century, Rogene had told him. The familiar high hit his brain cells and he started to relax, his senses swimming.

Finally.

Wiping his wet hands off on his braies, Dùghlas came and sat by his side. "By God's teeth, friend, yer fascination with things sent up an arse hasn't stopped surprising me in the whole moon we have been traveling together." Rolling his eyes, David offered the uisge. Dùghlas drank, croaked, and handed it back to him. "The things I remember ye wishing up my arse were a tree branch when we slept in the woods and it was too wet to kindle. A wet cloth when I tried to wipe the vomit off yer face after ye got drunk. And...oh, 'tis the best one yet, one of the rocks ye've been chasing and slamming yer hand into. The whole seven-foot-long rock." Dùghlas shook his head and laughed.

David drank more, chasing that numbness he needed. "Well, you can now add 'go fuck yourself' to the list."

"Ah." Dùghlas pulled the map out from under David's foot. "'Tis a good one. I prefer pleasuring myself to shoving things into my body that dinna belong there."

David chuckled and toasted to that. "You're not wrong there." He drank more.

"Where do ye want to go next?" Dùghlas asked, staring at the map. "Man, I'm glad ye understand this child's drawing and can orient yerself. 'Tis ogham to me."

"Well," David said, "I don't know. This is the last rock I know of."

"There are more," Dùghlas said. "The Picts were everywhere. They conquered Dál Riata, too, at some point. Perhaps yer rocks are somewhere in Galloway or even England. But I'll tell ye one thing. Be careful. Dinna ask folk about them. Dinna talk about them to someone ye dinna ken. And if ye can help it, dinna go near them longer than necessary."

David gulped more of the uisge, his head already spinning pleasantly. The wind from the sea gusted stronger now, throwing the long strands of his dark-blond hair, which he hadn't cut in three years, into his eyes. A few raindrops fell on his face and on the map, but he registered them only distantly. Scotland and rain. That had been his life for what felt like forever.

"Why? Would faeries make me disappear?" He drank more. He needed more of that warm burning in his stomach, to chase the cold of the wind and the rain away. He'd already stopped caring that the rain might ruin his precious map. A few more gulps of alcohol, and he'd stop caring that he was stuck in the Middle Ages. That was what he was going for.

"Nae." Dùghlas frowned. "But there's folk that dinna take people who believe in such things kindly. Especially priests."

David nodded. A sweet light-headedness tricked him into thinking he had no dark thoughts, that he was joyous and light and fun. Everything he wasn't when sober.

"We should go," Dùghlas said, then rolled up David's map and handed it to him. "The farmhouse down there"—he pointed at a croft—"mayhap they'll take us in."

David stood up, swaying, and pointed two fingers at his friend like Elvis. "Yeah, man. I'm glad you're traveling with me. You keep me out of trouble."

As they walked down the hill, David balancing over the worn-out, ancient rocks that indicated ancient ramparts, Dùghlas said, "Ye're glad? 'Tis a nice change from wishing things up my arse and telling me to go and pleasure myself."

Black clouds darkened the world. Rain intensified, and David was blinking water away. He was almost there, almost in that oblivious state where he could tolerate his miserable life and where the obnoxious, self-deprecating voice in his head was silent. But something bothered him. As he stepped over one wet, moss-covered step, his foot slipped a little, but he regained his balance.

"Careful," said Dùghlas.

"Thanks for the warning, man. I've been nothing but careful for three years."

Dùghlas frowned, a question born in his eyes at the mention of three years, but he withdrew, sighed, shook his head, and resumed walking.

They reached their horses, which were tethered to a bush at the bottom of the hill, and rode to the farm through what was now a true downpour. It was a typical Highland croft, with low stone walls and a thatched roof. They banged at the door, and a man opened it. He was in his fifties, short with a gray beard, a tired, weathered face, and a thin, pointy nose. The impression of a skull filled David's drunken mind.

"Maybe we should find another place," he whispered into

Dùghlas's ear, but based on the man's deepening frown, he had probably said it too loudly.

Dùghlas waved his hand at David as if to shoo him. "Friend," he said to the old farmer, "we are looking for shelter for the night in this weather. We are happy to do work for ye in exchange."

The man's lips thinned, and his chin moved forward as he looked at the ground and pushed the door to close it. But Dùghlas laid his hand on the door and stopped him. "Any work. Please."

The man's milky eyes were tired. "I can use two pairs of strong hands."

"Good," Dùghlas said.

"As long as ye dinna mind a leper in the house."

Dùghlas froze. "A leper?"

David shook his head. Leprosy was a common, incurable disease in the Middle Ages. David didn't know much about medicine, but he knew that it was a bacterial infection, treatable in the twenty-first century by antibiotics. But it was a slow and painful death sentence in the Middle Ages. If he and Dùghlas were careful about hygiene, they should be fine. And David always had a cake of soap with him. Plus, uisge would help to disinfect...if he had any left.

"We don't mind," said David. "We can sleep in your stables."

The man nodded. "If ye clean them, feed the horses, and cut the firewood, ye may."

Dùghlas looked at David with big, angry eyes. As a medieval man, he was terrified of leprosy. Maybe David should be, too.

"My friend here will," Dùghlas said.

"Good." The man stepped aside and let them come in. "My wife just made dinner."

As they entered, the scent of woodsmoke, unwashed bodies, and overcooked pottage hung in the room. There was a hearth in the middle of the house. The dirt-packed floor was covered with reeds, except for a healthy circle around the hearth so that any sparks wouldn't start a fire.

In the golden semidarkness, smoke hung under the thatched ceiling like a rainless cloud, and David's eyes started to burn. But even with the only light coming from the flames in the hearth, he could see the woman. She was bent over the cauldron, her back as round as a wheel. Her face was illuminated by fire, and there were the clear signs of long untreated leprosy.

As David stood by the door, blinking raindrops and smoke away, he drunkenly thought this must be where the old witches from fairy tales came from.

Her deep-set eyes were milky, the skin on her face dark and purple and hugging her skull like papier-mâché. She held the long, wooden ladle in her hand with three dark, rotting fingers. She watched David with a frown, her cloudy eyes menacing.

Dùghlas cleared his throat. "Good day."

David felt an urge to add *madam*, but stopped himself.

"Good day," she replied. "Supper isna ready yet."

"I'll show ye the stables," said the man. As they walked back into the torrential rain, the old man led the way through the yard of the farm. "My name is Padean, and my wife is Peigi. We are farmers. I lived in Carlisle before. I am a Scot, though," he added defensively.

He showed them the stables, gave them two shovels and two axes. David and Dùghlas worked for a couple of hours. The scent of manure and freshly cut wood were rich in David's nostrils. Physical work sobered him somewhat. When all was done, they went back into the hut.

"All done?" asked Peigi, still leaning over the cauldron.

"Aye," Dùghlas said, and put his sword against the wall by the door.

"Pottage?" she asked.

"Thanks." David unbuckled his own sheath with his sword that was held by his girdle and proceeded to sit at the table next to the hearth.

Padean took another ladle and poured the pottage into two clay bowls. He put the bowls in front of David and Dùghlas. The steam of something hot and freshly cooked tickled David's nostrils, and while Dùghlas introduced them, David shoved spoon after spoon into his mouth. The thick soup was mainly barley with a few root vegetables, but it was the best thing David had tasted in days. Padean poured two more bowls for himself and Peigi. He put them on the table, then came to help her stand up and led her to sit next to him, shielding her away. David glanced at Padean's hand as the man ate and noticed his fingers were dark, too. He hadn't escaped the disease.

For a while, the little house was filled with the crackling wood, the drum of rain against the thatch, the slurping of pottage, and the wind howling in the slits of the door. Halfway through the meal, Padean said, "Ye two are brave men. Nae everyone would come into a house with lepers. They say, 'tis God's punishment, a corruption of the very soul. Dunadd Fort helps to keep people away, and the Cambel tacksmen are kind enough not to bother us or put a too heavy of a strain for rent and produce. What brings ye two here?"

David relaxed, warm and full. He stood up and removed his wet *leine croich*. His long hair, gathered at the back in a tail, still dripped with water.

"Do you mind if I let it dry?" he asked as he stood up.

"Aye, lad," said Padean. "Do so."

"I look for faerie stones," David said as he stood by the fire with his *leine croich* hanging from his hands. "The ones that are up there—"

He stopped because the woman gasped, and the slurping stopped, and the only sounds were of rain and fire and wind.

"Leave," said the woman. Her voice was like a thunder strike. "Get out now."

Dùghlas chuckled. "Please, 'tis nothing. My friend is just curious—"

The woman turned to David, her face dark under her hood.

"'Tis a curse. Those stones are a curse. The same curse that hit me. 'Tis the faeries' fault, all their fault that God is punishing me, and now my husband. Leave before ye bring death to us!"

"Peigi," said Padean placatingly, "the lads have nowhere to go. It rains and there're nae other farms nearby. Come now, calm down, they can just go to the stables—"

"Nae, ye fool. I already brought the curse on ye. This man is just another one sent by God." She looked straight at David. "Up there, Dunadd hill, is the stone with the foot. But 'tis nae what ye've been looking for, aye, lad? Or ye wouldna have asked. Ye've been searching for the stone with the hand, aye?"

Mumbling angry curses, something along the lines of *I told ye nae to tell folk the wrong things*, Dùghlas stood up from the table and came to the fire, quickly rubbing his hands. His tunic, his hair, and his shoes were still wet, and David knew his friend didn't want to go out into the rain any more than he did.

David slowly picked up his *leine croich*. "Yes. I was looking for a hand."

The woman laughed hysterically. "Ye fool. 'Tis nae in the open like that, facing the sky, looking over the country. 'Tis in a place darker than night, where nightmares are born."

Even drunk, David felt a chill go through him. He stood, holding the wet *leine croich* that weighed as much as a sheep. "You know where it is?" he asked.

"Shut up," murmured Dùghlas as he put the baldric back on.

"I ken," Peigi said, narrowing her eyes at him. "But I wilna tell ye. I follow God's path. Only when my soul is healed, will my body heal."

He looked helplessly at Dùghlas, who shrugged. David shook his head, attempting to make his drunken head work faster.

Padean took David by his elbow and led him to the door. "Ye must go. Ye are upsetting her."

David picked up his sword. "Where then?"

But she didn't reply. Disappointment weighed at David as Padean opened the door and gently pushed him and Dùghlas out into the gray, muddy rain. Water poured over them as Padean led them firmly to the farm gates.

"Where is the stone with the hand?" David asked.

Padean pushed them out of the low gate and closed it, creating a barrier between him and David and Dùghlas. Then he sighed and shook his head, looking down.

"'Tis in Carlisle Castle," he said. "I was born here, but as a lad, I was brought to my uncle, the mason who worked on the castle dungeon. I remember seeing that stone—the handprint, the odd carvings of waves and a tunnel or something similar. 'Tis odd and pagan and shouldna be talked about by God-fearing Christians," he added with anger.

Carlisle...David thought. English territory. His next destination.

Padean's eyes softened. "If ye think about going there, lad, be careful. The castle is probably still well guarded. But I remember a way in. See, as a young lad, I fell in love with Peigi. She lived in the town, but I wasna allowed to leave the keep after dark. So I sneaked out. On the northwestern side of the curtain wall, the stones form a sort of stairway. They stand out a wee bit. The enemy wilna notice that, only them who kens 'tis there. My uncle, a Cambel, told me about it, to help me see my love. So mayhap it will help ye in yer search. Ye helped us with the stables and the firewood. We didna give ye shelter. 'Tis the very least I can do."

Then he turned, and, slouching like a question mark, returned to the sick love of his life. The girl for whom he'd spent his youth climbing the castle walls. Look where love had gotten them. David shuddered.

Sighing, he took out his map. Rain still poured, but he hoped to make the mark quick enough for moisture not to destroy it. He laid the parchment on top of the stone wall surrounding the farm, then took out a quill and a small jar of ink Rogene had given him so that he would write to her.

His sister was a dictator. What did she expect from a

dyslexic who could barely write with pen and paper, let alone with quill and ink? He hadn't written her in two years. He hadn't seen Paul, his nephew, for two years. David had left Eilean Donan Castle when Paul was about two months old.

He missed Rogene and Paul and thought of them often. Paul would already be a toddler, walking and babbling. He was a sweet baby, and his sister and Angus couldn't get enough of their son.

With a quill, he made a cross where Carlisle was, approximately. Rain poured on top of it, and it smudged. "How long till Carlisle?" he asked.

"About one week on horseback," Dùghlas said. "But I am nae coming with ye."

David put away the map so that it wouldn't be destroyed by the rain. "What?"

Dùghlas sighed heavily. "I canna set foot on English land, man. And I do need to get back to my own business, as much as I enjoyed this odd adventure with ye."

David frowned. He wished he could convince Dùghlas to keep traveling with him and helping him, but he knew the man had his own life, his own agenda, and his own mission. As with all relationships for David, this was only temporary. No woman, man, or child could keep him here.

With regret, he squeezed Dùghlas's shoulder. "I am sorry to hear that, buddy. As annoying as you are, I would rather make this insane journey with you than without you. You kept me safe. You taught me how to survive. You..." His throat caught. This was no use. Why was he being emotional when there was no way for him to make any connections in this age that he hated so much?

Dùghlas's rifle-scope eyes were sharp on him again as he squeezed David's shoulder.

"Dinna dismiss friendships so quickly, man," Dùghlas said. "Whatever ye look for in those stones...mayhap 'tis nae there at all. Mayhap, if ye accepted whatever life is throwing at ye, ye'd realize ye already have all ye need. They are just rocks, after all."

David shook his head. The man had no idea what he was talking about. They hugged, rain pouring over them as if from a bucket. Wind cut through David like a knife. Then they went their separate ways.

As Dùghlas's horse grew smaller in the distance to the north, swallowed in the Scottish landscape like another dark spot of moss, David huddled in his *leine croich*. Loneliness crept into him with the wet coldness of the Highlands. Wondering if he would ever get back to Chicago, he led his horse south to Carlisle.

There, in the dungeons of the castle, somewhere where nightmares were born, could be his way back through time.

His way home.

CHAPTER 2

AYR, Scotland
Three days later...

ANNA MACDONALD STEPPED ONTO THE DARK, WET SAND AND walked as far away from the sea as she could. She stood on the mainland of Scotland for the first time in her life.

The beach was littered with rocks and seaweed washed onto the shore like rags from a shipwreck she couldn't see. As her clan bustled about, carrying chests, provisions, and weapons from the three birlinns, she took a long breath. She inhaled air full of the sharpness of seaweed, the ocean, and wet sand.

Finally, her life could begin. Finally, her father needed her.

After seven years of silence, her wait was over.

Uncle Aulay came to stand next to her, his hand casually on the pommel of his claymore at his waist, his eyes on a group of horse riders approaching them from the rocky hills that bordered the beach.

"Stay close, lass," he said.

Colum came to stand on her other side. He was as tall as Aulay, but where Aulay was like a dependable boulder, big and muscular, a seasoned warrior with short, silvery hair and a beard, Colum was like a wolf, dark and lean and alert, his sharp eyes on the approaching group. She had been ecstatic when, after a year of imprisonment with the English, Colum had been freed by Uncle Aulay and other clansmen in 1307. And even though he'd returned different—somber and sad, not the beloved, humorous, kind war hero she'd known—she still loved him.

Anna reached into the hidden pocket of her long, angel-sleeved red dress and gripped the handle of the knife that Colum had given her for the journey. For the past seven years, she'd never swum again. But she had trained with knives and swords.

Colum cocked his head, the strands of his dark shoulder-length hair playing in the wind. "Do ye think 'tis the Bruce's men bringing the horses? They come from the direction of the town of Ayr, as agreed."

"I hope so," Aulay said and looked back at his men, who were still unloading the three birlinns. "Stop, lads."

They stopped immediately, putting down whatever they were carrying in an instant. The forty or so MacDonald clansmen moved into formation around their laird, Anna, and Colum. Forty fierce faces were hard, focused on the group of horsemen.

When one of the approaching men raised his hand and cried that they were from Ayr and brought horses for Anna's journey, the MacDonalds relaxed, and the men resumed unloading the ships.

After a while, they started loading the horses. Anna fastened her sleeping roll to the brown Highland pony she was going to ride. She was a beautiful white mare. Her summer fur was soft and smooth, the scent of it dusty and warm. The sea whispered rhythmically as waves crashed onto the beach, but Anna would never be enchanted by the water's song again. As men worked, talking to one another, occasional commands and warnings sounded. She kept throwing glances at the outline of the church of Ayr, the tallest building in a short mass of roofs at the edge of the coast up north, blue and foggy in the distance.

"He isna still there, is he?" she asked Aulay, who came to her horse with a heavier sack and fastened it to the other side of the saddle.

He'd been so heartbroken since Leitis had died. Seven years did not seem to have dulled the pain much.

Anna remembered that horrible night, one month after *Tagradh* had returned and brought her father to her. Leitis had gone into labor. It had been a little early, but it was the longest she'd ever gone in pregnancy, and there was much hope but also dread in the whole castle. She remembered standing in front of Aulay and Leitis's bedchamber. Aulay's hand lay on the door handle, but he hesitated, solemn, fire from the torches casting dancing shadows on his face, his eyes dark and burning. He breathed quickly, no doubt terrified, hopeful, and dreading the worst all at the same time. Leitis was moaning from behind the door.

He'd crossed himself and gone in, and Anna had sat by the door for what felt like forever, her arms wrapped around her knees, listening to Leitis's moans, then agonizing, heart-wrenching yells of pain that escalated like a terrible song to a high pitch and then silenced.

Anna had stood, shaking, and pressed her ear to the door, desperately listening for a newborn's cry. A squeak. But moments flew by, her breath rushed in and out, and no cry came. She leaned against the wall and slid down until she sat on the floor. Tears filled her eyes. No. There must be some explanation. She couldn't have lost Aunt Leitis. The only mother she'd ever known.

Soon, the door had opened, and Aulay had walked out, his great shoulders hunched, his head bowed.

"She's gone, Anna," he croaked.

He'd walked out a different man. A man with a hole in his heart.

Aulay looked in the direction of her gaze, his eyes dark under his eyebrows. They always had that sadness in them since that night. She wished he could meet someone again, mayhap find a new wife to fill that hole in his heart. Unmarried lasses and widows on Islay all looked at him with admiration and longing. Some of them were more straightforward than others, but he refused everyone.

"Nae, lass." He tightened the belt over the travel sack. "The king took Ayr a few moons ago. Now he's waiting for ye in Stirling."

Waiting for ye... Her father was *waiting* for her.

She exhaled a shaky breath as she tied a knot over the sleeping roll. The news had come a sennight ago, changing her life forever. "I canna believe he finally called for me, Uncle. I dinna want to disappoint him."

Aulay's eyes softened, became like liquid obsidian.

"Lass, 'tis impossible. Ye're a treasure for yer father, and yer husband will be verra lucky to have ye."

Her husband...that was another thing she couldn't quite believe, even though she'd been preparing for a marriage ever since Bruce had appeared in Islay seven years ago and told her she needed to become a proper lady. That was exactly what she'd done.

For him.

And yet, the thought of a man she'd never seen becoming her husband, getting full control over her life, made her stomach twist. But she shoved that thought away and pressed out a smile for her uncle, like a proper noble lady would.

In an hour, twenty MacDonald men were on horseback and traveling northeast to Stirling. Another twenty had been left behind to guard the ships and trade with Ayr and wait for Aulay and Colum to return after Anna's wedding.

The town of Ayr was soon behind them, and they rode into the woods. The trees rising into the sky were sparse at first but grew thicker the deeper they went. Dead leaves mixed with undergrowth, grass and ferns covered the ground. Rotting logs lay here and there, moss growing on them like fur.

The late May air was full of birdsong, the rustling of leaves and branches in the wind, and the soft hoofbeats of two dozen horses. Anna breathed in the earthy, herbal air of the woods, not unlike Bridgend Woods on Islay. She wished she could send the horse galloping down the footworn path and enjoy the speed, the air, the feeling of a powerful animal's body moving under her. But, of course, princesses, even bastard ones, didn't do such things.

Would her new husband allow her to ride like the wind? She knew next to nothing about him.

"Have ye met Sir Philip Mowbray, Uncle?" she asked Aulay, who rode by her side.

He gave her a reassuring smile, the corners of his eyes wrinkling. "Nae, sweet."

She bit her lip. "Did ye hear anything about him?"

"He's a Scot, though, obviously, he is on England's side. I imagine he is a capable and accomplished man. He wouldna have been made constable of the most strategically important castle England had taken in Scotland." Aulay chuckled. "And only a smart and ambitious man would make the kind of deal he has made with the king."

Accomplished, smart, ambitious... That would be her husband. She shook her head once, one corner of her mouth curving up. "The kind who would give Stirling to Bruce without a fight to marry the king's bastart daughter."

"Aye," said Aulay. "In exactly twenty-six days, on John the Baptist, your marriage to Sir Philip will bring Stirling back into Scottish hands. Ye are very important to Scotland, dear. And to yer father."

She exhaled slowly. This was what she'd been waiting for ever since she met her father seven years ago. To be by his side, to be appreciated and loved by him, to be important to him. Like a true princess, she had the power to save Scotland. To save many lives.

This was worth marrying a man she'd never met. This was a worthy cause.

Besides, they'd live somewhere in the Lowlands, like Carrick. Her dowry would be some gold and an estate there. So she would be able to see him more often. She'd visit her father's court. He'd visit her and Philip, hunt with him, eat at the feasts she'd throw for him, spend time with his grandchildren. Her heart squeezed in hope and anticipation. They'd discuss everything, talk about their lives, and do their best to catch up all the years they'd lost.

"Should we hurry, Uncle?" she asked. "Are we nae supposed to be introduced to each other sooner? And the dowry negotiation...the marriage contract..."

Truth was, she couldn't wait to spend more time with Robert the Bruce, and there would be plenty of reasons to do so before the wedding. The sooner she got there, the sooner she could see her father.

"'Tis still only two days until Stirling, sweet," he said. "We have plenty—"

Something thin and dark whooshed past Anna and hit the tree with a *thunk*.

An arrow.

A horse neighed. More arrows flew. Men yelled. Someone yelped and fell off his horse.

"Ambush!" yelled Aulay. "Protect Anna!"

"Goddamn it," cursed Colum as he rode next to her. His shield was on his right arm, and he put his horse between Anna and the arrows, his eyes darting, looking for the source of the threat.

But arrows came from everywhere, and the archers were impossible to spot in the woods.

Aulay was on her other side, swinging his shield as arrows flew at him and stuck in the wood.

Anna clenched the reins, squeezing the horse's sides. Everything within her screamed to run, to flee. MacDonald men screamed, wounded and dying. Horses neighed in fear and pain as arrows hit them.

"I canna see them!" yelled Aulay. "Where, God's arse, are they?"

And then they came. First, the thundering sound of dozens of galloping horses, and then the path behind them darkened as more horsemen than Anna could count charged them.

"Ride, Anna," Aulay yelled, unsheathing his claymore. "Go!"

She lost all feeling of self, only the vibration of the ground that reverberated in her gut like a tuning fork.

"Go!" Colum yelled and hit her horse's side.

A force kicked her as her horse launched. The reins in her hands felt spiderweb-thin, her ears were ringing from the noise, and somehow, even with her mind as thick as sheep's fleece, her thighs knew how to move to keep the horse riding hard.

"Hya!" she heard herself call.

Her own voice was strange, foreign. The green and brown of the woods flashed to her right and to her left, and the cool air scratched her heated cheeks.

Whoever it was, they'd come for her. They must have found out about the secret deal between the Bruce and Mowbray.

No. She wouldn't let them take her. Not when she almost had what she had always wanted.

A father.

Hooves thundered against the ground behind her and she looked over her shoulder. A dozen of them followed her, warriors in *léintean-croich*, with chain mail coifs on their heads. They leaned low over their horses, their eyes on her, like a pack of wolves hunting prey.

Their leader was an older man, his receding hairline gray and shaggy. But he was an important man—he rode a big war horse, and he was the only one wearing chain mail over his *leine croich*.

She kicked her horse's sides with her heels and whipped the reins, and the horse sped up.

"Come on, lass, come on!" she murmured.

Her thighs burned, and her lungs were tight.

"Hya! Hya!" she kept crying.

But a dark shape slowly advanced to her right, and as she turned, she saw the leader of the pack riding next to her.

"Stop, lass, or I will stop ye," he yelled.

One hand holding the reins, she reached with the other one to the knife hidden in her pocket and took it out. "Ye try and ye will be sorry."

He grinned, flashing a row of white teeth, and reached out to her rein. She stabbed his gloved hand but scratched only the leather of the armor. At the same time, another rider came up on her left, and another on her right.

They were faster, and they positioned themselves in front of her horse, forcing it to slow down.

No! No!

Anna spurred the mare on, but it had nowhere to go, and it neighed, confused, as desperate as she. Then the man reached for her hand that held the knife.

She couldn't let her father down now that he finally needed her. Now that she finally had a chance to have the life she'd always wanted, the one where an illegitimate lass had a father who loved her.

Her back hurting, she reached out and stabbed the bastard in the thigh. His braies opened in a long, bloody gash. The man growled in pain but didn't stop. She drew her arm back for another stab, but he hit her hand with his shield.

The blow cracked something in her hand, pain kicking the air out of her lungs, and the knife flew. Then he grabbed her and hauled her from her horse. The pommel of his saddle dug into her stomach as she lay in front of him, thrown over his horse.

"Nae!" she screamed. "Let me go."

"Shut up, ye bitch," the man said. "Ye're mine now."

Anna roared, fury overtaking her in a fiery wave, and bit into the man's thigh. He screamed in pain, the horse neighed and shied, and then a hard blow burst against her head.

As she sank into a painful, rocking darkness, there was one thought left.

She still had time.

Wherever he was taking her, she would find a way to escape.

She'd save Scotland and make her father proud.

CHAPTER 3

Woods near Carlisle, Borderlands
Ten days later...

Someone's clothes flashed between the trees. Friend or foe? David stopped and waited, Daisy's reins in his hands.

He couldn't see the clothes anymore between the branches and the tree trunks. He listened. Birds chirped and wind rustled leaves above him in the crowns of trees. Daisy breathed softly behind him.

His horse heard the man before David did. She snorted and pulled back, and before David could react, a dark figure appeared next to him and something sharp and cold was pressed to his throat.

"Dinna move," said a cool, male voice.

Right. *Friend or foe my ass.* There were no friends here, in the middle of the woods. Everyone was an enemy unless proven otherwise. Especially in the Borderlands, where England and Scotland had raided each other for generations.

David raised his hands in a placating gesture and looked to

the left without moving his neck, trying to see who his attacker was. "I don't mean any harm."

He was a warrior, David saw, a Highlander likely, based on his accent and his clothes. At least he wasn't English, small mercy. David had fought for the Mackenzies and for his sister, and he fully supported Bruce's cause for independence. Most Highlanders did, too. That made the English David's enemy, at least in this time.

"Are ye a local?" the man asked.

"No. I'm on my way to Carlisle."

The man cocked his head and narrowed his eyes, assessing David.

"To Carlisle? Why?"

"I have business in the castle."

"What business?"

Slowly, being aware of the cool, sharp edge about to break his skin, David turned to look at the man. He was tall and muscular. Sharp bone structure, high cheekbones, dark shoulder-length hair framed his bearded face. Dark eyes under long and full eyebrows were narrowed at him, watching his every movement. A recent cut crossed his temple.

He was dressed in a tunic, and boiled leather armor—a cuirass—covered his chest. The armor was expensive for a Highlander, and the sword that threatened to kill David was a claymore.

"Just let me pass," David said. "I don't want trouble."

"Tell me what ye want in the castle, and I'll see if I let ye go."

David frowned. "What is the castle to you?"

"I want in."

"So we both want in," David said thoughtfully, and the two of them stared at each other. "But I'm guessing the English don't want you in, do they?"

The Highlander's nostrils flared quickly as he inhaled and pressed the blade deeper into David's skin.

"I know a way in," David said quickly. "A secret one."

The Highlander's eyes widened in surprise, but swiftly narrowed into a threatening glare. "If ye are trying to fool me—"

"I'm not. I'm telling the truth."

"He's a Mackenzie," came another voice from the right. "Look, Colum, there's a Mackenzie mountain in flames on the cross guard."

David slowly turned his head; another Highlander stood with his sword unsheathed. He was younger and leaner. Blond hair was wild around his face, and a short beard covered his chin.

"I am a Mackenzie," David said. He was already used to identifying himself as belonging to the clan, even if he didn't quite feel that he had the right to truly belong. "I'm the brother of Rogene Mackenzie, the laird's wife."

The sword in Colum's hand withdrew a bit, and the sharp ping at David's throat relaxed.

"Ye're Angus's brother-in-law?" Colum asked. "Why havena I met ye before?"

Relief eased the tension in David's chest. "I've been traveling for the past two years. You know my sister?"

"Aye, I had the privilege to meet Lady Rogene."

David's heart squeezed. "When did you see her?"

"One year past."

"And my nephew? Was he well?"

"Aye, the wee lad was strong and in a good health."

David couldn't stop the grin. "Good. Well, maybe you can lower your sword, then, Colum? And we can talk like friends."

Colum glanced at his companion.

"Come now, lower the sword," said the young Highlander. "MacDonalds and Mackenzies are friends."

So they were MacDonalds. David had seen some of them at the Highland games near Eilean Donan three years ago, but not Colum. He knew Mackenzies sold fleece through the vast trade network of the Lord of Islay. The clan was powerful and rich, their ships and their warriors fear-inducing.

"Dinna ye dare trust him, Colum," came another voice as a

third Highlander stepped from behind a tree. He was older than the first one and bald with a long beard, broad-shouldered and barrel-chested. "Mayhap he killed a Mackenzie and took his claymore. Anyone can say he's a brother of the laird's wife. The world is full of oath-breakers."

At the word "oath-breaker," Colum's face became a pale, stony mask. Slowly, Colum lowered his sword, his eyes like burning coals on the older man. "Ye have something to say, Marcas, say it."

In the three years that David had been living in the Highlands, he'd learned there was little that Highlanders valued more than honor and loyalty. An oath-breaker was a man who broke both. What had Colum done?

"Ye ken I have much to say to ye, pup. Ye ken I dinna trust ye and will never trust ye after ye broke yer oath to yer laird and to yer clan and took the English side."

The English side? David narrowed his eyes at Colum. He needed to be careful with someone who could switch to the enemy side and then back. Marcas had a point. Who knew what Colum was capable of and what side he really was on?

"Marcas—" the young Highlander said, but Colum took a step closer and raised his sword, pointing it at Marcas.

"Ye dinna ken what ye speak of," Colum said. "People make mistakes, and God kens I will be paying for this one for the rest of my life. I swore my allegiance to the King of Scots, and I will die serving my king, my clan, and Scotland."

Marcas spat on the ground, looking like he'd just smelled rotten fish. "I guess we will have to wait and see."

Colum shook his head. "Either ye trust me or ye dinna." He pointed with his sword to the south. "Because out there, when we're in the castle and there are only three of us and the enemy all around us, there will be nae time for doubt. We have to have each other's backs, and if ye dinna trust me to have yers, then how can we survive and rescue her?"

Marcas's face distorted in contempt, and he shook his head.

"This was a mistake. I shouldna have agreed to go into the midst of the enemy with an oath-breaker. I will tell the laird the mission has failed." He looked at the young Highlander. "Are ye coming, Iàcob?"

The blond Highlander looked between the two of them, blinking, then his eyes went hard. "Nae. I am staying with the lord. Everyone deserves a second chance, and ye canna leave the lass in peril."

The lass in peril... Was there a woman trapped in the castle?

"We wilna. Aulay and the Bruce will gather more troops fer a rescue. Going in with three men is a stupid plan, anyway."

"I am staying. If the plan works, I will have a chance to prove myself. If it doesna, I will die saving a lass, serving my clan and my country."

"Suit yerself." The older man threw a last, hard look at Colum and a menacing one at David and walked away. After a few minutes, the sound of a horse galloping into the distance.

David's stomach growled louder. He looked at the two men. "I'm not a robber, and I didn't kill anyone to get this sword. Angus gave it to me himself, along with Daisy, my horse, and this armor."

Colum and Iàcob exchanged a look and Colum put his sword back into the sheath on his belt. "Mayhap. Marcas is right nae to trust everyone, but we did just lose a man and ye said something about getting inside the castle. Tie yer horse here. We set camp, but horses canna reach it. Ye're hungry. We feed ye, we talk, and ye tell me what I need to ken."

Should David really be doing this? Did he even know what he was walking into? He missed Dùghlas. Two heads were better than one. Dùghlas would have probably told him not to go, to find an excuse to leave. What reason did he have to trust Colum and Iàcob if even their own man had just left?

But if they were breaking into the castle, to save a lass or whatever, they could work together to get in. David didn't need to trust them for the rest of his life, just one day. This could be his only chance to find the rock.

He just needed to be careful.

He nodded and tied Daisy by a juicy patch of grass, then followed Colum towards a hill that became a cliff. They climbed a narrow path, and it sharply turned in to a sort of a corridor that opened to a flat space hidden from the woods by rock formations and bushes that grew from the stone. There was a small cave, and in that cave a small campfire burned below a field cauldron. Something gurgled beyond the cave, and when David walked twenty or so steps to the right of the entrance, he saw a small waterfall that fed a thirty-foot-wide round pond, which fed a brook that disappeared into a slit between rocks.

"Good place for a camp," David said, his mind returning to the campfire and something delicious burbling in the cauldron.

"Aye," Colum said as he sat at the campfire and poured some pottage into a wooden bowl and handed it to David.

David curled one hand around the warm bowl and, like a true medieval man, half ate, half drank the thick soup that had the salty taste of smoked bacon and a few roughly cut root vegetables and wild mushrooms. The liquid spread warmth into his body. Colum handed him a piece of torn bread, and David soaked it in the pottage and ate, gathering the last bits of the soup.

They sat around the fire, the other men eating at a regular, nonstarving pace. The cave around them was probably ten feet high, and there was plenty of room for the smoke to leave the space. There were two sleeping rolls on the floor and a couple of canvas bags leaned against the rough granite walls. There was little to see in the darkness of the back.

When David finished, Colum offered him another bowl and he couldn't say no.

Finally, Colum set his own bowl aside and wiped his mouth with the back of his hand. "So, how did ye find out about the secret passage into the castle?"

David drank a mouthful of soup. "I met a man on the road who told me about it."

"And why did he tell ye that?"

David took another sip. "He owed me for the work I did on his farm. He knew I was looking for something that's in Carlisle Castle."

"What are ye looking for?" said Colum, narrowing his eyes at him.

His mind raced. He couldn't tell them about the rocks, but he needed to give some explanation for why he had to get into the castle. He chewed the last of the springy mushrooms.

"Treasure," he said. "The English took treasure that belongs to my clan. I am looking for it."

Colum's face changed into a grimace of disbelief. "Alone?"

David scoffed. "And you want to get a prisoner out with just the two of you?"

Colum exchanged a long look with Iàcob. "Fair enough. Only, there wilna be two of us nae more."

David knew it would be safer to enter enemy territory with a couple of Highland warriors at his side, but he was still not sure if he could trust them. "Maybe. Maybe not. Tell me first, who is the lass you are trying to break free?"

Colum poured water from his horn into a cup and handed it to David. David took it and drank. "If I tell ye, ye must ken 'tis a sign of significant trust. 'Tis a secret, only known to a close circle of people."

"I will keep this secret."

"'Tis my cousin, Anna," Colum said. "She's the daughter of my deceased aunt Julianna, who was supposed to marry Robert the Bruce nineteen years ago."

David felt his eyebrows crawl to his hair. "Is she Robert the Bruce's daughter?"

"Aye. Bastart daughter. My aunt and he never got a chance to wed, even though the intention and the agreement of the families was there. Julianna died shortly after the birth. Anna must wed the constable of Stirling Castle in sixteen days, on John the Baptist. Her wedding will ensure Philip hands the castle to the Bruce without a fight. She was kidnapped ten days ago by Dugald MacDowell, an old enemy of the Bruce. We are sure he did it for revenge. The king's men ravaged MacDowell's lands, Galloway, and forced him out because he had killed Robert's two brothers."

Through the years, between Rogene's teachings and news from the front, David had gotten a pretty good understanding of Scottish politics and knew which clans were pro-Bruce and which pro-England. "Right. MacDowells have always been on the English side."

"Aye. He wants to stop the wedding so that Bruce doesna get Stirling easily. But we must retrieve her. We must save her, Scotland, and our king."

David took a long sigh. The last thing he wanted was to get involved in the political games and wars of medieval people. He didn't wish Anna any harm, and he would be glad to help her, but his main focus was on finding his rock. Could he do both?

"As ye ken," Colum said, "my clan is rich. Ye will be paid handsomely in gold for yer help."

"Why was it just the three of you? Now two."

"Because Carlisle is very hard to take by force," said Ìacob. "Bruce tried a few moons ago, and didna succeed. Besieging it again would only leave his forces weaker. And he's already besieging Stirling. First plan is to sneak her out secretly, smartly, like true Highlanders. If it doesna work, my uncle Aulay, chief of clan, will bring a larger force against Carlisle and Bruce will help him. There is nae guarantee this will work, either. So. Will ye help us get into the castle and retrieve my cousin?"

David thought about the map of Scotland and how he had no other leads as to where the time traveling rocks could be. If this paid off and the rock in the dungeons sent him back to his own time, then all the rest wouldn't matter. And if it didn't work, he'd have a handsome sum of gold from the MacDonalds, which would help him with his search and allow him to keep moving rather than having to earn his coin offering labor.

"Yeah," he said. "I'm in. I'll help you get your princess."

And hopefully travel in time. Maybe he was becoming a true Highlander, because in his head he added, *or die trying.*

"Good," said Colum. "We move tonight. Now tell me about that way in."

CHAPTER 4

CARLISLE CASTLE, the same night

ANNA DIDN'T KNOW HOW MUCH TIME HAD PASSED.

Darkness had become her everything.

Darkness was her very blood, her very breath. Her very existence.

Darkness was her bed, her guard, and her nightmare. It smelled like an outhouse, it sounded like a scream, and it looked like death. It felt like cold, wet stone and tasted like mold.

When Dugald MacDowell and his band had brought her to Carlisle, she'd thought they'd put her into a dungeon.

They did worse.

Dugald had dragged her down the stairs, down the narrow corridor between a stone wall and a grid of iron bars with several dungeon chambers. But he opened none of the iron doors. Fire kept jumping off the rough stone walls, off the iron bars like the spirits of those who'd died here long ago. She kept trying to free her hand, but he was too strong, and she was too hungry and thirsty and weak.

Then, at the end of the corridor, he opened a heavy door, and inside was a small, round room. He dragged her to a hole in the floor at its center. Cold death breathed at her from its endless nothing. Guards brought torches, and they spilled orange light on the stone floor and walls that came together above their heads in a round ceiling.

But the only spot in the room where light didn't reach was the hole. Like an entrance into another world.

The world of nightmares.

There was a mechanism over the hole, like that above a well, with a pulley and a thick chain with a hook at its end.

"What—" she had started, but it was quite clear what it was.

"An oubliette, lass," Dugald had said. "The only way out is death."

She had heard of oubliettes. An invention of Normans, it was a place cut out deep in the rock. A place where prisoners were put and forgotten. The French word "*oublier*" meant "forget."

No one came out of there alive.

As they pushed her towards the small hole, she kept fighting, futile of course. Then, holding on to the chain, she'd been lowered into a tomb that smelled like decay and madness.

Since then, she'd seen light only a handful of times. High above her, a circle of orange and gold appeared, hurting her eyes, and bread and water were lowered down to her in a bucket. The screeching of the chain was like a song of freedom. The only connection to the world of the living.

At first, she held on to her pride. She was the daughter of a king, after all. A MacDonald, her ancestors were Scottish and Viking warriors. She drew strength from them, invisible and yet always present in her blood. She wouldn't beg. She wouldn't scream and she wouldn't show her enemies a crack of weakness.

Looking for a way out, she felt the walls around her over and over, spinning in endless circles. Holding on to a drop of hope, she scratched them; her fingernails broke and she sucked on her salty blood. Her world was endless, and yet it was only a pocket made of stone.

There was no blanket, no bed, and no chair. Shivering, she lay on the hard, cold, wet rock, praying. Praying for her father and her clan to come for her.

Then praying to keep her pride and to not scream.

Then praying for death.

Dark madness seeped inside her drop by drop, breath by breath. She fought it with all she had left. Her memories. All the light she could get was in her mind.

What could she hold on to? What were the best moments of her life? Swimming in the sea—before she'd almost drowned and couldn't even think about putting a foot into it. Meeting her father. The freedom of running around with the children of Islay, feeling the wind in her hair and the rare Scottish sun kissing her cheeks. Inhaling the air full of the scents of the sea, and heather, and moss. Clan gatherings in the great hall of Finlaggan Castle, where everyone knew each other. Private jokes. Old Celtic songs. Her uncle Aulay telling stories. MacDonald traders talking of faraway lands—of Galicia and the caliphate and Norway, of Flanders and the Baltics and France. Minstrels, singing stories of King Arthur and Lancelot, of Tristan and Isolde.

But through that, always, she'd been waiting. Waiting for her father to ask her to come. Waiting for her life to begin.

Had she lived at all?

Her life may be over before it truly began. She'd been a lady, saved herself for marriage. She'd given up things that brought her joy. She'd left her family behind to marry a man she'd never met to make her father proud.

And for what? To end up a prisoner, to die in an endless stone jail that smelled of her own excrement and felt like a grave?

Why hadn't she allowed herself to be free? There was that lad on Islay who had fancied her and tried to kiss her once. She should have let him. She'd die a virgin and would never know a man's lips on hers. She'd never love like those heroines of great legends loved. She'd never know the joy of growing a life inside her and holding her bairn in her arms.

A sudden light made her eyes hurt, but she kept them open, struggling to see. They came from some symbols on the floor, glowing blue and brown. Strangely, the air filled with the scent of lavender and grass, freshly cut.

No doubt she had gone insane. But she still had to see what was going on.

The glow shed light on a woman in a green cloak with long red hair.

That was it. Madness must have swallowed Anna's mind.

The woman's face was barely visible in the dim glow. She smiled. "Dinna be afraid, lass. Hold on to yer hope. Someone is coming for ye. David, a man from another time. He'll be yer protector. And ye will need to protect him also."

Anna was losing her mind, but even the presence of her hallucination was a comfort. She wasn't alone. She could talk to someone.

"Who are ye?" Anna asked. "Are ye a saint?"

The woman giggled. "I'm nae saint, lass. My name is Sìneag, and I open a tunnel through the river of time and let people pass."

The river of time? Let people pass? Anna had never heard of such a thing. She was definitely going mad.

Sìneag continued. "I wish I could let ye pass through the stone and escape yer prison, but yer one true love is already coming for ye. He's coming."

Then she was gone. The glow faded, leaving the symbols of a wave and a circle with a straight line through it burned in Anna's mind like scars. She was shaking, looking around.

"Sìneag!" she called. "Sìneag! Please, don't go! Please…"

Then there was a sound. The screech of the door and voices and the circle of light appeared high above her. A torch and someone's head, dark against the light.

"Are ye still alive?" It was Dugald MacDowell's voice.

"Go to hell!" she screamed.

He laughed. The metallic clanking of the chain followed, and the bucket was lowered to her. "Yer last meal, lass. I shouldna bother with ye nae more. Bruce wilna be king for much longer. A ship is sent to Ireland full of gold and armor and weapons to restart an invasion on Bruce while he's busy playing sieges."

She barely registered that as the bucket clunked against the floor and she threw herself on it, wild with hunger and thirst, hands searching for the bread and the water that must be inside.

As she shoved the stale, moldy bread into her mouth, the world became dark again. This was the last bread she'd ever have. With darkness came despair. Her stupid mind was going insane, sending her futile hope for a rescue.

Her soul was shrinking, corrupted and dying. Dugald's torture was working.

Worst was, with every moment she passed here her father needed her less and less. She was only worth something to him if she could marry Philip. So what would be the point of being alive and being rescued if he didn't need her anymore?

It would be too late once the wedding date passed and the most important castle of Scotland remained in England's possession, making their victory a terrifying reality.

CARLISLE CASTLE, THE SAME NIGHT

"WELL, DAVID OF CLAN MACKENZIE," WHISPERED COLUM behind David's back. "Where is that way up ye talked about?"

David's real last name was Wakeley, but he was used to the shield of the Mackenzie name that he'd adopted three years ago.

Iàcob hemmed and scratched his chin. The moon peeked out from behind a cloud and spilled silvery light onto the wall. Their horses were hidden, tied behind a bush twenty feet or so away.

The town of Carlisle behind them slept. Padean had told him it was on the northwestern side of the curtain wall. He'd said the stones stood out a little bit and formed some sort of...

Steps. He saw them.

"It's a stairway," David whispered, watching the pattern in the wall. "Do you both see, the stones protrude out a bit—not much, but just enough to be able to very carefully step on them."

"Aye," Colum said. "But they're tiny."

"Aye," echoed Iàcob. "They may support my weight, but Colum's...and yers..."

David looked up. Twenty feet up, fire from what must be a torch moved. Three or four male voices sounded, then a laugh.

"Sentinels," whispered Colum.

An owl hooted in a small grove to their right. The town lay about three hundred yards away, its roofs black against the sky. Several church towers loomed over the town. A dog barked and a woman's voice shouted an angry tirade. The air was sweet with woodsmoke, cow dung, flowers, and plants in bloom. It was a good night, not too dark and not too light. All conditions were perfect for their mission.

Whether they would find Anna and whether David would find Sìneag's stone was another question.

The voices from above grew quieter and moved into the distance.

"They are gone," Colum said. "Let us go."

David nodded. With his stomach plastered to the wall, he stepped on the first stone. Slowly, he moved higher, rock by rock. The rough stone scratched his cheek, the scent of dust in his nostrils. His fingers hurt from trying to grab on to each step but finding little purchase. He looked back and Colum followed him, struggling as much. Iàcob came after.

Dry mortar and crumbled rock fell from under his fingers, skittering into the darkness. With nothing to hold on to, he could rely only on his balance and his legs to keep him from following the rocks. The higher he went, the weaker his knees felt.

Don't look down.

He kept going.

When he reached the parapet, he stopped and peered over its edge. The sentinels with torches were about fifty feet down the wall. He climbed one more step, jumped over the parapet, and crouched. A few moments later, shoes rustled behind him, and as he turned his head, Colum and Iàcob landed, too.

Behind them, there was an exit with the ramparts leading down into the inner bailey.

"Let's go," said David, pointing.

But Colum's eyes were on the torches. "Nae. We must kill them or they may see us."

"Ye dinna have to *kill* the English to prove yer loyalty," said Iàcob. "The way down is free."

Sorrow flashed for a moment in Colum's eyes and, once again, David wondered what had happened to him. If David found the rock in the castle, he may never know.

"Aye," said Colum. "Let's go."

They crossed the wall path and climbed down, silent as night. It was quiet in the inner bailey. No one was there, among the timber buildings with thatched roofs. Keeping to the buildings, they made their way from house to house until they reached the main keep, a square, three-floor tower.

"Let's go to the dungeons," David suggested as the three of them eyed the single heavy door.

The dungeon was where Padean had told him he'd seen the rock and likely where they'd find a prisoner, as well. The men nodded. Colum listened by the door, then slowly opened it. Typical of main keeps, the first floor was essentially a storage room with weapons, firewood, and food. In the corner was a staircase leading down.

They hurried as silently as they could. As Colum opened the door at the end of the flight of stairs, David saw two guards sitting around a small, round table. One of them had his chin on his chest, and the other one's head was leaning against the wall. Both were snoring.

David had expected to fight, but these two were sleeping. Like two dark shadows, the Highlanders came from behind him and, without a word, cut the throats of the guards. Used to violence in the Middle Ages, David still watched in shock as life pumped out of the guards in dark gushes.

With his sword out, darkened by blood, Colum walked to the next door. "Come on, Mackenzie. We're lucky to be alive by now."

The next room was a dungeon. A long corridor held a row of cells behind iron bars to the left. All appeared empty. While Colum went ahead with a torch, David took another torch and walked into the first cell, carefully lighting the floor.

Nothing. Just a smooth, dusty floor with no flat rocks and no carvings and no handprints. David stood looking helplessly around him in the empty cell.

"What are ye waiting for?" said Iàcob behind him. "She isna here. Hurry."

The screech of metal hinges down the corridor told David Colum must have reached another door. Colum checked the rest of the five cells one by one. None of them had the rock. With a sinking feeling of failure, David hurried after them.

They walked into a strange empty room with a round hole in the middle of the floor and something that looked like a well mechanism. Colum was leaning over the hole with his torch.

"Anna?" he called.

"Aye, I am here," came a weak female voice. "Who is there?"

She was down there, in a hole, with no way out. He looked down there, too, and it must have been ten feet down that he saw a female face peering at them. The stench of death and feces made bile rise in his stomach. What kind of animals would do that to a human being?

"'Tis Colum. We came to get ye out of here."

"Let me get her," said David. "I have been told about the oubliette."

He still hadn't found the stone; he hadn't found his way out. Padean may have lied to him, but he didn't think so. The place where nightmares are born, he remembered Peigi's words. If the stone was anywhere in the castle, it must be down there.

"There's no time to think it over, Colum," David said sternly. "Lower me."

"Aye," Colum said through gritted teeth.

David held on to the chain and Colum lowered him down. The screeching of the chain was like the call of a gargoyle for the master of darkness.

His torch attached to the chain above him, he plunged lower and lower into a prison of stone. Anna clung to the wall and shielded her eyes against the light, blocking his view of her face. She was a small, thin figure with dark hair in a mass of filthy knots.

When his feet landed on a smooth rock and he looked down, the floor seemed to tilt under him.

He was standing on the time traveling rock. Frantically, he looked around, moving the chain with the firelight. "Sìneag! Sìneag!"

"What are ye doing, man?" hissed Colum from above. "Take Anna and get the hell out of there."

He was shaking. What were the chances Colum's mission and his own would lead to one place, the oubliette.

"Sìneag!" he cried.

There was the handprint, and he sank to his knees and slammed his hand into it. Nothing happened. With desperation eating his heart, he slammed it again. And again. And again. His palm stung and burned.

"What are ye doing?" called Iàcob.

"Are ye David?" Anna asked.

He looked up at her. She wasn't shielding her face anymore, but looking at him with big, dark eyes. Under the smudges of dirt and grime, her features were sharp and elegant, like a fox's. Large, slightly slanted eyes with long eyelashes were open wide, in shock or in fear. She had full lips and a sensual mouth. High cheekbones protruded from under her pale skin, and her thin nose was turned up slightly at the tip, just enough to give the impression of an innocent girl.

He stood up, the turmoil in his chest raging between yet another disappointment and feeling sorry for her. And he was embarrassed he'd been screaming like an idiot when this girl clearly had been traumatized, mistreated, and hurt.

He looked at the rock for the last time. It wasn't his chance this time. Then he stretched out his hand to her. "I'm David. Come with me, we must hurry."

Anna grinned the most gorgeous smile and came to him. "David?" she asked with a chuckle.

As he wrapped his hand around her thin waist, he frowned. "Yes, David. How did you know that, by the way?"

Holding her tightly, he grabbed the chain with his other hand. She wrapped her arms around his neck. As Colum raised the chain up, Anna repeated "David?" and laughed.

And laughed.

And laughed.

It was a hysterical laughter. Insane. She sounded like a madwoman. Through the giggles, she was saying something about the river of time and Sìneag, and she kept laughing, snorting, crying.

With every word that came out of her mouth like sobs, "David... River of time... Tunnel... Sìneag..." frost formed around David's vertebrae.

"What do you mean?" he kept asking.

But she didn't reply. The girl had probably lost her mind after ten days in the oubliette. When he and she stood on the floor of the room, Colum briefly hugged her and pressed his hand against her mouth to shut her up. Surprisingly, she did. Only, as she looked around, a haze clouded her eyes, and it was as though the life had been blown out of her. She began shaking and almost fell, but David picked her up.

"We must run," Colum said.

David nodded, hauled her over his shoulder, and with swords unsheathed, they ran through the corridor and up the stairs and from building to building of the inner bailey. By some miracle, they managed to get to the gates and open them and run to their horses.

But as they reached their horses, their luck ran out.

"Stop!" someone cried from above. David boosted Anna into a sitting position on his horse and climbed up behind her. Once Colum and Iàcob had climbed onto their own horses, they galloped.

More angry yells and cries followed, and David looked back. Not thirty feet away, at least ten horsemen pursued them, death in their eyes.

CHAPTER 5

THEY GALLOPED through the dark town, winding through narrow streets. Anna was like a limp sack of potatoes in front of him, but at least she was alive.

He forced himself to stop wondering how she knew about Sìneag, and what chance there was that he'd been sent to rescue a princess who sat right on top of one of the time travel rocks.

And that the way home for him was still closed.

He needed to stop thinking about that. It was all about survival now. About escaping the enemy and saving the girl.

As they galloped into a small square, horsemen spilled into it from all four directions, blocking any way out. One- and two-story timber-framed houses surrounded them. David's, Colum's, and Ìacob's horses crowded together in the center and a dozen warriors surrounded them, going in circles. Based on the red surcoats with three golden lions, they were English. More men must have been sent to cut them off, to trap them neatly in this exact spot. His palms covered in icy, slick sweat. The warriors all unsheathed their swords, and David did so, too, although he held Daisy's reins with one hand, his arm encircling Anna.

Colum, never taking his eyes off the Englishmen, leaned closer to David. "Ìacob and I will give ye an opening. Ride for yer life, for the life of my cousin and for Scotland, do ye hear me? Ride to where we met and wait for us."

"I will."

"If we dinna arrive by morning, ye must take Anna to Bruce. To Stirling."

"No! I can't take her—"

"Promise me. If we dinna come by the morn, take her to Stirling!"

"Colum, I'm not a knight in shining armor. I need to keep looking for the—"

"Give me yer word!"

She was lifeless against his chest. What chance did he even stand, alone, with a girl who was so shaken she couldn't move?

Any chance he could give her. He couldn't just leave her unprotected in a dangerous medieval world. "Okay. You have my word."

What had he gotten himself into?

At a sudden cry from the surrounding horsemen, the enemy attacked. The little square filled with the sound of metal screeching against metal, horses' hooves on stone, men yelling and grunting.

David maneuvered as best he could, shielding Anna from the warriors. It was hard to wield his sword when he couldn't use the left side of his body and his legs, but he managed to wound one warrior, then another.

"Be ready!" yelled Colum.

There were seven horsemen left, and Colum and Iàcob kept fighting. But more hooves sounded in the distance. They had to get out of here.

Colum spurred his horse towards three horsemen, yelling a war cry. The horses snorted in fear and backed away, opening a street.

Opening an exit.

"Now!" yelled Colum, attacking the next horseman with his sword.

Steel glistened in the moonlight as David called, "Hya, Daisy!" He dug his heels into her sides, and she launched. He had to grip the reins and work his legs hard to keep himself and Anna from flying off.

Colum's and Ìacob's horses followed him. They rode hard, zigzagging between narrow streets full of stone- and timber-framed houses.

"Split now!" yelled Colum behind him. David turned Daisy to gallop to the right, and he heard Colum's horse ride away. When he looked back, the street was empty.

He rode in the direction of the city gate. A few more long minutes passed, where his heart and Daisy's drumming hooves were all he could hear. As the gate came into sight, he heard hoofbeats behind him. Men screamed for him to stop. Arrows flew.

"Close the gate!" came the cries.

The huge, heavy doors of the gate started to close, and he spurred Daisy on.

"Come on, girl! Come on!" he yelled, digging his heels into her sides.

They flew through the narrowing gap, and the doors shut behind them with a clang.

He kept spurring Daisy forward, his lungs burning. He couldn't feel his hand that held Anna anymore. Her hair was in his face, tickling him. The moon came out and illuminated the field between the woods and Carlisle. He looked over his shoulder.

Riders. At least a dozen of them. They were several yards behind, thanks to having to reopen the gate, but they were gaining on him.

A few excruciating minutes later, he and Anna and Daisy flew into the blissful darkness of the woods. His ears were ringing, full of the rumble of the hooves, the rustle of the trees, and his own heavy breathing.

He reined Daisy in a different direction, hoping to lose their followers in the trees. After some time, he could hear nothing but the soft night sounds of the forest—owls hooting, small animals burrowing in the leaves. Finally, they arrived at the gathering of bushes and boulders where their little camp was.

They would wait at the cave, as agreed. Colum and Ìacob could have escaped when the gate was reopened. They could still find their way back here.

He dismounted and, holding Anna in place on his horse's back, hid Daisy in a small grove surrounded by bushes and let her graze. Once the horse was tethered, he helped Anna dismount, as well. The arm he'd held her with tingled and he shook it to let blood flow again. Anna blinked, frowned, and looked at him lucidly for the first time.

Then she opened her mouth and screamed. Her shrill yell pierced the air like a siren.

David lurched to her and covered her mouth with one hand, the other arm holding her tightly.

"Shh!" he hissed, but she kept fighting, wriggling, kicking, and trying to bite his fingers. "I'm David. I'm with Colum, your cousin. I saved you, remember?"

She bit him and he yelled and weakened his grip. She wriggled free like a fish and ran.

"Fuck!" he cursed and lunged after her.

He caught her after a few steps and fell with her to the ground, pinning her under him. She screamed again, and he clamped his hand over her mouth.

And then he heard them. The hooves.

The English...or the MacDowells...

The enemy.

"Not a sound," he told her as he dragged her into a two-foot-deep gully under the roots of a tree.

He lay on top of her to shield her from the enemy. She watched him with wide, frightened eyes, and he couldn't breathe. The sounds of the hooves of several horsemen sounded right above them.

She was so beautiful, her eyes big and long-lashed, and almost translucent. She was breathing hard under him; he felt her chest rising and falling quickly.

The hooves slowly faded into the distance, and after a few moments, David knew they were alone again.

"If I remove my hand," he whispered, "will you promise not to fucking scream? I'm on your side. I'm the one who rescued you, remember? I'm the one Colum asked to bring you to safety."

She nodded. He nodded, too, and let go of her mouth. She didn't scream, just stared at him like a frightened animal.

"Okay," he said. "Good."

He sat up and let go of her completely. Slowly, she sat up, too, still staring at him.

"Are you all right?" he asked. "Can you walk? Or ride?"

She cleared her throat. "Aye."

"Good. Then there's a hiding place nearby. I'm supposed to take you there to wait for Colum and Ìacob. Come on."

He stood and stretched out his hand to her. She took it, reluctantly, and they walked to the cave, which was about a hundred feet away. Her hand was trembling, and he squeezed it reassuringly.

With a bitter taste in his mouth, he watched Anna's proud profile. Despite having been kidnapped, despite having been imprisoned in darkness and isolation, her back was straight and her head was held high.

He liked her.

Of course he liked her. Right, Sìneag? Why else had he found her on top of a time traveling rock, blabbering about Sìneag and the river of time?

Why else was he stuck with this pretty princess, with no way to return to his own time?

CHAPTER 6

ANNA HUGGED her knees in front of the fire. She couldn't stop the tremors that racked her body. The cave around her was the echo of the stone coffin she'd spent an eternity in, and only firelight chased the darkness away.

She supposed David thought it was quiet. But to Anna, everything around her was alive with sound. The murmur of leaves in the wind, the distant snapping of twigs, mosquitoes buzzing, owls hooting, hedgehogs rustling about. Somewhere very far away, a deer bellowed a mating call, sounding like a creature from another world.

It was both scary and reassuring. Hearing all that meant she wasn't in the oubliette anymore. She was free.

But after days of complete silence, the gurgling of the waterfall outside of the cave and the water starting to boil in the cauldron scraped against her senses like laundry against a rock.

David, her savior, sat a step away, his gaze wandering between the fire, her, and the darkness beyond the mouth of the cave. He had descended into the oubliette like an angel casting light into darkness, and from then on everything was a blur. It was as though her sanity had finally snapped and broken. Or what was left of it, especially after her vision of Sìneag.

What had she told Anna? Her one true love was coming for her. No, surely not. That was such an odd thing to say in an oubliette, down in the belly of solid rock. And there was no way anyone could have been down there with her. She must have imagined it. Was she still having visions now? She'd never seen David before in her life and had never heard of him.

"Who are ye?" she asked.

He looked sharply at her. "David. I told you. Don't you remember?"

If Sìneag was only a vision, how had Anna known his name before they met?

"Aye. Ye did. I am nae always sure anymore what was real and what wasna. Where do ye come from, David?"

A cringe she barely caught crossed his face as he looked away. "I'm with clan Mackenzie. My sister is the laird's wife."

"Oh. Yer accent... I've never heard it before. Is that a Mackenzie accent?"

His square jaw worked under his short beard. For the first time, she noticed he was handsome. Very handsome, actually. Straight, chiseled features, warm brown eyes, dark-blond hair in waves to his shoulders. He was tall and muscular and broad. His arms and shoulders were huge under his tunic, and his muscles moved as he fingered a twig in his hands.

"No, it's not a Mackenzie accent."

"Then where is it from?"

He cocked his head at her. "Is this an interrogation? How is my accent relevant? I just saved you from a torture chamber and from a chase, risking my own life and my own...goals. How about a thank you?"

The outburst was odd and not very chivalrous, but it did the opposite of what he had intended. He didn't intimidate her, and he didn't make her shrink and tremble in gratitude.

She straightened her back. "If I was such a nuisance to yer goals, I imagine there is something ye are getting in return for helping my clan, are ye nae?"

He sighed and looked into the fire again. "Yes. But I didn't sign up to bring you all the way to Stirling."

Stirling... Where her father and her future husband waited for her. Where she was now free to go. She'd do anything for her father.

"How long until John the Baptist?" she asked.

His eyes softened. "Sixteen days."

She was supposed to meet her betrothed one week before the wedding in a secret feast. If she didn't show up by then, Philip would become worried and might rethink the whole deal with her father.

She nodded. "How long from here to Stirling?"

"It should be about a hundred miles," he murmured thoughtfully, looking into space. "So, five...six days on horseback."

When he looked at her again, warmth washed over her. She realized she wasn't shaking anymore. A warm, calm feeling radiated through her. She nodded and unhooked her arms from her knees and tucked her legs under her.

There was enough time. Hope bloomed in her chest. Plenty of time to make it to Stirling. Still, it didn't mean she could relax and rest. The enemy was still out there, searching for her. "We should leave right away in the morning."

"We?" He cocked his eyebrow. "I am waiting for Colum and Iàcob to arrive by the morning. Then you can leave with them."

"Ye're right," she said and threw a twig into the fire. "'Tis best for me to wait for my clansmen. I dinna ken ye at all."

Handsome or not, she couldn't trust him yet, not fully. If life had taught her anything in the past few days, it was that enemies could be anywhere.

"Yes, ma'am," David said and looked into the cauldron. "Water is boiling. You still hungry? You should eat something warm." He pulled three parsnips, dry fish, and a small sack of oats out of a travel sack. "How are you feeling?"

His care for her warmed her and brought color and heat to her cheeks. She reached out and took the oats, pouring some into the cauldron. The scent of them, even dry oats, made her stomach growl. Even though she'd eaten the moldy bread earlier, after days in the oubliette, she could eat a cow.

"I'm all right, I thank ye," she said. "I wouldna mind more to eat, aye."

David took out a field knife and began peeling the parsnips. Anna threw dry fish into the cauldron and the sharp scent of the sea steamed out at her. Just like back on Islay. Nostalgia stung her like a needle. She was far away from home, in the place where she'd been waiting for her life to begin.

Had it? Certainly not in the way she'd imagined.

David peeled a long strand of parsnip skin off and looked at her. "Are you really Robert the Bruce's daughter?"

She frowned. "Aye. Of course I'm really his daughter. Didna ye ken?"

His gaze slowly went up and down her body. "Yeah, I did. I guess I just didn't give it much thought that I've been in the presence of a princess all this time."

Something playful danced in his eyes, and the ice in her bones began thawing.

"I'm nae really a princess," she said. "I'm a bastart, as ye must ken, too. My father has a legitimate daughter, Marjorie. She's the princess."

"You're still a princess to me," he said with a grin and peeled off another strand.

For the first time in what felt like forever, a lightness soared in her chest and the corners of her mouth crawled into a small smile. Who was this man? His manners, his voice, his accent were so different from anyone she'd ever met in her life. She hadn't traveled much, but she had seen and met people from different corners of the world through the trade network of clan MacDonald.

And yet, never in her life had she met anyone like him. And no one ever said to her she was a princess. To everyone, she was a bastard. A royal bastard from the age of twelve. But still, a bastard. Some looked at her like she were a dirty rag. Some looked at her like she didn't exist.

No one said she was a princess.

David finished peeling one parsnip and threw it into the boiling water. "Do you love your fiancé?"

She shifted, took a twig, and started drawing something in the dust on the floor. "I havena met him yet." She watched as David's hands moved slower. His gaze was dark and heavy on her. "My king needs me to do my duty for him and for my country. Love doesna matter."

David gave a quick nod and peeled faster. "You're right. It doesn't matter for me, either. I'm not looking for it."

His voice was odd, distant, and low.

"What are ye looking for?" she asked.

He threw the parsnip into the water and met her gaze. It was hard and direct and full of resolve. "For a way out. To go where I can be proud of myself. Where I can be myself."

Anna blinked. She knew what it was like to push the true self down and away.

He picked up the last parsnip and drew his knife under the skin and pulled, watching the pale strip separate. "You've been in captivity for a few days. I've been in captivity for years. And I'm still living in it. And all I want is a way out."

Something about it rang a tune in her very soul. "What does that mean, David? I dinna see ye in shackles. How are ye in captivity?"

He shook his head and looked down at the parsnip. "You wouldn't understand. You were born here, and this is all the life you know. You're at home here. I'll never be."

He threw the last parsnip into the cauldron, picked up another, smaller cauldron, and stood. "I'll get some water from the waterfall to boil, for drinking."

As Anna watched his tall, strong frame disappear behind the corner of the mouth of the cave, she frowned. He was wrong that she didn't understand him. Being a bastard, she hadn't felt at home one day in her life. She'd always needed to make an effort for people to love her and accept her. Love from her clan was never a given.

It was conditional.

And she didn't even know if Robert the Bruce really wanted *her*, or if she was just a pawn in his political games.

Even though she hoped he would love her for herself, she suspected it was the latter, and yet she was ready to do anything for him.

What else could a bastard do?

CHAPTER 7

AFTER THEY'D EATEN, Anna went to the pond to wash. Moonlight sparkled in the waterfall like stars. A cake of soap David had given her in one hand and what he had called a toothbrush in the other, she stood, listening to the gurgling water and breathing the air. The griminess and the dirt were like a sickness on her skin, the smell of her own excrement still lingered on her dress, and she shook herself into action, eager to feel clean.

She took her rich, red dress off. The warm June breeze tickled her through her white linen shift, and she rejoiced in feeling the wind. Wind was freedom.

She took off her shoes and undid the lace garters that held her hose under her knees and removed them. The grass, stones, and a few twigs were sharp and yet pleasing against her bare feet.

She knelt before the pool and soaked her hose and her dress in it, watching the dark fabric thicken and sink. She foamed David's soap, inhaling the pleasant scent. What kind of a traveler bothered to have soap with him? And an expensive one, clearly imported from Galicia or France. It smelled like heather and something else, something herbal and sweet. She rubbed the soap against the fabric and ground the dress against a rock at the edge of the pool.

What did she really know about David? Where was he going, what was that way out he was seeking? How had he come to find her cousin and Iàcob? What was it that they had promised him for helping them rescue her from the castle?

Soon, she finished with her dress, twisted water out of the heavy fabric as best she could, and hung it on the branches of a bush growing by the water. Then she did the same with the pair of hose. She looked back at the cave. She knew David wouldn't come out as she'd told him she'd wash herself.

But still, there was something exciting about knowing that all that would separate them would be just a few steps from the cave to the pool of water.

To keep something dry, she decided to wash her undertunic later when her dress was dry. It wasn't as soiled as her dress, but her body needed to be washed.

She dragged her shift over her head and laid it on the ground. Goose bumps covered her bare skin, but she stood and breathed, absorbing the feel of crisp air on her flesh. With the cake of soap in her hand, she went into the water to her waist. It was cold, but not as cold as the sea at Islay, and the sharp coolness and the soft mud of the bottom were welcome against her aching body.

The last time she'd swum in the sea was seven years ago, the day she'd met her father. Busy with the education of a noble lady and terrified the sea would try to kill her again, she didn't dare. But she was safe here—rock surrounded the pool on all sides and there was no strong current.

Pouring water over her shoulders and back felt divine. As she slid the cake of soap along her skin, the flower-scented lather washed the nightmares away together with the dirt and the grime. She cleaned her hair, pulling knots apart with her soapy fingers as best she could and scrubbing her scalp.

She could breathe again. Dipping into the water was like coming back home to her true self and putting back the broken pieces of her soul.

There was a sudden rustle of branches, and Anna yelped. Her

head turned to the bushes and undergrowth that grew around the entrance to the pond, by the rocks.

In a moment, David ran out of the cave with his sword drawn.

From the bushes, a squirrel appeared and ran, crossing the open ground between the boulders like a furry lightning bolt.

David's eyes fell on her. She was standing in the water, naked, her hair clinging to her like a second skin. The moon came out and water shimmered in her hair and on her breasts.

Eyes dark, mouth open, David stared at her like a wolf scenting a deer.

"You look like a sea goddess," he murmured.

She should cover herself. She should tell him to stop staring and to go away. But she was not ashamed to be naked before him. In fact, she felt warmer and warmer, as though he'd set an oven ablaze within her. The pure lust and adoration in his eyes made her skin tingle. His sword was drawn for her, to protect her.

Her protector... Something melted deep within her, and an invisible force pulled her to him. She knew a proper lady should be ashamed. But she ached to be near him, skin to skin, breath to breath, heartbeat to heartbeat.

Not long ago, she'd felt her life was over before it had begun. Now there was a glorious warrior with a strange accent and muscles like stones. A warrior who had rescued her. And, based on a large bulge between his legs, he wanted her.

She was alive, and she could have him. She could give in to temptation and experience life before it ended.

She could tell him to remove his clothes and join her. She could glide her palms over his hard chest, over his corded arms that had held her so tightly and kept her safe.

A strong gust of wind rustled the bushes. She shivered, and the moment was swept away like a cloud of smoke.

David shook his head and turned around. "Get dressed."

She didn't move. "David..."

"Get dressed," he barked. "My body may enjoy what I see, but I'd never be interested in you."

Rejection stung. He'd never be interested in her? He was a fool. No, not him. She was a fool.

She marched through the water, splashes resounding. "Go to hell."

She stepped onto the shore, shoved his damned soap and his damned toothbrush into his hand. She picked up her shift and forced it over her head. It clung to her wet skin and was still smelly, but she didn't care.

"Ye're delusional, David," she whispered angrily. "'Tis me who will never be interested in ye. I'm engaged to an important man, while I dinna even ken who ye truly are." She thrust her feet into her shoes and picked up her wet dress and her pair of hose. "Something is very odd about ye, and 'tis just a matter of time before I find out what 'tis."

His eyes darkened with hurt. She didn't care. His rejection still burned. He'd just called her a sea goddess and then he said he wasn't interested? He was a fool. She pointed her finger at him. "Actually, I dinna even need ye to protect me. I ken how to fight, I'm a MacDonald. 'Tis one advantage of growing up as someone who isna important—ye can do anything ye want. I wanted to learn to fight like a lad."

She marched into the cave and stretched her dress on a boulder next to the fire, then her stockings. As she did, she heard David come in and put his sword back into the sheath.

"My aunt Leitis was like a mother to me," she said as she poured hot water into a bowl and sat by the fire with her hands curled around it. "My uncle Aulay, the laird, was like a father. They gave me as much love as they could, given I wasna theirs. But they also didna think I needed to be brought up as a lady. Nae as strictly as my cousin. So I had freedom. I ken how to swim, how to fight with swords and shoot an arrow."

"Good. But that's not enough to make it to Stirling alone," said David.

"I ken many things, more than ye imagine. The only thing I dinna ken is the way to Stirling. And when Colum comes, I wilna need ye, anyway."

Colum... Oh God. Where was he? With every moment that passed, it was harder to imagine he was alive... A shiver of worry washed over her. Using a cup, she scooped some warm water from the cauldron and drank it. The warmth settled pleasantly in her stomach. As she looked at David over her steaming cup, she thought she saw hurt in his eyes.

But he quickly hid it behind a grim look.

CHAPTER 8

"You should sleep," David said as he stood up and walked to the mouth of the cave, looking into the darkness. They had eaten and Anna had warmed up, so David let the last fire die, not wanting to attract any more attention than necessary.

The night was quiet. The moon hung low before it hid behind the cave. It must be around 2 or 3 a.m., David estimated. "The sun will rise in a few hours."

She was in her ankle-length shift, grayish and brown in places. She was so thin, with her cheeks hollowed out and dark circles under her eyes. He clenched his fists at the thought of how little her captors must have fed her, how hungry she must have been all that time. Her long hair was clean now and still wet, and her face, no longer grimy, was beautiful, her skin translucent.

The image of her, naked and wet and shimmering in the moonlight, like a sleek Celtic goddess of the sea, had been burned into his mind forever. Her perfect small, round breasts with nipples that were dark pink and puckered from the cold. The curve of her narrow waist flowing into rounded hips, the shallow belly button on a too-flat stomach.

God, he wanted her. He felt the stirrings of desire even now.

At twenty-one, he was still a virgin. Would she laugh at him if he told her?

"I'll keep watch," he told her, swallowing hard, then walked to his things and found his bedroll.

She watched him undo the straps and roll out a stag skin for her by the dead campfire, then unroll a thick, wool blanket and hand it to her. The stag had been killed by Angus and the blanket knitted by Rogene for him, their blessing for his journey two years ago. The stag skin kept the wool dry and provided insulation for sleeping on the ground.

Anna took the blanket and murmured a thank you without looking at him. She looked sheepish. Perhaps she was sorry for saying *I wilna need ye, anyway*.

She sure needed him now. But he didn't blame her. He had been ogling her when he should have turned away and given her privacy. He just couldn't stop looking. She must be the most beautiful girl he'd ever seen. And telling her he would never be interested was the biggest lie of his life. She had no idea how close he had been to ripping his clothes off and running through the water to her.

Anna wrapped herself in the blanket and lay on the stag skin on her side. She closed her eyes, and he had an odd longing to be that fabric, to wrap himself around her and keep her warm. She tucked one arm under her head and cuddled into the blanket deeper. He sat by her side, facing the mouth of the cave, watching and listening.

He hoped she would get some rest, but she kept rustling, shifting her legs, moving. Then shaking. When she began whimpering and grimacing, as though in pain, he shifted to her. "Anna, are you all right?"

She opened her eyes and looked around. "I canna sleep."

"You're safe. I'll keep you safe. I have my sword right here."

"'Tis nae the swords and nae men I'm afraid of," she whispered, "'tis the dark."

He brought a few more dry branches and kindling, took out

his high-carbon fire steel, and struck a sharp edge of chert several times until sparks flew into the kindling. Even though he knew a fire might bring the English to them, he couldn't stand seeing her like this.

The girl had just been tortured for days. She probably had PTSD. With the fire going, he sat back cross-legged and shifted closer to her. "Do you want to put your head here?" he put his hand on his thigh. She frowned and looked at him dubiously. "You're not alone," he said. "I'm with you. I won't let darkness take you."

She nodded and cuddled deeper into the blanket. He hated to see her looking defeated and scared.

As she moved closer to him, their hands touched and their eyes met. Her lips were pink and plush, and she had just her undertunic on. How would she taste if he kissed her?

He'd had one girlfriend back in high school—Jessica, a beautiful, popular girl. He'd been a jock. Sports had always been easy for him, and because of his dyslexia he never had good grades. Often, he'd been teased that he wasn't the smartest, even by some of the teachers.

He'd let them put him in a convenient box: dumb jock. Even Jess thought that. She hadn't wanted to lose her virginity until she was eighteen, and so they did a lot of oral and hands.

But the Instagram-perfect Jessica paled in comparison to Anna's raw beauty. Their eyes were still locked, their lips so close, their breaths mixing...

In the next moment, she pulled away.

"Don't be afraid," David said. "I won't touch you."

"I'm nae afraid. And nae ye wilna touch me. I'll have a husband soon."

Right. A husband. Yet another reason for David not to act on his desires. Besides, he didn't want to fall in love or get someone pregnant in the Middle Ages. Leaving a child fatherless and a woman without support was unthinkable. And sooner or later, he'd find the way back to the future or die trying. He didn't want to feel any more trapped here.

Anna laid her head on his thigh, the weight of it pleasant on his leg. He felt the warm dampness of her hair through his linen braies. He longed to stroke her head.

"What do you know about him?" he asked. "Your future husband."

"I ken he's a Scot. He's nae a young man. And I hear he's a man of honor. But he is allied with our enemy."

"Are you worried?"

"If he's a kind man, 'tis all that matters." She was silent for a moment. "Do ye have a betrothed? A wife?"

"No."

The closest he'd had to a fiancée or a wife had been Jess. They'd been together for three years. Perhaps, in medieval terms, she was a bit of a princess. Jess wanted to be an influencer, and even in high school she had built a big social media following.

How could he explain that to Anna?

"But I used to have one," he said. "For three years I"—he tried to think of the right term—"courted her."

"Oh." He felt Anna shift, her shoulder tense against his thigh. "Who was she?"

"She was...a noble lady, I guess."

"Ye guess?" She laughed. "She either is or isna."

"Well, then, yes, she was. But it didn't work out."

Jess was a smart girl, but she'd never shown it on social media, trying to fit into the image of a pretty girl who talked about brands, makeup, and wellness. She didn't think she needed a college degree to be successful. To her, success was about the number of followers she had. She'd listened to podcasts and read books about entrepreneurs, so David knew there was more to her than that.

He often wondered if the popular-girl image was armor she'd put on to protect herself. To steer everyone away from seeing that underneath was someone who desperately needed to feel loved. That adoration and admiration from her fans was an attempt to gain the love she didn't feel for herself.

"It's the first time I've told anyone about her," he said.

"Why did it nae work out? Didna yer clans arrange the marriage?"

Truth was, when they'd graduated, Jessica had decided to go on a global lifestyle tour. He'd been heading to Northwestern. It was an amicable separation. They'd ticked each other's boxes for a while in high school. He was her jock. She was his prom queen. After graduation, their performance was over.

"She didn't want it anymore, and I let her go," David said.

"Did ye love her?"

"I don't think I've ever been in love with anyone. Not yet."

In the golden darkness, she turned to look at him and their eyes locked. A question was in them, but before she could ask it, he said softly, "You should try to go to sleep. I'll watch over you."

She turned away from him, facing the fire. "What do ye do if ye canna sleep, David?"

He chuckled bitterly. "Recently? I drink. It's the only way to reach oblivion."

"Uisge?"

"Yeah. But before, when I was home, I used to read books. Um, stories." Even though reading had been a struggle, he'd always loved the escape novels provided.

"I like that. Can ye tell me one?"

Tell her one...what could he tell her? Something medieval, something she'd understand and that wouldn't make her ask too many questions... Maybe *The Princess Bride*? Rogene and his cousins had loved the movie. No, something that she might know, as well. A familiar story would comfort her.

Then he knew.

"Long, long ago, in the place called Cornwall, there was once a young prince named Tristan. He had lost his parents and King Mark of Cornwall raised him like his own. Tristan became King Mark's most loyal and honorable warrior. That is why he sent

Tristan to Ireland to bring to him Isolde, the fairest and most beautiful princess. The marriage would bring peace and end a long war between their two kingdoms."

"Mhm..." she mumbled sleepily. "I ken that story...but nae how ye tell it. Please continue. Tell me what happened."

"Tristan successfully reached Ireland. But when he saw Isolde, he fell in love with her. She was not just beautiful, she was everything. Smart, kind, and as courageous as a warrior. No matter how much Tristan resisted and tried to stay away from Isolde, on the way back to Cornwall, Isolde fell in love with him, too. Both knew they could never be together. Isolde was bound to be King Mark's bride, and Tristan could never betray his adoptive father. Honoring his word and putting the king's trust above everything, Tristan brought Isolde to his king. And just like Tristan couldn't break his word, Isolde couldn't be selfish. Her marriage would bring peace between their kingdoms and save many lives. So Isolde married the king."

"Aye..." mumbled Anna as she nestled against his thigh. "What else would the lass do?"

David chuckled. He ached to touch her smooth cheek, to run his fingers through her hair. "But she never stopped loving Tristan, and he never stopped loving her."

Anna's breathing was even and heavy now. "Didna Tristan die?"

David swallowed a hard knot as he watched the flames. "Yes, he died. To him, it was a better fate than loving a woman he could never have."

CHAPTER 9

THE LIGHTENING SKY was visible in a space between the mouth of the cave and the boulders hiding the entrance. Anna stirred on David's lap, bringing tingling over his thigh. His leg was numb from reduced blood circulation, but he hadn't dared to move, not wanting to disturb Anna's sleep. She needed it.

She turned her head, one black-lashed eye squinting up at him. Her cheeks were flushed from sleep and her full lips were relaxed.

He grinned at her. "How did you sleep?"

She wiped her mouth and sat up by his side and stretched her arms, arching her torso. He looked away as her breasts protruded through the fabric. "Well," she said, looking around. "I havena slept much since MacDowell put me in the oubliette. It was always so cold and so wet I could barely sleep at all. Any sign of Colum and Iàcob?"

He felt his face fall. "Not yet."

She sighed and threw a long, worried gaze at the mouth of the cave. Thoughtfully, she gathered her long, wavy hair, which was now dry, and brushed it with her fingers. She looked more rested and healthier and even more stunning, with her shiny eyes the color of dark honey and some color to her cheeks.

David stood and stretched; his legs were tired from sitting in one position for hours, but seeing her rested was well worth it.

He cleared his throat. "I'll go and check on Daisy. My horse..." he added when she looked at him with a puzzled expression. "We'll need more firewood to cook breakfast."

She nodded. "Aye, thanks. I'll get dressed; my gown must be at least somewhat dry by now."

David picked up his sword in the sheath and put it around his waist, then made his way between the boulders and down the small, steep path. Before he could step off the path, he froze.

Only five feet away, spread between the trees, was a camp. It was so close, David could see the seams on the field tents, the scars on the faces and hands of the men sleeping under them. He could hear the crackling of a small campfire. The horses were grazing thirty steps away, Daisy among them...

Right in front of David, three steps away, with his back to him, a single man sat at the campfire. He was sleeping, his head hanging between his shoulders. Birds chirped cheerfully in the green canopy high above. The scent of woodsmoke reached his nostrils, mixed with the scents of decaying wood, plants, and morning dew.

David stopped breathing, frozen like a statue, praying Anna wouldn't make a sound or decide to come down. A woodpecker tapped somewhere nearby.

As soundlessly as he could, his eyes never leaving the sleeping sentry, he backed up the path to Anna. This must be the search party. They had probably stopped until light to keep looking.

If David and Anna didn't leave now, they would find them.

When he was out of sight of the camp, he ran up the path and into the cave. Anna was in her red princess dress. The long, angel sleeves were draped with fur, and now that it was clean, he saw crimson flower patterns. It was torn in places and faded stains still remained, but it suited her so well, and highlighted her proud stature.

Their eyes locked and she didn't move, either. Color

reddened her cheeks. She was a true princess, this one. Something about her seemed otherworldly, like Liv Tyler in *The Lord of the Rings*... Damned Sìneag. Did she have to put the most beautiful woman he'd ever seen in front of him? If Sìneag thought Anna was the woman destined for him, she was probably right. And perhaps now, after meeting Anna, the time traveling rocks would finally work.

He'd avoided any relationships here, even though he'd met pretty young women in this age. Drunken, he'd allowed himself to be seduced by a willing farmer's daughter, but made sure to keep to only oral sex as he didn't want to get anyone pregnant. Apparently, many medieval women weren't used to receiving oral sex, and after he'd brought them pleasure, many didn't want to let him go.

But never with any woman had he felt this flutter, this pull at his very soul, that he had when he looked at Anna. Like the world was brighter, and the ground under his feet was shifting and light.

He'd bet this was exactly what Sìneag had wanted. Bringing him to the woman he could fall for.

Well, he wouldn't let himself do that. He could admire her, but he wouldn't touch her.

"We must leave," he said as he bent down and started to hastily put things into his bedroll. "The enemy is camping right under our doorstep."

Anna gasped and jumped to gather the field cauldron and the utensils into the traveling sack.

"And they have my horse."

"Nae!"

"Yeah. We can't wait for Colum and Ìacob anymore." He tied the strings around the bedroll, and when Anna handed him his travel pack, he tied the roll to the bottom. "If the enemy has my horse, they know we're nearby, so we need to trick them and go in a different direction than Stirling."

David put the pack on his shoulders. It was his own invention he'd made before setting out on his journey, his own back-pack to carry on his shoulders.

"Ayr," Anna said. "'Tis west and under my father's command."

"Okay," David said and walked to the path. "Just quietly."

"I'll go alone, David," she said behind his back, and he turned to her. She was eyeing him coolly. "Ye made it clear ye have yer own path ye need to follow, and I dinna want to be a burden. If ye can lend me a knife, I'll protect myself."

David frowned. There was no reason for him to be worried about her. To be worried about the deal between the Bruce and Philip Mowbray. It wasn't his battle. He was a modern-day American, thrown into the midst of a war that wasn't his to fight. He hadn't even paid much attention to the historical details when Rogene had told him about the outcome of the war. He remembered the English would attack Stirling, but Bruce would win, although he didn't know when and how it was connected to Anna's wedding. Rogene had told him something important, but he just couldn't remember.

Either way, there was no reason for him not to give Anna a weapon, the rest of his silver, and some provisions and let her go and resume his search. He liked her, but there was no future for them.

But he couldn't leave her alone. He couldn't live with himself if he didn't make sure she was safe.

It was probably the same part of him that had tried to stop Rogene from touching the time traveling stone. The part that had picked up a sword and fought for the Mackenzies in the battles with clan Ross. The protector in him.

"I won't leave you alone, Anna. I won't let you get harmed."

To his surprise, relief relaxed her face. Her eyes sparkled, and a small smile stretched her lips.

"All right. Then let's go to Ayr. We can lose our pursuers and get horses and help to safely reach Stirling."

David nodded. "Okay. Let's go. Very, very quietly."

What had he agreed to? David asked himself as they made their way down the path.

When they reached the base of the hill, the camp was still sleeping. But the sentry was now awake. Still sitting with his back to them, he was curled over a bowl in his hands, slurping a pottage. David turned to Anna and put his finger to his lips. She nodded.

They crept to the left, behind the sentry. David's eyes never left the man's back, watching every time his hand raised and lowered the spoon. The forest floor was covered with old leaves, grass, and flowers, and David was careful to avoid stepping on twigs and branches.

A squirrel darted across his path just as he was about to put his foot down. He jumped back and something snapped under his foot like an explosion.

The forest froze as the sentry stilled, the spoon halfway to his mouth. "Fuck!" David muttered silently under his breath. Freaking squirrels!

The sentry turned his head and looked straight at David.

As his eyes widened, something red and black flashed in David's peripheral vision. A thick piece of fallen branch in her hand, Anna lunged as the sentry was standing up, his hand to his sword. She swung the branch and hit him on the back of the head with a dull *thunk*.

A man in the nearest tent stirred but didn't wake.

The sentry swayed a little but didn't fall, and as he turned to Anna, David threw himself at the man, wrapping his arm around the sentry's neck in a choke hold. The man's hands grabbed at David's arm as he grunted and groaned. In a minute or so, he relaxed in David's grip and David let him softly fall on the ground.

Someone stirred in the farther tent and sat up.

David looked at Anna, and they ran as quickly and as silently as they could.

CHAPTER 10

ANNA HELD her breath as the hooves of the English horses thundered above them. The scent of earth enveloped her. She saw a few white maggots crawling under the roots of the tree growing at the edge of the ditch she and David hid in. Sunlight flickered over their heads as the riders passed. David's arms were warm and reassuring around her shoulders. His touch gave her strength. She was exhausted and wanted to lie down and sleep for a long, long time. She was still tired from hunger and thirst and was still chased by the darkness.

Perhaps she always would be.

But David helped. The sun helped, and being in the open air, breathing the scents of the forest and of nature, helped. They had been walking for a while, and it was after midday that they had heard them chase after them and hidden here.

After the English passed, she looked at David. He had such handsome, warm brown eyes and a face that belonged on tapestries and in the stories of minstrels.

Breaking eye contact, he looked up and waited. "I think they're gone," he whispered.

"Aye," she said.

"Let's make camp here. You need to eat and rest. You look a little pale."

She sighed. "I admit, the thought of a rest sounds good. But I want to make haste to Ayr and arrive there as soon as possible."

"We will. Now that they've passed, I don't think they'll return here soon, so we're probably safe for the moment. I hear a stream. Maybe there's fish. I'll roast it, and it'll do you good."

They climbed out of the ditch and found a good place for a camp. While Anna was making a fire, David brought her a trout that he'd already gutted and cleaned. The sharp scent of fresh fish hit her nostrils, and even though it was raw, her stomach growled. While he put it onto a stick to cook over the fire, she drank from a vessel made of a ram's horn. He had pushed his sleeves up, and the muscles on his strong forearms moved as he worked. She had an odd urge to run her fingers lightly over them.

"Trout," she said and closed the cap of the drinking horn. "'Tis a verra nice one. On Islay, my uncle Aulay took me fishing on Loch Gorm with Colum and my cousin Seoras. That was before I ever met my father." She chuckled. "My other cousin Laoghaire, always a noble lady, stayed with my aunt Leitis and sewed dresses from silks that had just arrived from the Mediterranean."

Worry about Colum was a constant tightness in her shoulders. Was he injured? Captured once again? Was he still alive? Were he and Iàcob trying to track her down? She admitted, David's presence brought her reassurance. He said her uncle Aulay was alive and with the Bruce, waiting for word from Colum about his secret rescue mission, ready to storm Carlisle if needed to free her.

David was struggling to put the stick through the fish's mouth and she came closer to him. "Ye're nae doing it right. Allow me." She reached for the fish.

"You want to smell like fish after all that effort you put into washing the dress?"

She chuckled. "Nothing will save the dress. And I'm hungry."

He shrugged and handed her the stick and the fish. Carefully, she navigated the sharp end through the trout's cold, slippery body.

"Please." She slid the stick through the side of the fish tail and handed it to him with a triumphant smile.

He cocked his head with respect and put the fish over the fire to cook. "Well done. So you weren't raised by Bruce?"

"Nae," she said. "My mother and Bruce were engaged, but she died not long after I was born, still unmarrit... I suppose he got caught in all the warfare... William Wallace. Then John Balliol. It was the year he became king that he came to Islay. And it wasn't even to see me. It was because he was running from the English and my uncle was hiding him. So I was raised by my uncle Aulay and my aunt Leitis. My cousins are more like siblings to me. Except Laoghaire." She chuckled, looking at her hands. "Laoghaire never liked me."

He chuckled, too. "I have a cousin like that, too. Liam. He always found some excuse to fight with me."

She pushed the fire around with a stick. "Aye. I ken what 'tis like. Are ye close with yer parents?"

"My parents died when I was five."

Anna watched him with different eyes now. She hadn't thought this handsome warrior could have a tragedy of his own. "I am sorry they're with God already, David."

"Yeah, thanks," he said. Picking up a twig, he started digging a hole in the ground. "I was raised by my aunt and uncle, too. My mom's sister. But they had four kids of their own, plus my sister, Rogene, and I. It was always so passive-aggressive. The sighs. The heavy looks. The implications that if it wasn't for us, their kids could have had new things instead of secondhand clothes."

Anna frowned. "What are secondhand clothes?"

He muttered something under his breath—she thought he cursed himself. "Just...um...things someone already wore."

"Oh. Aye, 'tis nae so good for nobles, but regular folks often get 'secondhand' clothes. I got many from Laoghaire. She's the legitimate daughter of my uncle Èoin."

He nodded. "They should have treated you like a legitimate daughter, too. It's not your fault your parents weren't there."

"And 'twasna yer fault, either," she said.

He looked at her for a long time, then grinned. "I didn't have the best of childhoods with them. I don't know why I'm in such a hurry to get back to them. It's not like they'll be missing me. One less mouth to feed. And my mouth ate a lot. I burned a lot of fuel playing football."

"Football?" She frowned.

He cursed again and shook his head. "What is it with me today? Loading you with all kinds of new words I shouldn't. Um. Football is just a game people like to play where I'm from. I was good at it, but it always left me even hungrier, so my aunt and uncle weren't thrilled about it."

"Well, Uncle Aulay and Aunt Leitis loved me," she said. "But still, they wanted bairns of their own. And I wanted my own ma and da. When Aunt Leitis got with child, they tended to forget about me. I dinna blame them. Everyone wants their own flesh and blood. A child that is part them and part the person they love. But it didna make it easy for me, to be wanted and loved at one moment and forgotten the next."

He nodded and gave her a sad smile. "I know, princess. I know."

Warmth spread through her chest as he looked at her with kindness, and she knew he understood her pain. The rest of the day passed by quickly as they kept talking about their cousins. David told her stories about how his cousins made jests and even humiliated him and his sister. She told him how Laoghaire made fun of her simple dresses, of her being friends with the children of shepherds and farmers, of her going to bed with dirt under her nails.

He was odd, using strange words she'd never heard, and his stories included objects and notions she didn't understand.

They ate the trout and the rest of his bread, and at night, he made a shelter from one of his blankets. As they settled down to sleep and he rolled out his bedroll, they both lay on it, and he pulled her closer to him. His body, big and hard and warm, was everything that was reassuring and good about the world as she dozed off in his arms.

She was warm, she was safe, and for the first time in days, there was no darkness haunting her.

There was only the scent of a man, and of woodsmoke and of grilled trout.

DAVID PEERED AT THE COAST NEAR AYR FROM BEHIND A DUNE. Anna, who was by his side, shook her head in disbelief.

"They're nae here," she murmured, her eyes on the sea. "Why is the ship nae here?"

David scanned the platter of the sea, leaden in the evening light. No ships. Not even to their right, where far ahead, the outline of the town of Ayr was visible.

"And you're sure they were supposed to stay here?"

"Aye." She pointed at some large rocks on the beach. Next to the rocks were about twenty tents. "Uncle Aulay helped me pack my horse by those rocks."

"Then who are they?"

Forty or so horses grazed at the edge of the beach where sparse grass started. Four dozen men sat around campfires, cooked, played dice games, trained on swords, and shot arrows at targets.

Anna's gaze was dark on the camp. "Who do ye think?"

He strained his eyes, watching for any signs of the enemy. From about a hundred feet away from them, all he could see were warriors in *léintean-croich*, some of them with linen and chain mail coifs on their heads. "MacDowells?"

"Aye. And they have yer horse." She pointed her chin at the horses.

"You're right," he said, eyeing his light-brown Highland pony. "Daisy is there."

She had been his companion these last two years and had gone with him north and south. She was somewhat shorter and sturdier than the other horses, and the middle of her mane had a sand-colored stripe.

For the past two days, traveling without Daisy, he'd missed her like a friend. Though having Anna by his side had been a pleasant distraction. The feeling he had around her reminded him of the few times he'd gotten high with his friends in Chicago.

He looked at Anna. The two days they had spent walking northeast had done her good. Under normal circumstances, she should have rested, drunk plenty of liquids, eaten a healthy diet, and slept a lot. But instead, she'd traveled on foot, built fires, gathered berries and mushrooms, and even killed a partridge.

But still, her cheeks had gained color, there was a brighter shine in her chocolate eyes, and she smiled more and more often while they walked and talked. The trembling, shell-shocked girl he'd fetched out of the depths of the oubliette was disappearing. She'd still clung to him tightly during the two nights they'd spent outdoors, in the darkness. But during the day, he thought, the freedom of the open road, the air, and nature had done her good.

Staring at the camp, she gasped.

David followed her gaze. "What?"

"Do ye see that older man in chain mail? He's shouting at someone."

"Yeah," David said.

He was in his forties, although his gray hair and beard aged him. He was clearly a strong man with broad shoulders and a thick neck. Stooping, the man gesticulated broadly, his face red, yelling at a younger warrior who stood with his neck hidden between his shoulders.

"Who is he?" David asked.

"The bastart who put me in the oubliette. Dugald MacDowell."

Anger flooded David's blood like intoxication. He wanted to hit the man for doing that to Anna.

"We should go," he said. "Now. Clearly, they're serious about finding you if even the chief of the clan and constable of the castle himself is after you."

Anna looked at the horses. "Aye. 'Tis only thirteen days left till John the Baptist, and only six until the day I am supposed to meet my betrothed."

David looked longingly at Daisy. He didn't just miss her. His map of Scotland and his writing tools were in the travel pouch attached to her saddle. "We need the horse."

Anna looked at the church tower peeking out of the distant outline of Ayr. "We can go into town and ask for help."

"We don't know if we'll meet anyone who can help."

"My clan could be in Ayr. They'll protect me. They'll take me to Stirling."

David felt his jaw work. How could he explain to her that the key out of this time was on his horse?

And going to Ayr...she was probably right. But the idea of letting her go so quickly made his chest hurt. Somehow, he was clinging to any opportunity to stay with her.

"They're not paying attention," he said. "Whatever Dugald is yelling about, everyone's looking." Almost all of the warriors were gathered around Dugald and the young warrior.

Anna was looking between the camp and the horses. They were far enough away from each other that if the MacDowells kept arguing, they may have a chance to get Daisy. Now the wind brought snippets of angry voices to David and her.

"All right," she said. "Ye're right. They are still arguing."

"Okay," David said. "Stay here. I'll get Daisy."

"Nae..."

"Stay here!" He took a breath. "Please, Anna. Listen to me.

Under no circumstances can they see you. I'll be careful, but even if they catch me, you run, okay?"

She sighed loudly. "Yer strange 'okay'... I never heard anyone use that word before, though ye say it often."

"Promise me."

She rolled her eyes. "Okay," she imitated him and they both grinned, and her smile sent a ray of sunlight straight into the middle of his chest.

He squeezed her shoulder as he passed by her, crouching. He stayed low as he moved to the horses behind the dunes. In about twenty feet, the dunes ended in a patch of sandy grassland. That became proper, albeit a little rocky, soil with short grass and underbrush.

When no dunes protected him from the sight of the MacDowells, he straightened, as though he had all the right in the world to be there, and calmly walked to the horses. Still about eighty feet separated him from the camp, and with every step he was closer to Daisy.

She raised her head and snorted, looking at him.

Steady, girl.

His feet were heavy; it was like walking through custard. He kept throwing sideways glances at the MacDowells, who were still arguing, and now someone had started a fistfight.

Good. They were yelling now. At each other.

Better.

He imagined one of them looking up and seeing him, pointing his finger, then all of them, already angry and blood-thirsty, running at him. Forty men against one. A single, cold slice of steel against his neck would end his life.

And he wouldn't be there to protect Anna.

But no one pointed. No one yelled in alarm.

Miraculously, he reached Daisy. The scent of horse manure was pungent in his nostrils as he patted his old friend, looking into her black, shiny eyes. She snorted softly as he stroked down the rough, warm fur of her nose. He was relieved to see that his traveling pouch was still attached to her, even though he had no idea if his map was still there.

"Hey, Daisy," he said softly as he untied the reins from the bush she'd been grazing on. "They didn't harm you, did they? Let's get out of here."

"Dinna move a muscle," someone said behind him.

His breath caught in his chest. Slowly, he turned his head. A man was pointing his sword at him. Where the hell had he come from? Was he guarding the horses? Goddamn it. The man put the tip of the sword against David's back.

"Ye're nae going anywhere."

CHAPTER 11

"Ye tried to steal a horse?" Dugald MacDowell said and guffawed, his eyes closing to slits from laughter. "Well done, man."

There was a fresh bruise under the eye of the younger man that Dugald had been yelling at earlier. Forty pairs of eyes were on David like shards of glass, and all he could think of was Anna. Please, God, or whoever could hear his prayer, make her leave. Let her not try to help him or stay and wait...just leave. David could stall them, do something for the MacDowells to linger here and give her time to run. She could go to Ayr and see if her clan was there, or if someone allied with Bruce would help her.

David stayed impassive. MacDowell was a bully and an abuser. He didn't have to put Anna into an oubliette. He could have kept her in a regular room. David had no tolerance for cruelty.

He crossed his arms over his chest. His sword had been taken away by the guard who'd caught him. He had no way of fighting his way out except with his fists. And he was one man against forty armed warriors.

When Dugald calmed down, David raised his eyes at him expectantly. "I didn't try to steal a horse," he said. "I tried to take my horse back that you stole. If you give me back what belongs to me, I'll be on my way."

Dugald had high cheekbones and a strong, square chin under his beard. The orange glow of the setting sun made his strong features even more pronounced. Wind moved his long, shaggy gray hair, and he narrowed his eyes at David.

"Ye ken I wilna give ye my horse."

"It's not your horse."

Dugald's face fell as he looked David up and down. "My men found it near Carlisle. Who are ye and what was your business there?"

"I'm David of clan Mackenzie. My business near Carlisle is none of your concern."

Dugald's face lost all humor. "A Mackenzie. A well-kent ally of Robert the Bruce, are ye nae? Bruce is a usurper who took my rightful lands of Galloway from me. Do ye see my problem with giving the horse back to my enemy's ally?" He licked his teeth under his closed mouth, his face rearranging into an echo of a snarl. "How did ye find my clan here?"

"I followed you."

"Why didna ye approach me like an honest man would? If ye're nae hiding anything, surely we could have resolved a misunderstanding. Instead, ye admit ye followed us and tried to steal yer own horse. Ye see my mistrust of yer story?"

"Mistrust or not, doesn't change things. I wanted my horse, I didn't think you'd give it to me willingly, and I didn't want to risk a fight."

"Ye didna want a fight, and yet a fight is what ye'll get."

He looked his men over. It was getting darker now, the sun halfway swallowed by the sea and spilling fiery light over the grim faces.

"Ye say one thing, I say another. There is nae way to ken the truth. I will tell ye what. An old tradition of resolving the dispute: ordeal by combat. Ye ken it?"

"Sure." But he didn't like the sound of it.

It was part of the medieval world David detested. He'd seen it used as a method of problem-solving among warriors. Two drunk guys couldn't agree who would sleep with a willing widow, so they fought, and the winner took the woman.

"Then if God is with ye, ye will win and ye may leave with yer horse, yer sword, and yer life. If I am right and ye're lying, God will be with my champion and let him win. What do ye say?"

David looked around at the men. He hadn't had daily combat training from the age of seven like warriors in this time had. He'd only started practicing sword fighting when he got here with Rogene three years ago. He'd been an athlete his whole life, so it helped him to learn faster, but he'd seen only three real battles, not like these guys. Constant fights and raids and clan feuds. What chance did he have? And what choice?

If he died today, at least it would be for the right cause. Protecting someone.

Not just someone. Anna.

Anna, who had been on top of Sìneag's rock. If that didn't tell him about destiny, what did?

"Sure," he said. "Let's decide if I'm telling the truth with swords and bloodshed. That seems reasonable."

Everyone frowned. Dugald's eyes bulged. "Are ye mocking me, lad?"

"I'm just agreeing with your terms, even though I don't want to. Come on. Give me my claymore and let's fight."

The sun has set now, and the sky was like blood set on fire and spilled over an indigo blanket.

Dugald chuckled. "Oh nae. I wilna fight. I will pick my champion, who will fight for me."

The men moved away and formed a circle around them. In the light of the campfire, a giant figure stepped into the circle, his face in shadow.

He was at least a head taller than David, who was six foot two. His shoulders meaty and broad, his arms like tree trunks, he moved towards David, chain mail clanking.

"'Tis Goiridh," said Dugald. "My best warrior."

With his long, swaggering stride and flexed arms, the man reminded David of thugs and gangsters from TV.

David imagined Goiridh lifting him up easily and snapping his vertebrae against his knee like a twig.

As the main fire illuminated one side of the giant's face, David's whole body froze, and the silence around him was absolute. It was as though even the waves shrank back, as terrified of Goiridh as David was.

The man was surprisingly good-looking, and David knew it was odd that he noticed that. But he guessed he expected the giant who'd surely kill him to be ugly, like a troll or an orc from a fantasy book. But women in the twenty-first century would have been all over this hunk as if he were The Rock. Somehow it made him even more terrifying.

Someone handed David his sword, and the weight felt like a stone dragging him to his death. The circle of men jeered, fist-pumping in the air as Goiridh set his feet wide apart, bulging thigh muscles stretching his braies. He took his sword with both hands, flames glistening off the blade.

Not feeling his arms, David raised his claymore to his shoulder, and all he could think of was *Please, let Anna not see this.*

"To the death," said Dugald, crossing his arms over his chest. "I hope yer horse is worth it."

"Dinna fash, lad," said Goiridh with a grin. "I'll make it quick. Ye wilna suffer long."

The antler handle of David's claymore was sleek from sweat and cold under his palms. He planted his feet wide apart, but he couldn't feel the hard ground. This wasn't his first fight. He'd fought and wounded and killed men before when he was protecting his pregnant sister and the clan that he had considered his. He'd been protecting his future nephew. He wasn't a coward. He wasn't running from a fight, and he wasn't going to let anyone bully him.

But he was shitting his pants now, looking up at Goiridh's

face, half of it illuminated by the fire, half in the darkness. In every way, he was stronger and a more capable warrior than David. He was older and taller and wore chain mail.

David didn't even have his *leine croich* on. It was rolled up in his traveling pack, back with Anna.

With a grunt, Goiridh attacked, swinging his claymore down and across. David stepped back, and the swoosh of the sword was like a windmill blade. Goiridh swung the sword across from the other side, aiming for David's neck. David blocked the hit and their swords met with a metallic clang. The impact reverberated into David's bone marrow, pushing David back like a bulldozer, his heels digging into the sand.

Goiridh thrust again, from the side, and David barely managed to deflect it. They slashed and struck and parried. Goiridh was always on the attack, always the unstoppable giant pushing his way through. David was always defending, dodging blows.

A cut on his shoulder, a close call on his thigh. Bruises and hits on his face and chest. He was panting, his sword as heavy as a boulder. How he was still alive, he didn't know.

The MacDowells cheered every time Goiridh struck and David stepped back.

And then, Goiridh seemed to grow tired of David not dying. With a roar, the giant barreled forward, launching strike after strike at David, using his sword like a hammer.

David took refuge under his sword, which was the only shield he had. The impact of those strikes could have cut through bone had his opponent reached any part of David's arm.

David took a few quick steps back, panting. Goiridh was panting now, too. Sweat covered his forehead, his teeth bared as he sucked in air.

David and Goiridh circled each other, David slashing a few times symbolically. But they were both tired and taking time to catch their breath. David's chest was on fire with the pain of bruises and hits and the long, exhausting exercise, his biceps and shoulders aching.

After a few minutes of this, Goiridh, seemingly recovered, launched at David. David stepped back. His foot caught on something, and he lost his balance and fell into the sand, right at the edge of the circle of warriors.

His hand landed on something hard and cold, shaped almost like a football.

A rock.

Goiridh charged at him, both arms raising his sword above his head, but David rolled out of the way and scrambled to his feet, the rock still in his hand. Under the jeers of the onlookers, he ran to the opposite side of the circle.

He wouldn't beat Goiridh. Not with a sword.

But he was still an athlete, the star quarterback.

He stopped and turned to Goiridh, who was a panting, fire-lit giant walking towards him in long strides, determined to finish this.

Moving the sword into his left hand, David took the rock in his right and imagined he was on a football field with his team. He had to throw the winning pass. "Go CATS!"

Using all the strength left in his body, he swung the rock back and threw it, aiming for the man's head.

It flew through the night air, hints of orange and red reflecting off its wet sides. It was like a comet, David thought oddly.

And then there was a thump and a crack of bone. Goiridh took two drunken steps and fell to the sand with a grunt and a thud. He lay on the beach like a log, his chain mail glistening with fiery gold.

Waves whooshed and murmured, crashing against the beach. Blood slowly poured from Goiridh's temple, feeding the sand in a black blot.

David stared at the man he had just killed.

Damn it.

Although he was relieved, he didn't like killing. He hated that people like him and like Goiridh had to listen to petty warlords who weren't interested in reason and wanted bloodshed.

"Sorry, Goiridh," he murmured. "I'm so sorry."

In the silence that followed, he felt every pair of eyes on him. Astonished, angry, antagonistic stares.

"Ye're sorry?" yelled Dugald. "Ye're *sorry*? He was my best warrior! My champion!"

David straightened his shoulders and looked at Dugald, who was watching him with wide eyes and a snarl.

"I didn't want the ordeal by combat. I didn't want it to be to the death. All I wanted was to get my horse back. I won. So, according to you, God showed you I told the truth."

Dugald's snarl became wild.

Some of the warriors put their hands on the hilts of their swords.

"Good night." David walked through the empty circle that served as the battle arena. He shouldered his way through the line of silent MacDowells, feeling their eyes on him like knives.

But before he could reach freedom, Dugald's voice pierced the air. "Kill him!"

Hands grabbed him, but he tore his sleeve out of their grasp and ran into the darkness. From in front of him two large silhouettes approached quickly, hooves thumping against the ground. Behind him, angry MacDowells yelled and ran after him.

"Get him!" he heard. "Kill him!"

He ran. Then the silhouettes became horses. Daisy, her light-brown coloring looking almost black in the darkness, and another horse—with Anna riding it.

"Hurry!" she cried.

He didn't hesitate. Putting his sword into its sheath, he climbed into Daisy's saddle, then looked back. Forty Scotsmen, their swords drawn, ran at them like a wave in a storm.

As Anna and he spurred their horses, arrows hit the ground around them as they galloped past the pasture. Anna must have untied the rest of the horses, as they were now running in all directions.

And as the wind blew into his face and the barely visible outline of the woods blackened against the sky, he was tempted to berate Anna for not leaving. But, if he was honest, he couldn't be happier that she'd broken their agreement.

CHAPTER 12

THE GALLOP WAS a wild ride in the darkness. The moon came out from time to time, light seeping through the branches of the woods like spiderwebs on the wind.

David didn't know where they were going, just away. Away from the sharp blades and the bared teeth and the savage eyes. Away from the man he'd killed and the pool of blood. Away from death.

The horses' hoofbeats drummed in his ears, and the black shapes of tree trunks flashed past on either side, as wide as Goiridh and as dark as his shadow. The forest was pungent with the scents of the trampled underbrush and moss and damp earth. Daisy's sweet scent and the movements of her strong body were comforting. But the darkness swaying before him in shades of indigo and charcoal and pewter made it feel like he was riding in a nightmare.

And, as though beaten from the ground by Daisy's hooves like sick music, his thoughts reverberated.

You killed him.

You killed him.

You killed him.

Though he'd always hated it, he'd learned to live with

killing during battles, knowing he had no choice if he wanted Rogene and other Mackenzies to survive. But he hadn't killed anyone for over two years now, and the weight of it was a shock.

After a while, he thought he heard a distant rumble of horses somewhere far behind. But when he looked back, there was nothing but darkness.

He hoped he was imagining it.

After a long, hard gallop, David felt that Daisy was getting tired. She was slowing down and beginning to stumble a bit, the steady rhythm of her gallop broken.

He looked back again and listened. But he heard nothing and saw no one chasing them.

"We need to stop," he called to Anna's dark shadow ahead of him through the drum of hooves.

"Aye," she responded, "my horse is tired. I think we lost them."

He brought Daisy to a halt. The poor thing was shaking her head, snorting. She needed a drink, some food, and rest.

They dismounted, and the ground swayed for a moment under David's feet. As he took Daisy's reins and walked with her into the darkness of the woods, away from the path, the night air cooled his sweaty body through his wet tunic.

"You promised," he said to Anna as she walked her own horse by his side. "You should have left."

Anna scoffed. "How about a thank ye, David? Didna I just save yer life?"

"But you should have left. We agreed if they get me, you run."

No response came from her. "I ken, aye. Ye're right. I agreed to it. But once they got ye, I just couldna. When I saw that man holding ye, when he called for more men to come, I...I guess I didna want ye to be captive like I was. I wouldna have wished it on anyone."

He shook his head and sighed. Somewhere deep in the

woods, an owl hooted. "You're a stubborn Highlander, aren't you?" he asked and chuckled.

She chuckled in return. "I'm the daughter of my clan. The daughter of my father."

"A Scottish princess." David felt his grin return, the same grin that he'd had for the past three days. "I don't know why I'm surprised."

A soft gurgling of water in the distance reached his ears, and Daisy raised her head, ears perked, sniffing the air.

"I hear water," Anna said.

"Yeah, me, too."

"I must say, David, I didna think ye'd come out of that fight alive. That man... Forgive me, but ye didna stand a chance against his sword. I thought surely I'd lose ye..." Her voice broke. "And I didna want to lose ye."

There was warmth in her voice that soothed David and made him breathe easier.

"I couldna watch. I went and freed the horses and took Daisy and another one. I was ready to run into the crowd and hit the bastart and get ye and then get the hell out. But when ye hit him with a rock and *killed* him..." Her voice was awed. "Ye killed him with a rock! I...where did ye learn to throw like that?"

"Um...football. I was the team captain, and the coach always said I had the best arm."

They came to the brook now, the scent of water and mud strong. Anna and David tethered the horses to the bushes growing at the side of the brook and the animals sank their muzzles and drank. Moonlight seeped through the canopy opening above the brook, making the water glisten like polished silver.

"I dinna ken what that means. Is that like the Highland games?"

Clan Mackenzie had organized the Highland games three years ago and invited different ally clans. There was tug-of-war and stone put and caber toss. David had enjoyed himself there—

it was the first time he'd forgotten he wanted to leave the Middle Ages. Until clan Ross had ambushed them right in the middle of the games and almost burned pregnant Rogene to death.

"Yeah. It's...a bit like the Highland games," he said. "Minus clan feuds and bloodshed. I'll start the fire. There's a good place for a camp." He pointed at a flat meadow surrounded by the trees five steps away from the brook.

Anna and he walked around gathering dry branches for the fire. "I was terrified for ye," Anna said. "But once we got away, I dinna think I've felt alive like this since...since before my father arrived in Islay seven years ago."

He picked up another branch and added it to the heap that he held against his body. "Why?"

"Before he became king and appeared in my life, I was just a nobleman's bastart. The clan took care of me and loved me, but if my father didna come to claim me, he didna need me and didna want me. No one cared about my education, about my manners, about my household skills. My cousin Laoghaire was groomed and trained from birth. Like every noble lady her valuable virginity will be sold to her future husband, and she will be an important link between clan MacDonald and her husband's clan. But I...I was no one. As a bastart, I dinna have a claim to anything. My value is defined by how much my father values me. And when he became king, I became more valuable to him—another daughter to forge alliances through marriage. It wasna good nae more for me to run around and swim and behave like a wild child. Suddenly, I had to be groomed and trained and taught just like Laoghaire. So that freedom I used to have, 'twas gone. And today, with ye, galloping away in the darkness, I felt it again. I've been feeling it for the past three days, more and more. Nae one kens where I am. Nae one demands for me to sit for hours at the loom and weave fabrics, make dresses, and go and argue with the cook."

Even through the darkness, he saw the pale, round outline of her face staring up at him.

"I liked the wild chase and the adventure," she said. "Even though I often felt alone and not needed, there was freedom in being a bastart, and I didna realize how much I miss it."

He walked to the middle of the clearing and threw the heap of firewood on the ground. As he sank to his knees and arranged the branches to build the fire, he said, "I understand more than you know. Since I came here, I realized how free I actually was back—"

She came to stand by his side and laid more branches next to his. "Came where?"

To this time, he wanted to say.

"To Eilean Donan," he said and added more branches. "To my sister. But I've been traveling for the past two years trying to find a way home."

"Where is home?" she asked. "I thought ye were from Eilean Donan. From Kintail."

"No." The firewood was ready now. He took the fire steel out of his belt pouch and struck it several times over the kindling. Bursts of orange sparks hurt his vision, then the small glow of fire ate at the dry grass and wood chips. Curling his hands around the kindling, he blew on it. As he watched the fire grow and expand, his mind raced. What should he tell her? What lie would satisfy her and wouldn't betray him?

Rogene had said she was a distant cousin of James "Black" Douglas, Robert the Bruce's most important lieutenant. But as their encounters had been close a few times, this lie was dangerous, as James could easily tell everyone the truth—that he'd never heard of Rogene and David and that they were imposters. Only a handful of people knew they were time travelers. And to the rest of the world, Rogene and David said they were from Ireland's Dingle Peninsula. This was the most western area Rogene could think of that the Highlanders would actually know. Dingle was a faraway land for medieval Highlanders, most of whom never went farther than fifteen miles from the village they were born in.

But, of course, for clan MacDonald, traders, and seafarers, it was not much of a distance at all.

Still, David could mention Dingle Peninsula to Anna now, and she'd likely believe him. But it wasn't that she'd catch him in a lie that stopped him. It was that he didn't want to lie to her at all. He felt so free with her, so much more like himself. Lying to Anna felt like blasphemy.

He placed larger pieces of wood above the burning kindling and watched small flames lick the branches. The comforting scent of smoke reached his nostrils. "It's far away. Back home, I was promised something, a big step forward. Something I've worked years for. But now I'm stuck here."

He looked at her over the fire. It was still small, but he already could see her face. Her eyes were big and glistening and beautiful. She sat down on the ground, her dress crimson in the light against the blackness behind her.

"What is freedom for ye?" she asked.

He swallowed and looked at the fire, thinking. "I actually don't know. I thought I knew, but now... Maybe it's because I never felt free, never felt at home. Maybe I'd always hoped if I achieved success, it would fix this emptiness inside of me. Stop me from knowing I'm never good enough. That there is always more out there—more to grab, more to conquer, more to own. More money, a better car, more success, more admiration...I always thought those things would make me feel like I'm worthy."

She frowned with a puzzled expression. "A car?"

"Did I say car?" He scratched the back of his head. "I meant cart."

He meant his college scholarship would be the answer, that he'd be successful and finally feel at home. But maybe he'd never feel that even in his own time. Even with all the money and success in the world.

As he looked at the beautiful girl over the growing fire, he thought that if freedom existed, what if it was with this girl who has no expectations of him? This girl who made him feel like himself?

He grinned at her, and she smiled back. He remembered his life back home—the daily football training, the exercises for dyslexia, the easily available clothes, never having to worry about catching your own food, gutting your own fish or rabbit. He remembered his friends and teammates who'd expected him to be dumb and to be like them.

Only he wasn't like them.

Maybe he wasn't supposed to be like anyone.

Maybe he was supposed to race his horse alongside a beautiful princess, feel the silvery moonlight and the wind on his face and the movement of the horse, and just be.

CHAPTER 13

AFTER A SHORT SLEEP, Anna woke up the next morning tightly wrapped in David's arms. She didn't move at first, absorbing the weight of his arm and his leg thrown over her, his heat against her back. She breathed in the fresh air and blinked as sunlight peered over the leaves and tickled her eyelids.

If she could, she would stay with him like this forever. She inhaled his manly scent, which set a deep longing within her that made her want to rub herself all over him, especially—and shamefully—*there*.

Her nightmares stayed away as long as he was near her. She felt safe with him. He had descended down into the bowels of her stone prison and stolen her from death.

But she couldn't stay like this. And she shouldn't. She was supposed to meet Sir Philip in five days, and she wasn't even sure where they were exactly.

When David woke up, they broke their fast, cleaned the horses, and kept going northwest. At midday, they stopped by a small loch to let the horses rest and graze. Anna caught a fish while David picked some mushrooms and wild strawberries. With the fish cooking over the campfire, she ate them with delight, and when she smudged her face with the red juice, David wet a kerchief and wiped her lips.

The strawberries were sweet and fruity on her tongue, and she wondered how his lips would taste if they wiped the juice away instead of the kerchief.

They kept on riding and talking, exchanging easy jests and stories of the past. She told him about Islay, about the castle, and about the people of her clan. About her aunt Leitis, who'd been like a mother to her.

About how when she'd died during the fifth and final stillbirth, her uncle Aulay had never been the same again.

Neither had Anna.

He told her about the feud between clan Mackenzie and clan Ross, about the battles that Euphemia of Ross had inflicted upon them. About his nephew, Paul, who had been born more than two years past and how, soon after Paul's birth, after he knew his sister was all right and whole, David had left on his journey.

He didn't talk about where he was from and only spoke in general about his family, his sister, and that football... Why couldn't he tell her anything about where he was born and where he grew up?

But she didn't want to press and question him. This peace and easiness between them, the trust that had grown like a fragile wee flower was too precious. She enjoyed his company, even though there was always that question at the back of her mind...

What was he hiding? Who was he really? Besides the man who had saved her and protected her and made her feel safe...

And alive.

In David's arms, she felt this burning inside, this lightness, as though a fish's swim bladder full of warm light had been put inside her stomach, as though she would lift off the ground and float higher and higher into the air like a butterfly.

Part of her dreaded meeting Philip Mowbray—the part that didn't want to separate from David.

By the evening, they had entered a swampy area. Sickly brown and yellow grass stretched around them like horses' manes as far as she could see. Several ribbons of smoke curled into the air in the far distance. There must be a village over there. Good. They could go there later to buy some provisions for the road.

They followed a worn path that was partly sunken in gray water. Trees and bushes grew here and there, though they were low, and stretched out along the ground, like the vegetation did on the highest mountains of Islay. A cloud hung above the swamp, and it rained a drizzly, misty fog as she and David struggled their way through.

But at the end of the day, the swamp ended. So did the rain, as though an invisible force had kept it over the swamp.

And when twilight came, they arrived at a strange collection of rocks on a hill, as though a giant had placed boulders the size of two-story houses, and moss and rain had made them sink into the ground. A river flowed nearby in a steady, dirty-green flow, with weeping willows cascading into the water.

Once they got closer, Anna saw they weren't really random rocks thrown into the ground as though by giants.

It was a ruin. A ruin of what must have been an ancient motte-and-bailey fortress. The broken stones grew from the earth like teeth, ivy and moss covering them like rot. It was quiet here. Birds didn't sing in the trees; the river didn't even gurgle. As they rode on, David's profile darkened, tensed. Did she smell a whiff of lavender?

"'Tis a good place for a rest," she said as they stopped the horses. It was a secluded space, formed by a half circle of the rocks and earth. "If anyone follows us, they wilna see us easily from the path."

"Yeah," David said, his eyes on the collection of rocks by the foot of the earthen slope leading up to the base of what once must have been the fortress. "We'll stay here."

As though enchanted, his gaze remained fixed on the rocks. He dismounted and slowly walked there and stood over the rocks, staring.

Anna didn't like it. Not a wee bit. With an alarm blaring in her chest like a war horn, she descended from her horse. Something about all this was familiar. But what?

Slowly, she walked the soft ground covered with short grass towards David. There were some carvings cut into the surface and a handprint in the rock. It was the same kind of rock that was on Islay, up in the ancient ruins. Everybody stayed away from it. Children were warned not to go anywhere near there because if they angered the faeries, the faeries would kidnap them and they would never return home.

Faeries were, of course, just superstitions, things of myths and legends. All who believed in God knew they were just stories.

Still...she had had that vision of a woman called Sìneag in the oubliette...

And then she knew what was familiar. The very same symbols glowed on the surface of the rock in the oubliette. The very same symbols that were on Islay.

Her memories of Sìneag, and the glowing symbols and how David rescued her were vague. But there was something about him slapping the rock and calling for Sìneag. She had thought this was her imagination, that she'd been sick from being alone and in the cold, damp darkness for so long.

But what if it wasn't?

"What is this rock?" she asked. "Why are ye looking at it like 'tis going to swallow ye whole?"

He didn't reply. He reached out to the rock but stopped, his hand an inch away from his body.

Then he dropped his hand and hid it behind his back and stepped away.

As he turned at her, the haunted look on his handsome face made her stomach drop. Why did she have the feeling she had almost lost him?

"Yeah," he said and backed away. "Let's stop for the night. Eat. Rest."

He looked like a ghost. And why did that scent of lavender, so strong now, turn her stomach upside down? "Tell me what's the matter!"

"Let's just start the fire..." He leaned down and picked up a branch, then stared at it as though it pulsed a miasma of pestilence. "I might even tell you."

CHAPTER 14

THE SKY above them was gray and fading to indigo as the daylight died in the west. David cut a stick into shavings to make kindling.

His hands hurt as he ran the knife along the bark of the birch branch over and over, watching the shavings separate and fall into the pile. They were all wrong. Too thin or too thick. The blade of the knife came dangerously close to his thumb holding the stick. His fingers shook as tension hardened his muscles and sinews. Sweat covered his face, droplets falling onto the shavings.

He fought the allure of the rock ten steps away. The tug had the force of a bulldozer, insistent and unstoppable. The smell of lavender made him sick. Was Sìneag somewhere nearby? Was she watching from behind one of the rocks or trees? Was she lurking in the bushes?

Was she finally opening the tunnel for him?

And if so, what the hell was he still doing here, cutting this goddamn stick?

The next slice of his knife tore a white-hot pain through his thumb. He grunted as a line of blood flowed from the cut.

He sucked it, the taste warm and salty.

"'Tis enough kindling, David," came Anna's worried voice as she rose from the travel sack she'd been rummaging through and came to him. "Dinna hurt yerself. Come, show me."

"It's nothing," he said with his thumb still in his mouth.

As she lowered herself in front of him, shielding the rock behind herself, he felt easier. He could drown in her big eyes, shiny and glistening, the long lashes, the arches of her eyebrows. Her high cheekbones and the delicate bone structure that gave that otherworldly look. Why did he keep searching for a faerie when he had *her* right by his side?

"Let me see," she insisted, and, as though enchanted, he stretched his hand out to her.

She took it gently in her hands, her touch like silk against his rough skin. As she looked down at his thumb, he couldn't turn his eyes away from her. She was by no means Instagram perfect. She had smooth skin, but the tiny, silvery traces from old blemishes, perhaps teenage acne, were visible on her chin.

They were like flecks on a panther's fur. Awe-striking.

A few scratches on her cheekbone, perhaps from the oubliette or from when she'd been kidnapped, were the battle markings of a warrior. The signs of her unbendable spirit shining through.

Her fingernails were chipped and partly torn off, with dark crusts. She must have tried to claw her way out of her prison.

How could he not admire her, stare in awe at her every hair, every eyelash, the very shadow she cast over the ground? He didn't know how light didn't glow through the pores of her skin. What was that dumb rock compared to this girl?

"The bleeding stopped," she said and met his gaze. Her lips were just an inch away. The pull to taste them was like the force of a storm pushing him in the back. "Let me put a bandage over it."

"Don't," he said. *Don't move*, he wanted to say.

He could swear she swayed just a little bit towards him, as though a wind pushed her forward. But she didn't move closer.

Instead, she rose to her feet. "I'll start the fire. Yer kindling is ready."

She went to the travel pouch and took out the fire steel. As she hit the carbon steel against the piece of flint, sparks flew and landed on the dry moss and shavings.

"That rock," she said as the kindling caught fire. "Have ye seen those before?"

He poured water he'd previously boiled from his uisge horn flask over his cut. He hadn't had uisge in days. The horse Anna had stolen had some provisions in the travel sack; perhaps there was some uisge he'd missed. He desperately needed some.

Strangely, he hadn't craved alcohol as much. Not until now. Not until the rock he'd been searching years for was right in front of him, and he wasn't doing anything to pass through it.

He opened the MacDowell travel sack and retrieved the cheese, which was a bit moldy and sweaty but still edible. A little loaf of stale bread. Dried fish. A small horn flask. He opened it...uisge... Part of him wanted to drink it, but he couldn't allow his mind to be clouded. Not tonight. He put the cork back in.

They wouldn't need to fish or hunt tonight. "Why?"

"Ye said ye'd tell me about that rock."

"Hmm." He wasn't sure he wanted to talk about the rock. It was bad enough it was staring at him like it had eyes. He definitely didn't want to think about. He didn't want to think, period.

He wanted oblivion.

"I have seen one before," Anna said as she propped a few bigger pieces of wood over the burning kindling.

She bent over and blew on it, her face glowing orange.

"Where?" he asked, frozen holding the pieces of bread and cheese. "The oubliette?"

"Aye, there." She straightened as the fire began burning well. "But we also have a rock like that on Islay."

Islay...it wasn't even on his map. He'd had no idea. He needed to put a cross on his map, which he'd been relieved to find was still in his travel pouch attached to Daisy's saddle.

"Really?" he asked. "And what do people say about these rocks?"

She came to him and took the triangle of cheese from him. "Old people believe there are faeries living near those rocks. That those faeries make people disappear. But most Christians know 'tis nonsense. Old tales. Why do they interest ye so much?"

He swallowed. She picked up the knife he'd carved kindling with and cut a piece of mold from the cheese and threw it into the fire. It hissed and smelled like pizza for a second.

Don't think about pizza. Pizza could be one touch of your hand against the rock away.

This could be the last time he'd see her. It smelled like lavender. He'd met a woman he could easily fall for—perhaps, as James said, Anna was the woman he was "destined" for. That was what Sìneag had wanted. But David had no idea. Sìneag had matched Rogene and Angus across time. Then Catrìona and James. Then Raghnall and Bryanna.

For David...

It could be Anna.

And the rock was right there.

His freedom was at his fingertips.

And now that it was, maybe he didn't need to hide anymore. He was tired of pretending, lying, being afraid of someone discovering he was a time traveler and doing something medieval, like torturing or killing him.

Most of all, he didn't want to keep lying to Anna.

Besides his sister, he'd never cared for anyone more than he did for Anna. What they'd lived through together in only four days was intense. They were bound now with more than just the goal of getting to Stirling.

He knew her. He related to her. He'd never felt so alive than he felt with her.

Maybe he would come to regret it, but he wanted to tell her the whole truth.

He hadn't told it to Dùghlas or anyone else besides the narrow circle of Mackenzies and Cambels who already knew the truth.

She'd be the first one.

He stood up, went to Daisy, and fetched the map, his ink, and his reed pen. As she chewed a bit of cheese, he went to her and unrolled the vellum, showing her the map.

"What is it?" she asked.

"Scotland."

"What are the crosses?" she asked.

"They are faerie rocks like these where we stand." He opened the jar of ink and dipped his reed quill and made a cross on Islay. "And we must be around here." He made a cross around what must be East-Northern Ayrshire, though it was hard to tell.

"Are there so many? And why are ye searching for them?" she asked.

He swallowed and sat in front of her, cross-legged, on the ground. It was cool now that the sun had set. He wanted to tell her, and yet uneasiness crippled him. She wouldn't believe him. She'd think he was insane. He'd lose her trust forever.

"Because what you heard is true," he said. "Faeries do make people disappear near them. Well, not faeries. One faerie. Her name is Sìneag. The rocks are for traveling in time. They're ancient Pictish rocks that open the river of time."

A heaviness at the back of his spine prickled. Was someone watching them? Sìneag? He looked around and saw nothing but the shadows of trees and bushes.

No Sìneag.

He looked back at Anna, who kept frowning at him, her eyes wide.

"People don't just disappear near those rocks," he said. "They travel through time. I'm one such time traveler, from the future."

She blinked and frowned, looking as though she wondered if she'd misheard him. In a moment, she might tell him he'd gone insane.

"I've been searching for a way to return to my time because I don't belong here. I'm stuck here, imprisoned, held back from living my life."

She didn't contradict him, didn't call him crazy or a demon caster, like Catrìona had called James. She looked at the rock and said, "Sìneag?"

And then words poured out of him. He told her about his parents, about Rogene, about dyslexia, about his struggle living in a family of geniuses. About football and about the scholarship to Northwestern that would finally allow him to live and to be something. Make something out of himself.

She listened.

"I don't remember Rogene saying anything about you playing a role in the Bruce's victory. But I may be wrong."

He sighed. Darkness had descended around them, and he could see one half of her face in shadows and one half in golden firelight.

"I dinna ken if I believe ye or nae," she said. "But I ken yer pain, David. The pain of never being good enough."

He swallowed. "Sìneag, she sends people through time to find the person destined for them. If I do indeed have such a person in this age, it's you, Anna. It's you."

She began shaking. "Sìneag...she's real, is she nae?"

"Yeah. She is."

Anna clenched her hands. "She came to me in the oubliette. I didna think she was real. I thought she was a vision. My insanity born of the darkness."

His heart ached for her. "Anna..."

"She told me the same thing. There's a man for ye, she said, David, and he'll save ye."

She went silent. Fire seethed in David's body, and yet his

mind told him to shut up, to withdraw, to go to the rock and put his hand into the handprint.

But his heart... Anna had changed everything. His heart knew it even if his mind refused to accept it.

Damned Sìneag. She was right. Right all along. Anna might be the woman for him.

If she wasn't getting married to someone else.

If that marriage wasn't intended to save Scotland.

And if she wasn't from the Middle Ages, a time from which he desperately wanted to escape.

Her chest rose and fell quickly under her red dress, and he was hopelessly trying to keep one memory at bay. The memory of her naked breasts glistening with water in the moonlight...

There she was, beautiful and brilliant, and not calling him crazy after the stuff he'd told her.

"I dinna ken if I believe ye," she repeated. "But I ken I dinna want to be with anyone but ye, David," she said.

As though overcome by a flood of feeling, his mind switched off. And he did what he'd wanted to do for days.

He leaned in and kissed her.

CHAPTER 15

His kiss was like velvet.

For the first time in her life, a man had put his lips on hers and was kissing her.

And it wasn't like anything she'd ever expected. David, with his hard angles and muscles and sharp jaw, wasn't at all rough or in a rush.

On the contrary, his lips touched hers like he was a cloud. Light and gentle. His smell reached her, and his taste was on her tongue...something delicious, masculine. Something that shot a bolt of fire straight through the middle of her body and down there, between her legs, where the feeling rested and grew and burned.

She didn't know anything about kisses. She didn't know much about men at all.

But she knew one thing.

She wanted more.

More of this mysterious man who talked of time travel and the future and football. Of success and universities and of potential.

He couldn't have confused her more. She didn't believe him.

And yet, everything he had told her about himself couldn't be more similar to what she felt about herself and the world.

Like him, she felt trapped. Like him, she had to constantly prove she was good enough and worthy. Like him, she'd been alone and unwanted for as long as she could remember.

And so, when he dipped his tongue into her mouth and brushed hers, she didn't pull back. She pushed against him as though an invisible force connected them.

His tongue, his delicious, sleek tongue worshipped and licked and stroked, stirring a storm of fire with every wicked movement.

His arms wrapped around her, bringing her to him in an iron-hard embrace. She clung to him, her arms around his neck, like a crab. She stroke his surprisingly silky hair, running it between her fingers.

His unshaven chin scratched her skin, which was strangely exciting.

But then his lips left hers, and she stared at him as he pulled away, panting. His eyes were dark on her. "I shouldn't have. You're not mine."

Not mine...

Och, how she wanted to be his.

But he was right. She was marrying another man. Someone she'd never met in her life. Someone the very thought of whom made her feel like she was suffocating and sad, like she was back in the oubliette.

She clenched the side of his tunic. "I thought I was about to die in that oubliette. I thought my life was over just before it began. I never got what I wanted in my life. Nae my father, nae my clan gave me that. To be wanted. To love and to be loved..." She shifted closer to him. "I may die tomorrow. My husband may be a cruel man, and there's nae a thing I can do about it once I'm his wife. But I ken ye're nae any of those things. And I ken I want ye. And for once in my life, I will get what I want."

His Adam's apple bobbed as he swallowed, a tortured look on his face.

"Ye," she said. "The rest of my life, I'll serve my husband, Scotland, and my father. Let this be one moment. One night where I can have what I want."

He studied her, not blinking, eyes dark and stirring a delicious feeling of danger in her blood. There was an ache behind his eyes, but also heat. As his gaze dropped to her mouth, she had a strange sensation of falling.

"Anna…" he said, his voice soft and warm and intimate.

Why didn't he move? Why didn't he kiss her again, wrap his arms around her like a tight cocoon? The hurt of rejection tightened her throat in a hot, painful clasp. He'd made her feel brave, made her want to take action and allow herself to live, but mayhap she had read him all wrong.

"Ye dinna want me?" She pushed away, trying to get out of his grip, but he held her.

"I do. Christ, Anna, you have no idea how much I want you," he growled and brought her to him. "It's taking my last drops of self-restraint not to tear that dress off you and show you how much you are wanted, and how much you'll be missing with your husband. This is your last chance to stop me. Tell me no and I'll never touch you again. Last chance, Anna."

For a moment, he didn't move, just kept staring at her with a gaze that brought an odd prickling all over her body, making every tiny hair on her skin stand up. Everything around them stilled and quieted, waiting for her. In that moment between the old world where Anna had been a miserable maiden and the new one where she'd be fallen but happy, the wind stopped rustling the leaves and branches, the crackling of fire quieted, and the only thing she could hear was her pulse thudding in her temples.

He gave her a choice. He gave her control. No one had done that in her life. And she'd never have it again, not as Philip's wife and not as the King of Scotland's daughter.

"I wilna say nae to ye, David. Show me what 'tis like to live and to be free. I'm saying aye."

His lips were on hers before she could take her next breath. His kiss was demanding, claiming her, just a wee bit short of being rough, and she leaned into him, clutching the tunic on his hard shoulders, then clasping his neck as she wanted more. His tongue was greedy, sweeping against hers, over and over again.

Mine, his kiss was saying. *Mine.*

She sagged against him, wanting that tongue everywhere. As she ground her pelvis against him, she felt something long and hard between his thighs.

Oh God, he was so hard for her already.

She knew what that meant. She'd seen animals mating on Islay, seen stallions covering mares. And even though she'd never seen a human male organ, she knew what this hardness meant.

And she liked it.

Heat rushed through her with every sweep and every bit of suction and pressure. She was squirming and rubbing against his solid body, against the hard length of him. She'd felt his body every night pressing against hers, and only now was she allowed to have what she wanted.

He moved his large, strong hands up her spine, spilling fire through her, doing something with her dress. The pleasure of his kiss, the heat of his body, his smell, and his closeness made her skin itch. The dress felt too tight, unnecessary. As though he read her thoughts, in a few moments, the dress was loose on her shoulders, and he tugged it down.

His mouth left hers and moved down her neck, leaving scorching traces of kisses. She dug her fingers into his silky hair and heard her own moan escape her throat. She didn't recognize her voice. It wasn't her. She wasn't the lass who wanted desperately to be legitimate, to be a noble in her father's court.

This was her. A true, wild spirit—a Highlander with a heart glowing like the sun, her body turned liquid and spilled through the world like she was one with it.

One with him.

He pushed her dress and her undertunic down her body, and, to her shock, cupped one naked breast and took it into his mouth. A burst of pleasure shot through her as his mouth tugged and nibbled and sucked her flesh, his tongue flicking her nipple, which hardened like a pebble, aching. She arched her back, and she may have called his name. She was half-oblivious.

As he moved to her other breast, still fondling the first one with his hand, she knew her logical mind was gone. It had evaporated in the heat of her desire.

And she liked it. She wanted more of this. Everywhere.

She ran her hands down his muscular chest and stomach and undid the girdle around his waist. As it fell on the ground with a soft thud, she pulled his tunic up, marveling at the hard surface of his body, the body of a warrior. She dragged his tunic over his shoulders, and his naked torso was like a warm stone against her sensitive nipples.

"You're so beautiful I can't breathe," he whispered as he looked down at her body, shamelessly, decadently, and she wanted him to have every inch of her. "God, you're the most beautiful girl I've ever seen."

Her throat clenched from emotion; she couldn't believe a man would say things like these about her.

And would want her so much…

He pushed her back down to lie on the sleeping roll, the soft fur of the stag skin like a caress against her naked back. He stretched over her, supporting himself with one arm. The skin of his bulging biceps gleamed with firelight as he leaned down and kissed her again.

His kiss was different now—urgent and deep and taking her, claiming for his own. As she was gliding her hands against him, he pushed down the rest of her clothes to her hips and then down along her legs, and the dark air of the evening caressed her naked body like he did.

His tongue kept making love to hers as his hand traveled

down her body, cupped a breast, and played with the nipple. Pleasure spilled through her chest like wine. He growled into her mouth as she arched her chest into him, wanting more of his touch, more of him over her, more...

When she thought she wouldn't be able to breathe anymore, his hand moved down her stomach, spreading liquid heat through her. And with every inch he came closer and closer to the very center of her, the place between her legs that throbbed and ached and burned with need. Then he was at her curls, and his fingers were spreading her folds, and as he touched her—right there—an intense jolt of pleasure shot through her like an arrow.

She gasped and jerked, and he intensified the kiss, murmuring into her mouth.

When he froze, letting her get used to the sensation, she ground herself against him, unable to wait, and he grinned into her mouth.

"I knew you'd love it, sweetheart," he whispered. "This is just the beginning."

"The beginning?" she murmured. "Och, David, I'm going to burst..."

"And I'll catch every part of you."

He started moving his finger against her there, as though gathering her pleasure, winding it up, and coiling it like thread on a spindle, concentrating on one, single spot. It was unbearable. It was magical. Like starlight and sparkles, the sweet cravings moved through her in a wild, primal dance. She moaned, clutching at him, moving her hips, fisting the fur of the stag skin.

She was opening up, unraveling, and the pleasure was bigger, and deeper, and swallowing her whole.

She knew she was at the edge of something...something spectacular. Something godly. And she'd fall over the edge and dissolve and...

Only, she didn't. He withdrew, and she gasped, disappointed and frustrated.

"David..." She looked at him.

He was watching her, his dark eyes a mix of predatory desire and reverence.

"I'm falling for you, Anna," he whispered, his voice rough and hoarse.

Falling for her... Her soul sang. Her body was exposed, naked, swimming in an ocean of pleasure. And now her heart and her soul were raw and aching from his words.

Because she was falling for him, too. And distantly, in the echo of her logical mind, she knew this was bad. This would ruin her. It may feel sweet and blissful now, but she'd pay for this happiness.

Before she could say anything, he had moved from her side and now hung over her like a gorgeous mountain. He kissed and nibbled and gently bit her breasts, and moved his mouth down her stomach, and she thought this would be it, this would be the moment he'd take her like a man took a woman, and she'd lose her virginity...

He moved further, kissing her stomach, then moving lower... and even lower.

She gasped and sat up when his lips were on the inner side of her thigh, embarrassed and worried he'd want to kiss her *there*. Animals didn't do that. She didn't know if it was something that people did at all.

But that was exactly what he did.

He spread her folds with his fingers, exposing her flesh to him, and covered her with his lips.

She cried out, unable to stop her shock and her pleasure. It was so wanton and soft and oh dear, dear God almighty, so good!

His tongue stroked her over and over, right where his fingers were before. She tried to recoil but had nowhere to go. He lifted her thigh over his shoulder while his other arm kept her in place. Heat like boiling honey spread through her blood from the center of her pleasure. She couldn't do anything but take it, dissolve in it, swim in it.

He growled like a hungry beast, licking and sucking and teasing her aching folds, as though knowing what she needed and giving it to her. Then she was shaking as if from fever, grinding herself against him, feeling her insides clenching with a strength she'd never known she had. And, as though blinded by the sun, she didn't know she had come to an abyss, until with one more flick of his capable tongue, she was falling.

Clenching viciously.

Burning with pleasure.

Opening up and spilling from the skies like rain.

And a lifetime later, when she was lying in his arms, covered with a blanket, and breathing, blissfully safe and happy surrounded by his scent and his hot body, she fell asleep with one thought.

Like someone addicted to uisge, this was a blissful happiness. But the more she drank of it, the more it would hurt when she had to stop.

CHAPTER 16

DAVID WATCHED Anna stir in his arms. He couldn't stop staring at her, drinking in every detail of her face, the way the morning sun left soft shadows under her long, dark eyelashes, the way her wavy hair lay on her shoulders. Her porcelain skin was delicate, her collarbones were graceful, and he ached to trace his lips along them, feeling every curve.

She opened her eyes and beamed at him, then nestled into his chest. He tugged her closer and kissed her head, inhaling the scent of her hair—sunshine, road dust, and an herbal scent that was all hers.

"Good morning," he murmured. "You look delicious."

"Good morning to ye," she said.

He kissed her lips, the taste of her succulent and intimate, and stirring desire in him yet again. Last night, she'd fallen asleep after he'd made her come, and he hadn't wanted to disturb her. She needed sleep, and even though he hadn't gotten his release, it was for the best. He hadn't been sure he'd be able to restrain himself much longer and not take her...

That would go against his promise to himself to never risk an unwanted pregnancy in the Middle Ages. And if he took her virginity, it could cause her in trouble in Stirling.

No. Last night was amazing, but it would be just one night.

He withdrew and brushed a strand of hair from her face. "I never wanted to please anyone like I wanted to please you. But this can't happen again, Anna." Her pretty smile disappeared, and he wanted to kick himself for it. "Not because I don't want to. Believe me, I do. I don't think I want anything more than to keep giving you orgasm after orgasm."

"Orgasm?" she said. "Oh…is that the sweet release…?"

He chuckled. He was a virgin, and so was she. Innocent and sweet and so tempting he couldn't stop touching her. "Yeah, that release. The thing is, I don't think I can restrain myself. I'm losing my head around you… And I can't take your virginity. I can't do that to you. I can't make proper love to you…the way I really want to."

He brought her closer into his hug. Her head was heavy on his biceps, and he could feel the whole length of her—her silky skin, her soft, warm hip against his leg. Her triangle of dark hair against his inner thigh.

Heat rushed to his cock, and he was getting hard.

She chuckled. "Are ye…"

He swallowed hard, staring at the curve of her breast barely covered by the blanket. "Princess, I'll never stop being ready for you. You're a treasure, you know that?"

She giggled and wriggled out of his embrace and stood up, covering her chest with her shift. "Well, in that case…" She turned her round, perfect ass to him, and he bit the back of his hand to suppress the burn of lust at the sight of it. Then she pulled her undertunic on and turned to him, her glorious body covered. "I'll go and wash up in the river. Then we must speak of that future ye told me about." His gaze fell on the time traveling rock twenty steps behind her, and all desire washed away. "I dinna think ye were in yer right mind. I wasna in my right mind when I saw Sìneag, so mayhap ye had a vision, too. Mayhap a fever dream. I need to ken more," she continued. "Understand more."

He sat up and curled his arms around his knees. The fresh morning wind smelled like damp grass and tickled his bare skin. "Yeah," he said, unable to look away from the rock. "You go. Bring some water, we need to boil it to drink."

"Why do ye always want to boil water? 'Tis odd." She picked up their traveling cauldron and gave him a soft peck on the nose.

"Because it purifies water of bacteria...of disease."

She chuckled and shook her head. "Yer strange notions."

As she disappeared behind a rock, he brushed his fingers through his hair and looked away from the stone.

The pull he'd felt yesterday was back. There it was, the way out he'd been seeking for so long. And there she was, the woman he was supposed to fall in love with, the woman who was destined for him. He could easily imagine his life with her. It had only been a few days since he'd met her, but he was falling for her, and he knew she was falling for him.

They fit together. They were the same despite being born centuries apart.

But he didn't want to fall in love with her. They had no future. And falling for her and then leaving her... God, he'd be condemning himself to a lifetime of heartache.

He stood up and began gathering branches, throwing glances at the rock. He picked up a long, dry branch and snapped it in half against his knee. Was this how Sìneag wanted it? To let people from different times fall in love with each other? People who could never be together in the long run? How could David's perfect match be engaged to another man?

On the other hand, Rogene had fallen in love with Angus, and he'd had a fiancée he didn't love. And Catrìona had intended to become a nun, and yet James, a police detective from Oxford, had changed her mind. And Bryanna had been a diabetic with only three insulin pens left—a death sentence in the Middle Ages—but she and Raghnall had made it work.

But none of them had this... The outcome of the Scottish-

English war was possibly in Anna's hands. And none of them had hated it here so much.

It was impossible for him and Anna. So he was still leaving...

Right?

He was not as sure anymore. What he wanted most right now were answers. And Sìneag was the only one who could give them.

Yes, he had lots of questions to ask her. How could she be so cruel? How could she put people in such impossible situations? Looking around, he yelled, "Sìneag! Sìneag! Show yourself! What, afraid to appear out of thin air? Show your Highland faerie magic in practice. You want food?"

He took the rest of the bread out of his pouch and put it on the rock, very careful not to touch the surface of the stone even with the tip of his pinkie. "Here, here's my offering."

But everything was silent around him. Birds sang in the trees. An animal snapped a twig in the bushes. The air was full of lavender, but now in the sunlight, he realized it was because there was a patch of lavender growing on the other side of the mound.

Desperation crawled in his chest like worms. "Sìneag!" he called.

He didn't want to leave Anna. He didn't like being away from her, not even for the brief time it was taking her to go to the river.

But he had to know if he had a choice. Maybe he'd never have a chance to leave, anyway, and he could stop being tormented about it. Or maybe the rock would work, and he could end this misery, this search now.

If Anna was the woman he was destined for, the rock must work now. Or maybe he should consider abandoning his quest and stay with her. Maybe he actually was entitled to happiness. But was their happiness worth breaking the course of history for?

He put his hand closer and closer to the handprint, both craving for it to glow and not wanting it to.

Something prickled at the base of his neck and he felt a strange warmth there. Someone was watching him.

Had Anna come back? A jolt of happiness leapt in his stomach and he turned.

But it wasn't Anna watching him from the bushes.

With a grimace of absolute disgust, a priest was staring at him, surrounded by about twenty men and women. They were villagers or farmers, poor, worn-out coifs on men's heads, wimples and headrails on the women. The priest wore a brown robe that was tied with a belt. He was in his fifties, with a broad nose and a clean-shaven face, a bald at the front head, and bushy gray eyebrows.

David turned to them and stood up. The priest and the rest of the people came from behind the bushes.

David gulped. He knew it wasn't a good thing to yell about faeries near a rock that might be considered magical. Especially not in front of devoted Catholics.

An angry murmur went through the crowd.

"Why were ye calling for a faerie?" asked the priest.

David just hoped Anna was still away by the river. "There are no faeries, everybody knows that. I was just kidding. Jesting," he corrected himself.

"He must be a Highlander," said one of the men. "His accent is very strange. Highlanders are wild. They still believe in faeries."

"Aye," said another man. "He slept near the old faerie rock that everybody in Kennifar kens nae to go near. Whoever does will be cursed. And now he's been casting a spell and calling for faeries."

With a sleek, cold horror David remembered Dùghald's warning. *There's folk that dinna take people who believe in such things kindly. Especially priests.*

"Aye," said another man, raising his pitchfork higher. "And

he's probably been at it for some time, since a few days past lepers arrived in the village. And everybody kens lepers' sickness is a curse from faeries and demons. A living death."

David chuckled uncomfortably. He threw a glance at his sword, which lay about ten steps away by his travel roll. Could he get to it in time to fend off this superstitious rabble? "It was just a joke," he said and took two steps towards the dead campfire. "A jest!"

The priest's eyes pierced him like the tines of the pitchfork. Slowly, he walked closer to David. "He is clearly a demon caster and will bring God's wrath on us. Get him!"

They ran at him while he dove for his sword. Hands grabbed him from all sides, clasping his arms and pushing him somewhere. He thrashed, trying to get away, while the priest started chanting a loud prayer.

David managed to free his arms several times, but there were too many of them.

As they drove him away through the swamp, under the priest's loud chanting, he kept looking back to make sure Anna wasn't there.

But from a flash of red cloth between the branches of the bushes, he knew she had seen him.

He only hoped she would keep going to Stirling and forget all about him.

CHAPTER 17

ANNA WATCHED the crowd drag David away. The sight was like a nightmare from which she couldn't awaken. Like a piece of her heart was cut out from her chest.

She knew that when David disappeared behind that grove of trees, the nightmares from the oubliette would come back. The thought was a lightning strike, holding her in its fiery, blinding power.

But she'd need to learn to live without him anyway. She'd need to learn to fight the nightmares without him in her life. Even though she still couldn't completely believe in time travel, he had told her he wanted to leave, that he couldn't stay.

And she was bound to marry another man.

Four days until Philip expected to meet her at Bruce's camp. What were they all thinking now? Was Colum alive? Did her father worry? Had he tried to send a rescue team? How long until they all thought she must be dead and that the wedding would never happen?

And even if she started on the journey to Stirling, she still had the MacDowells and the English looking for her...

Still, she needed to go and fulfil her duty. And even though she'd sinned with David last night, she was still a virgin. She could keep that event like a wonderful memory that would warm her like a hot coal for the rest of her life.

But she didn't want to go. What she wanted to do—what she must do—was to save David like he'd saved her. Even if it meant risking her life again.

She quickly gathered their things, packed them onto her horse, and mounted, leading Daisy after her. Slowly, she followed the tracks of the mob, and when she saw the first houses of the village, she dismounted and hitched the horses to a pole.

The village was not big, perhaps two hundred houses altogether. The houses were timber-framed with thatched roofs, and the streets were dirt-packed and muddy in places. Chickens and geese ran around, dogs barked, children ran and played, men cut firewood and carried sacks, baskets, and barrels, and women cleaned and did household chores. Wearing a rich dress but looking as dirty and disheveled as a wandering beggar, she got odd gazes from people. She ignored them and followed the sound of raised voices, praying she wouldn't be too late.

When she reached the market square, there was a crowd. A stone church was the tallest building, its tower rising far above the simple village homes.

Some tents and stalls encircled the square, but in the center of the open space was a platform with three stocks, and David was in one of them. Her heart dropped into her feet. How she hated seeing him helpless like that, his dark-blond head poking through the hole between his hands as he looked around the crowd, his handsome face stoic and courageous.

The crowd was yelling at him and shaking their fists. They threw vegetable shavings and waste at him, and some sort of gray goo slowly crawled down his hair and face. Anna's fists clenched. He didn't deserve this. Mayhap he *was* a time traveler who spoke to faeries, but even so, he hadn't caused any harm to them. What could she do to save him?

The brown-robed priest standing next to him wore an expensive gold cross and had a gold ring on one finger. He was in his fifties, with a broad nose and a clean-shaven face, a balding head, and bushy gray eyebrows.

He raised his hand and the crowd silenced. "Men and women of Kennifar, what we have witnessed must be known to ye. This Highlander was calling for faeries at the faerie rock. We saw him give an offering."

The crowd gasped.

"Witcher!" someone yelled and threw a chicken bone at David.

Anna wanted to hit the man.

"The common thing to do," said the priest, "is to make the offender confess and ask for forgiveness. But first we all want to know why ye were calling for a faerie, Highlander."

"I ken why!" yelled a woman in the crowd. "'Tis he who brought the lepers to the village!"

The crowd parted like the sea for Moses and five lepers were let into the center by the platform. Everyone formed a circle around them at least ten steps away.

"Aye, this is proof," said another man. "At the same time as he was calling for faeries."

David was saying something, but his words were swallowed by the uproar of the crowd.

"Why were ye trying to put a curse on the village?" yelled the priest, and the crowd's roar died down.

David shook his head. "I didn't put any curse on your village. Leprosy is not a curse, it's a disease that originates from bacteria."

Oh nae, David, this wasn't the time for strange words and theories!

"What is bacteria?" asked the priest.

"They're germs—tiny and invisible—and they make milk turn into cheese or mold grow on old food."

A chicken squawking several houses down was the loudest sound for several seconds as the crowd gaped.

"So ye called the invisible demons that cause flesh to rot and cause leprosy!" shouted the priest, red-faced and shaking.

The crowd roared. Men and women surged towards the platform, still avoiding the lepers as though there was an invisible glass dome around them. People brushed past her, shoved her. The scents of smoked meat and woodsmoke mixed with the odors of sweat and fear, making her stomach turn.

"Death to the demon caster!" the villagers called.

"He cursed us!"

"Kill him!"

Rocks flew at David, and Anna watched, helpless, clenching her fists. What could she do? Most of the rocks hit the wooden stocks, but one hit him in the head, and a trickle of blood crawled down his face.

The priest raised his arms. "Calm down! Calm down, good people! Calm down."

The crowd silenced yet again, and the priest turned to David. "Do ye swear and confess on the Bible that ye have been calling for a faerie to bring evil on the village?"

Anna's hand shot to her throat. He was in an impossible situation. He couldn't agree to what he didn't do—it would mean certain death. And they'd never believe him if he told them the truth. She had to think of something! But all she could do was feel her stomach knot painfully and watch the tragedy unfolding.

"I will do no such thing," said David. "I called the faerie for my personal reasons that have nothing to do with the village."

For his personal reasons that had nothing to do with the village... She knew those reasons. And she did believe he was from another time now, she realized. It was the only explanation for David's strange words, strange accent, strange behavior.

And he wanted to go back to his time. He wanted to leave her. After all the nice words he'd said... Calling her his princess... Telling her how he wanted her...how she was the most beautiful woman he'd ever seen.

Yet the moment she went to get water, he was going to leave

her because he had finally found the rock. Anger and hurt spread through her like wildfire. What did she expect? He'd never promised her anything. He'd told her he'd leave eventually. He'd told her that was what he wanted.

Still, it hurt. Because she didn't want to ever separate from him. She didn't want to marry Sir Philip. If she was to marry anyone, she wanted it to be David.

The crowd groaned. "Ah. So ye confess ye called a faerie after all," said the priest.

David sighed and said nothing.

The priest looked over the crowd. "I sentence him to death by drowning with the first light of the morrow."

Anna's heart plummeted in her chest.

The man she was falling for may die because of her. He would likely be nowhere near this village if he hadn't saved her from Carlisle and then promised to take her to Stirling.

Devastation weighed on her like a stone. But she couldn't just sit and wait for it to happen. She had to free him.

CHAPTER 18

ANNA WATCHED David's prison with a heavy feeling of trepidation. To keep the usual market trade going, they had moved him from the stocks to a shed next to the market square.

Gaps between the worn-out boards would let in a bit of light. But it was a prison nonetheless, and she knew what it was like to be in one.

Even if they would never be together, she needed to save him, needed to know he was free and alive. Even if he would be alive in another time.

The wind picked up and brought the scent of smoke from the households. The onlookers had left the market square when David had been dragged into the shed, and the merchants and farmers were setting up their stalls around the place. There were booths with fish—smoked, dried, or fresh—oats, live chickens and geese, kitchen utensils, clay and glass pots and jars, knives and trenchers. The blacksmith set out his swords, scramasaxes, scissors, tweezers, and other metalwork. Another merchant laid out red, blue, and ochre silks and linens. Merchants called out for customers to take a look at their things.

"Cloth!" cried one.

"Tanned leather!" came another call.

Slowly, people arrived to browse the displays. The square filled with laughter and conversation. A minstrel started playing a lute and singing the ballad of Tristan and Isolde. Anna's heart ached. That was the story that had helped her go to sleep that first night of freedom. Her first night with David.

Like Tristan and Isolde, their growing love was doomed.

But, unlike Isolde, she was determined to not let the man she loved die.

As more and more people came to the market square, it started to feel crowded. But the five lepers sat near the church, and like water parting around a rock in a stream, people stayed at least ten steps away from them. There was almost a perfect circle of emptiness around them. People were afraid of the miasma that came from the lepers. If they inhaled it, they could get sick themselves. And there was no cure.

Anna watched the five of them, with a single wooden cup set before them. They begged for alms, stretching out their cupped hands. Two of them had dark, almost black fingers, and one had only two fingers left. Their faces were bluish or violet, looking like stones were set under their skin, making it uneven. This was the corruption of the sickness that God had sent to them. It started in their souls and then ravaged their bodies.

In big towns and burghs, like Carlisle or Edinburgh, they wouldn't be allowed in until a certain day of the week and time, when they could come in and ask for alms. But this was a small village, and no one would stop them.

No one gave them any alms or food. People were too afraid of the curse, of the corruption.

Well, Anna wasn't. She knew David hadn't brought the miasma on them. And they needed to eat something. She went to the new horse and got some of the silver that she'd found in MacDowell purse attached to its saddle. Then she bought some fresh bannocks, cheese, and smoked herring from the merchants, as well as some weak ale. With that, she went to the lepers. There were three men and two women, all different ages, probably, but looking like dead, dried-out bodies that moved.

Standing alone in the circle of emptiness, neither with the villagers nor with the sick, she felt awkward, and she knew people were staring.

The five lepers were staring also, wide-eyed.

"Alms?" said one of the men, hopeful. His nose had a dark tip that looked like dried wood.

"Aye," she said and sank to her knees. "Alms."

She gave each of them a bannock and cheese and poured the weak ale for them. They grabbed the food like starving people, which, she was sure, they were. They smelled like sickness and death, and she knew she was probably breathing in that miasma that might kill her, too. But if that was God's will, so be it. She couldn't let these people starve.

Handing out the five clay cups, she asked, "Where do ye come from, good people?"

One of the women stopped chewing and looked at her. "Lass, ye shouldna talk to us."

"Dinna fash about me," Anna said and smiled. "I just want to ken about ye."

"I am from Edinburgh," the woman answered. "So is my father." She pointed at the older man who held his bannock with only two fingers.

Anna sent a silent prayer to God to ease the man's pain. Whatever God had planned for him, she hoped the man wouldn't suffer much more.

"I come from Carlisle," said the younger man with an English accent.

The other two were from Galloway.

"How did ye come together?" asked Anna as she watched the third man drink the ale thirstily.

"'Tis better we lepers stay together when everyone shies away from us," said the woman. "Doesna matter if ye're English or

Scot when ye're a leper. Nae one wants ye anyway. And everyone is equal to God."

Anna nodded. She was so right. Everyone was equal to God and to his plan. David was as much an outsider right now as these lepers, even though he wasn't sick. But he had called for faeries, and that scared folk. What kind of plan did God have for her and David, to have brought such disparate souls together in this seemingly cursed way?

As she watched the lepers eating and the people still avoiding them, she got an idea. She glanced at the shed where David was kept.

Aye, that might just work.

"Would ye good people be willing to help me?" She put four shillings in their cup, and the five of them stopped eating and drinking. That would buy them fresh bread for a month. "I promise, 'tis easy. I just need ye to move from here"—she pointed to the shed where two guards stood next to the door and chatted casually—"to there."

The lepers exchanged glances, and the woman shrugged and looked at Anna. "Aye. I dinna see why nae. Doesna matter where we sit."

Anna grinned, hope fluttering in her chest. "Thank ye. And if one of ye can steal the key ring"—she placed two more shillings into the cup—"I'd be most grateful."

The woman nodded. "We can live for a year on this if we eat sparingly," she whispered. "And if one of us doesna die before."

Anna's heart ached for them. She promised herself once she reached her father, she'd talk to him about creating more leper hospitals. There were several next to big cities, where lepers were taken care of, and their suffering was eased until they died one day. But there weren't enough. Especially not after the Wars of Independence that devastated the country.

But she would change this. Even if she needed to spend some of her own dowry that her father had promised, she'd make her husband help.

She stepped away and nodded to them and blended with the crowd.

She watched them finish their food and gather their things and slowly make their way to David's shed. The crowd shifted around them as they moved, always leaving a large gap between themselves and the sick. Then, to the guards' surprise, the lepers sat right by the shed, leaning against its walls.

Anna moved closer and watched. One of the guards blinked rapidly; the other scratched one hand with the other. Both took several quick steps back.

The younger one eyed the streets leading out of the market square. The older one's knee bounced. "Leave!" he yelled, making a clumsy gesture with his arm. "Ye canna sit here."

"Make us," said the old man, the one who looked the worst.

"Aye," said the younger guard, taking a tentative step forward and putting his hand on the sword at his waist. "Ye think we're afraid of ye? We're nae afraid of ye."

"Aye, ye're afraid of us," said the woman. "Canna ye smell the leper miasma? The corruption in our souls, the punishment God has sent us?"

"I will end yer punishment!" yelled the older guard as he took five decisive steps forward, drew his sword, and pointed it at the woman.

The young English leper was now behind the man's back, and Anna held her breath as he reached out and took the key ring from the man's girdle.

With every step heavy and her skin sweaty, Anna made her way to them.

"Try and ye will be drowned like that man ye're guarding," said the old man.

Anna came to stand by the young leper, who handed her the key. Both guards had their backs to her. But people were stopping to see what was going on. While the lepers and the guards argued, she went to the door. Her hands shook as she inserted the large, iron key into the hole.

Aware of more and more people stopping to watch the argument between the guards and the lepers, she struggled to turn the thick, heavy key. "David," she whispered.

"Anna?" She heard him and saw a shadow move between the slits in the planks.

"I'm here, I'm getting ye out..."

The key finally turned with a clank, and she threw the door open. He stood before her, his eyes staring in wonder at her. His hands were still in shackles, but he could run.

"Come on." Anna made a wide, sweeping gesture for him to come closer.

He rushed to her, whole and alive and so dear. His dark-blond hair was like a crow's nest over his head. His eyes wet and glistening.

"Guards!" cried someone.

The two guards looked back and gasped. She grabbed David's hand and they ran...but only three steps. Then a force jerked her back, and David's hand disappeared from hers.

"Anna!" David cried as they shoved him back into the shed and the door was closed again.

"Leave, ye silly woman!" yelled one of the guards. "Leave before ye're drowned in the river with yer man!"

"Leave, lass!" cried the lepers. "Run!"

The crowd was pushing her, furious faces flashing. She was numb, her body tingling with fatigue as she ran. And as she untied both horses, climbed her horse, and spurred it forward, with Daisy following them, she felt like an abyss was opening under the horse's hooves.

But he wasn't dead yet. And she wouldn't just give up.

CHAPTER 19

DAVID TORE a piece of straw and threw the shredded bits on the dirt-packed floor. The sharp edges of the shackles bit painfully into his wrists. He was grateful they hadn't put his hands behind his back, at least.

Outside, the village was loud with people's voices, merchants calling for people to check their goods, dogs barking, horses neighing, children giggling and crying. He slumped to the cold ground, leaning against the wall of the shed, the wood hard against the back of his head.

He'd been so close to escaping. How in the world had Anna pulled off opening the jail door? What a wonderful, beautiful, and resourceful woman. Even after the horrors of the oubliette, she hadn't run when he was in trouble. She could have left for Stirling, especially knowing the truth about him. She might be thinking the same thing as the rest of the medieval world.

That he was a demon caster. A faerie friend. An outsider.

Well. What had changed? He'd been in a medieval jail for the past three years.

Today, it had just gotten much smaller. It had shrunk to the size of a shed.

This might be it, folks. This might be it. He might very well be dead tomorrow. Dùghlas had warned him about watching his mouth, but he hadn't paid enough attention, hadn't taken it seriously.

Story of his life.

He breathed in the dusty, earthy air of the shed, filling his lungs.

If he died tomorrow, his imagined life would go unlived. Even though, he had to admit, his actual life wasn't that bad. He'd loved playing football, had fun on his high school team back in Chicago. He'd loved his sister, his aunt and uncle and his cousins, despite the problems there.

He even remembered his parents a little. His mom showing him picture books with castles and reading him the fairy tale of *Puss in Boots*. His dad had done science experiments with him—he remembered how excited he'd been watching dry ice bubble and fill the sink with fog.

He picked up another straw and crumbled it in his hands.

Anna... Just her name, just the thought of her prickled his skin, making his heart beat faster. Perhaps all the hardships and struggles he'd been through were worth it so that he could meet her and get to know her. So that he could have one night with her, skin against skin, in his arms.

Did he have any regrets? Yes. He wished he could see Rogene, Angus, and Paul one last time. Wished he could see Anna again. Tell her he was falling in love with her. That she was the one.

To hell with it, he'd make proper love to her, have his first time with the girl he loved. He wanted to feel himself buried deep within her. Feel her quiver and see her mindless with plea-sure. Every one of her orgasms would be his. He wanted all of them, a lifetime of them.

Was his life in this medieval reality so bad?

Yeah, it was hard...and dangerous. But it was his own fault that he'd ended up here. He hadn't believed Rogene about time travel. He'd grabbed her arm when she'd traveled through time. Sìneag hadn't sent him here. She'd been as surprised as he was.

And if he hadn't come through time, he wouldn't have had time with his sister. Wouldn't have shared this world that was so important to her. Wouldn't have seen his nephew.

And he would never have met Anna.

As he stood up, sadness weighed on him, and he rolled his shoulders and stretched his neck.

He was lucky to be part of clan Mackenzie. They'd taken him in like one of their own. When he'd left Eilean Donan Castle, going on his adventure, Rogene had asked him to write to her, but writing was a struggle for him, especially with the quill and the ink.

Still, he should have tried. His only family in the world would never know what had happened to him. If he survived, by some miracle, he would make an effort and write to her.

He walked around and kicked at the dirt-packed floor with his shoes, tiny clouds of dust rising and playing in the beams of sunlight.

"I didn't do too bad, did I?" he asked himself out loud.

This was a pretty incredible adventure he was on. Only a handful of people had experienced it.

And now that he'd met a woman he cared about, he wanted more. More time with her. More time with his family. More time to appreciate the life he had rather than wanting something different.

No, he wasn't done yet. He wanted to live. He still had so much to do, to say, to experience. To give—his love and his loyalty and his protection. He still needed to see Anna through to Stirling, even if it meant her marrying another man. He would do anything for her.

He stood up and looked at the door. Desperation and fury tore him apart. His fists clenched, and with a roar, he ran at the door and hit it with his shoulder.

Pain burst through his bones as the door rattled, and he got kicked back by the hit. The guards yelled at him from the other side of the door. "What are ye doing, ye fool?"

It didn't work, but what did he expect? He couldn't just sit and wait for his death. He had to do something. He walked back and ran at the door again. More pain tore at him. More rattling, and he thought that perhaps he heard a hopeful crack of wood.

Again.

And again.

And again he stepped back and ran and hit the closed door. The guards yelled at him. Then laughed.

And he got angrier and angrier and more desperate.

This was how he'd been feeling for the past three years—trapped and mindlessly flinging himself against a closed door.

He was just breaking his own bones.

Not the door.

He stopped and slowly slid down the rough wall until he reached the floor. With his shoulder burning and aching, he didn't feel the tears, only that something wet was falling on his hands.

His struggle would end tomorrow at dawn.

CHAPTER 20

THE KEY CLANKED in the hole and the door to David's jail opened. A crowd of people stood silent and dark against the predawn sky. A guard came in carrying a torch that hurt David's eyes and brought the scent of smoke and steel.

The man grasped David by the elbow and led him out of his prison into the silent crowd. They eyed him with a quiet, dark apprehension. He was the source of the menace, the illness that God had brought into their midst. He had called the faeries, and God was punishing them all because of him.

Here it was. In this era of violence and misogynistic views and extreme religiosity, it was only a matter of time before his strangeness, his outlandishness would kill him.

How could he ever stay here?

Only for Anna. For Anna, he would...perhaps.

He searched the crowd for her face, to ensure that she hadn't been harmed after she'd tried to free him. To see her one last time and know she'd be with him in his final moments. Maybe he could cry out a message for her to deliver to Rogene. That he loved his sister and he was sorry.

Maybe he could tell Anna that he loved her.

That she was a treasure, and she should know it every day of

146

her life. That her worth didn't depend on the approval of her father or her political usefulness for Scotland.

That he loved her the way she was. And she should love herself.

But he didn't see her among the dark faces.

Then the priest came. "'Tis time," he said. "Let us go to the river."

The procession was quiet and solemn. As they walked, the sky kept brightening and he kept searching for Anna, looking into the dark streets they were passing. Once they left the village, he hoped to see her hiding behind a bush or a tree.

But there was no sign of her. Eventually, they came to an old wooden bridge that crossed the river. The crowd stopped on the riverbank. The priest gave a man a sack, and he put a rock inside. Then he passed it on to the next person. One by one, the villagers filled the sack with rocks, and with every single one, David's heart grew heavier until he had to look away.

The sun must have risen now behind a gray blanket of clouds. The river was a broad, steady current flowing like liquid iron. The other bank was full of bushes and trees and grassland. It smelled like river water and morning dew and old mud.

When the sack was full, the guard took it and shoved David to walk on the old bridge. Weathered wooden planks shook under their feet, and he could see water moving quickly through the gaps.

When the priest and one of his guards stood with him between them in the middle of the bridge, David looked into the sky. The cheerful singing of birds grated against his nerves. Water gurgled quietly, steadily...menacingly. These might be the last things he would hear.

He didn't want to die. His life was being taken from him so early, so unfairly. Anger was a fiery force inside him.

But he didn't want to spend his last moments in anger. He wanted to spend them thinking of Anna. And his sister. And what an extraordinary life he'd lived. What an adventure he'd had. He wanted to be grateful for the time he'd been given.

While the priest was reading something in Latin from the Bible and making the sign of the cross over him, David tuned him out. He didn't want to hear his jailor's words. He wanted to remember Anna's laughter and see her smiling face in his mind for the last time.

"Ye will be given the mercy to confess yer sins before death," said the priest finally.

The guard leaned down, and as he tried to put the rope around David's ankles, David kicked him, the rope flying out into the river like a snake. The guard rose, his jaw set, and drew his arm back. David ducked, but not fast enough, and the punch exploded through his head with a crack of bone. Disoriented, he wavered, only distantly registering that the guard tied another rope around his ankles.

Desperation cocooned David, heavy and dark.

"Would ye like to confess, son?" asked the priest.

With bile rising in his throat, blinking to clear his blurred vision, David said, "I would, if I had done anything to deserve this death. In my life, I always tried to do the right thing. Yes, I lied to stay alive, but that didn't harm anyone. I killed men in battles to keep my sister and my nephew safe. To help the clan that accepted me as their own. But I didn't do anything to you and this village. So it will be you who'll need to confess to the sin of wrongly judging me and killing an innocent man."

The priest sighed heavily and shook his head while the guard undid David's shackles. "The cuffs are made of iron and expensive," he murmured. "They will be used for the next prisoner."

Even with his head still swimming and his arms heavy and his legs tied, David pushed the guard, hoping to topple him over the railing and into the river. But the guard took two steps back and punched David in the stomach. The hit kicked all air out of David's body. The force threw him back, and unable to move his legs, he fell, the wood creaking under him, pain radiating through his back.

The guard sat on top of David and grabbed his wrists, holding them in a tight grip. "Ye son of a whore. Help me, Father! Tie the rope!"

With all the strength he had left in his arms, David wrestled to bring his wrists to his mouth. Raising his head, he sank his teeth into the guard's fingers, tasting salty blood.

The guard growled but didn't let go. The priest sank to his knees, smelling like dust and old urine and unwashed body, and tied the rope around David's wrists, binding him completely. Helpless rage thundered through him as the guard made an attempt to straighten David's arms along his body. David wriggled and wrestled, but now even the priest held him against the ground.

"Dinna struggle, son," the priest cried angrily. "'Tis God's will. Ye canna do anything about it. Ye dinna want to confess, so I will give ye yer last rites. May the Lord in his love and mercy help ye with the grace of the Holy Spirit. May the Lord who frees ye from sin save ye and raise ye up."

The guard wrestled a rope around David's body, tying his arms to his torso, then pulled him up to stand and brought him to the edge of the bridge.

"Ahhhhhhh!" David roared, screaming while the priest read the Bible in Latin and made crosses at David. "Let me go! You have an innocent man! Argghhh!"

The crowd murmured. "Witcher..." he thought he'd heard. "Hell..."

The guard put a noose around his neck, then attached it to the sack full of rocks that the villagers had filled earlier. It weighed on David's neck, hurting his shoulders.

David was still thrashing and wriggling when the guard pushed him closer to the wooden railing. There was a gap where the wood was broken and river rushed below with no barrier.

This was it.

He was tied up in a cocoon of death. The medieval world had caught him, physically and emotionally.

Finally he felt a push from behind, and with words of the priest still filling his ears, he fell, head down as the sack of rocks pulled him. The iron-gray water sped up to meet him. He took a huge mouthful of air.

A wet slap against his head.

A shock of cold.

Weightlessness.

Muffled gurgling in his ears.

And then the sack pulled him to his death.

As though time slowed, Anna watched David's body fly into the water. She was on the other side of the river, and downstream, hiding in the bushes on the bank.

It must have been very quick, just a moment, mayhap two rapid blinks of her eyes.

A loud splash and he was gone.

And she was gone, too. With David's body hitting the surface of the river, it was her soul that broke into myriad shards.

And they were sinking with him.

Fear for him warred with fury at the priest who was standing so calmly next to the guard. The solemn crowd on the opposite side of the river seemed to cheer up and start talking with one another. As the priest and the guard walked back, there were even relieved smiles. They were thinking, with David gone, the threat to their village had ended. The faeries wouldn't be called upon to bring sickness and curses. Demons wouldn't be tempted to come and steal and lurk around, killing livestock, spoiling milk, bringing disease and taking babies' lives.

Heart racing, she looked into the water. She needed to act. Her knife was in her hand. The people wouldn't see her from here...most likely.

And yet, here it was, the strong current that could bring death not just to David, but to her, as well.

Her feet were icy cold as she stepped in, her chest hurting. The current tugged at her feet like the hands of kelpies. The memory of the last time she was swimming gripped her. She remembered the impossible strength of the sea current twisting her lungs, choking her. She shook, and she couldn't feel her legs and arms.

But she couldn't give in to this. She had to act or David would die.

Anna walked into the river, careful and quick, mindful of the villagers. She took a lungful of air into her painfully tight chest and dove. It was cold and dark, but she kept her eyes open, looking for David.

The water was muddy and green, and bubbles moved up from her undertunic and her hair. She was weightless, letting the water carry her, play with her, be her friend. Not the evil current that would take her to her death.

And there, among the river plants and stones covered with moss and bottom mud, a light shape wavered. She worked her arms faster. Her lungs began burning. She hadn't had any practice holding her breath underwater for the past seven years. Three more lunges, and she saw David struggling and wriggling his body like a giant worm. The sack of rocks was doing its work —holding him at the bottom.

Her lungs burning, she began sawing through the rope with her knife. It didn't go easily. The rope kept escaping the knife underwater. She held it tightly with one hand, working the knife back and forth with the other. David's eyes were wide and anguished. He must be at his last breath. The scorching of her own lungs meant she didn't have much time left, either.

Finally her knife sliced through the last threads of rope, and she grabbed David and pushed herself and him up. God, he was heavy, and he didn't move at all, but she needed to bring his head above the water and let him breathe. She pushed and kicked with her legs, propelling the two of them up. The river above her was getting lighter and lighter the higher she went. As she and David emerged into the air, Anna gulped it into her lungs, gasping and coughing and spitting out water.

But he didn't.

The river kept pulling them downstream, and David sank underwater again. She was still holding him, his head just above the surface, but his neck was limp.

Oh nae!

Was she too late?

Anna didn't have much time, and she didn't have the energy to carry a heavy warrior like David and swim upstream towards the horses. She had to work with the river. She let it carry them downstream while swimming towards the shore. Even if she had to walk back some distance to retrieve the horses, at least they'd be out of the water.

An excruciatingly long time later, she felt the rocky, muddy shore under her feet. She took David by the tunic and dragged him until he was lying on the ground. A quick glance at the opposite bank showed her the villagers were gone. Small mercy.

But that wouldn't matter if David was dead.

Strands of wet hair were plastered to his face. His eyes were closed. He was pale.

He was not breathing.

She put her ear to his chest. Fear sliced through her stomach when she didn't hear any heartbeat.

"Damn ye!" she cried and hit him with all her might in the chest. He had to spit out water that filled his lungs. Nothing.

She turned him to his side and started hitting him with her fist against his chest.

Nothing.

"David!" She kept hitting and hitting. "Dinna leave me. Breathe, goddamn ye! Breathe!"

Slam. Slam. Slam.

Nothing.

CHAPTER 21

PAIN BURST through David's chest, and he coughed out a stream of water...or maybe vomited. A desperate, gut-wrenching need for air gripped him, and he gasped, sucking oxygen into his burning throat.

It hurt to breathe. He kept coughing and gasping...coughing and gasping.

And retching again.

Through blurry vision, he saw a lead-gray sky and Anna's face, wet and worried.

"David, 'tis all right... I'm here... Ye're alive..."

He was alive?

Last thing he remembered was the fall into the river, the weight pulling him down, holding him under the rushing water. The terror, the helplessness, the absolute agony of being bound with no ability to free himself. The dirty, dark-green river water, the bubbles floating up all around him.

The panic, all-consuming.

The anger. At them. At the world. At himself.

The pain of holding the air and wanting to breathe and not being able to.

Then a vision of Anna swimming to him like a mermaid. The

sight of her had warmed him, even if he knew it was likely a fantasy in his dying mind, a manifestation of his desire to see her one last time. And he couldn't hold it off anymore. The agonizing, burning sensation of sucking water into his lungs.

He hugged her, marveling at the freedom of his hands. She must have cut his bonds. He was shaking violently, his chest still on fire with pain.

"'Tis all right," she murmured into his ear soothingly. "Ye're safe. They're gone."

"I thought this would be my death," he said, his throat hurting and his voice rasping.

She pulled back and cupped his face. He could see her better now. Her long, dark eyelashes were glued together with water, her eyes bloodshot from searching for him underwater, but still beautiful, dark and glistening.

"My mermaid," he whispered. "You brought me back to life. You risked your life once again for me."

She smiled, her teeth white against reddened lips. "Ye would have done the same for me."

Somewhere in the distance, thunder rolled. He looked up at the dark sky. On the horizon, a black storm cloud was rolling in. He waited, letting his body breathe and adjust. Letting himself feel alive again. The scent of river water was in his nostrils and he was cold. Cold was good. Pain meant he was still alive.

"God, it's so good to breathe," he said.

She nodded. "Aye, 'tis. But we must go. It will rain soon, and we better find a shelter and warm ye. Ye didna die from drowning, but ye may still die from fever. Can ye stand?"

He nodded, and she helped him stand. He was dizzy and wavered, but she pulled him close against her side and let him wrap his arm around her. They walked through the bushes up the stream until she found their horses. She gave him his cloak to wrap around himself and walked behind the bushes to strip off her shift and put on her dry dress.

Then she helped him climb onto Daisy, and they galloped away.

They kept going northwest, towards Stirling. The wind was picking up, and the trees and bushes swayed violently, bent to the ground as though by an invisible hand. Rain drizzled at first, then poured. It came from the sea in the west and chased them like an army. Thunder rolled louder and closer. Lightning flashed.

But David was feeling better and better, coming back to life. He kept reminding himself that he didn't die. Thank God, he didn't die. His whole body was tired but alive, sensitive to every blow of the wind, the rustle of leaves, the drum of Daisy's hooves.

Soon, he saw a house to his left through the gray mist of rain.

"Look!" He turned to Anna and pointed. "Let's ask for shelter there."

They should avoid people, really. But what choice did they have with the storm on their heels and nothing but fields and woods and hills around them? At least they were a good distance from the village now.

As they came closer, he saw it was a farm, though the fields were overgrown with wild plants and flowers. There was no smoke rising from the smoke hole in the roof. They dismounted, completely drenched, and led the horses into the empty stables. The roof leaked in one place, but it was a decent enough shelter and the horses would be fine here. There was some hay and even tools to clean their hooves and coats.

"I'll tend to them later," Anna said. "We need to get warm, eat, and rest."

He clapped Daisy's back. "Thank you for saving me yet again, old friend," he whispered to her, giving both horses hay and water.

David took his sleeping roll, his traveling purse, and his sword. He drew the weapon as they walked out. Even if there were no signs of life, it didn't mean bandits weren't hiding there. They crossed the small courtyard and David slowly opened the heavy door and peered inside the house. The shutters were drawn and there was little light. It was quiet and smelled dusty and a little moldy.

"I think it's empty," David said. "Wait here a minute."

He stepped in and moved slowly through the house, his back to the wall. Rain drummed against the thatch above. The outline of a bed was visible against the wall to his left. There was a fireplace where people must have cooked and even a stack of wood. He heard the rhythmic sound of droplets hitting the wood and thought the roof must be leaking here, too.

It was empty.

He nodded to Anna, and she came in. He lit the fire in the fireplace, grateful for a dry, warm shelter. When there was light in the house, he looked around. Herbs and mushrooms hung on strings in the corner. Smoked fish was suspended high above the fire.

There was also a table where the family must have cooked and eaten, six chairs around it. Three chests stood open and empty. Given the state of the fields, they must have left months ago.

He wondered why. Maybe they couldn't pay the rent anymore and the lord hadn't found anyone to replace them. Life was tough in the Middle Ages.

He ached to remove his wet clothes—they were clingy and heavy and cold. Standing by the fire, he unfastened the cloak and pulled up his tunic. He hung it and the cloak on the backs of two chairs and pushed them closer to the fire. He wanted to dry his braies, too, but he turned to Anna to see what she thought of that. He didn't want her to feel uncomfortable.

He found her standing and staring at him, her eyes slowly walking up and down his naked torso.

"You like what you see?" he asked.

Her looking at him made blood rush to his cock. Not long

ago, he'd been the one staring at her naked while she'd been bathing.

"Um…" she said and swallowed hard. "Aye. Ye're…ye're…" Her breath seemed to catch. "Ye're very handsome, David."

He grinned. "Thanks."

Her red dress was wet from the rain, but it wasn't soaked through. Her cheeks glowing, she turned away from him. "Ye must eat," she said as she busied herself with retrieving the rest of the bread they had in their travel pouch. "The MacDowells even had a small horn flask of uisge."

He had forgotten about the uisge…

To his surprise, he realized he still didn't want any, even after being nearly drowned. He didn't want oblivion. But he didn't know why.

Maybe it had something to do with the Highland princess who had saved his life twice already.

She put the loaf of bread on the table and the remnants of the cheese. They sat and ate, throwing smiles at each other. Thunder was roaring above them. Rain battered against the house, and wind wailed through the gaps around the door and the window shutters.

But all he could see was how the fire was reflected in Anna's glossy, wet hair and how her eyes shone when she looked at him. And how dimples formed in her cheeks when she smiled at him shyly.

When they had eaten, he stretched his hand out to her over the table and she took it.

He stood up and gently pulled her up to stand before him.

They had nowhere to go. The world outside had been shut down by the storm. The wedding…it would happen later. As far as he was concerned, ten days was so far in the future it didn't exist.

There was only the two of them. And his soul was connected to hers.

He drew her to him by her waist. Her dress was damp against

his naked torso. "You know what will warm a man better than fire?" he asked her.

Her eyes were like pools of night before him. Endless and liquid and breathtaking.

"What?" she asked.

"This."

He kissed her. Her mouth tasted like strawberries and something flowery and her...like heaven. Her plush, full lips, her sleek tongue as he lashed his against it over and over, were an ache in his blood. Who needed uisge when he had this? When she kissed him like she wanted to meld their mouths, their bodies, into one?

Her body, strong and wet and pliable, was pressed against him. She was his treasure, his salvation, and she was in his arms.

"You're wet," he whispered against her lips. "Let's dry your dress."

"Aye..."

As he undid the laces at her back, her dress became free, and he pulled it down. Her skin was pale and glistened in the firelight.

As her dress fell and pooled around her feet on the floor, her small breasts, perfect and round, were right there, touching him, skin to skin. He could feel her hard nipples pressed against his chest. Christ, he was getting excited, wanting her like he'd never wanted anyone before.

"Anna, I want you," he said. "I want to tease you and taste you and bring you orgasm after orgasm..."

He wanted more, actually. In the jail, he'd been craving more from her.

But he had no right. He'd need to stop. Her whole future depended on her virginity.

"I want to do the same to ye," Anna whispered.

He felt his erection jerk and he groaned. "Oh, Christ... Come here..."

He picked her up, cursing as he felt her hot, sleek folds press against his hard stomach as he carried her to bed. He laid her on the bed and pinned her hands above her head and marveled at her, looking at the length of her gorgeous body, small and feminine and delicate and strong. He kissed her again, tasting every nuance of her mouth, his hand traveling down the length of her body. He caressed her breasts and teased them just the way she'd liked last time. She was soft and round and warm under his hand. She was squirming and moaning into his mouth, and he knew she was excited.

His balls ached from desire for her. His hand moved down, and when he reached her soft curls, she gasped and her legs fell open for him. He knew now she was made for him, and he was made for her. His soul sang when he was by her side.

And he wanted to give her the world. Bring her every pleasure, every joy, every desire she wanted.

His fingers spread her folds and touched the soft, luscious sex of her, searching for and finding her clit. The moan of pleasure she gave into his mouth was like an explosion of need in his veins. Her legs fell even farther open, and she moved her pelvis, searching for, needing more of his touch.

He loved it. God, having her so open and so hot for him.

He withdrew and pulled down his braies, and as he stood before her, completely naked and erect, her eyes were wide on his penis. "Oh... David..." she gasped.

But it wasn't fear, it was...

Desire.

She wanted him.

But he couldn't have her.

"No, sweetheart. We'll only fool around. I can't take your virginity, and we both know it."

She didn't reply, only sat up and put her hands on his sides and pulled him down on top of her. "I almost lost ye. Twice," she whispered and kissed him with her hot, wet mouth. "Our days together are ending. Ye're the man for me, David. Only I canna be with ye for the rest of my life. So at least give me this. Be my first. Let me imagine ye'll be my only."

He groaned. "I really want to... You have no idea. But I can't..."

"There are ways that my virginity can be faked," she whispered. "I'll pay the price later. Take me. Make me yers."

Her words were his undoing. He'd been dreaming of her, imagining this, craving it for days. He'd regretted not doing this earlier. He'd show her how much he loved her.

"You'd be my first, too," he whispered.

And she kissed him harder, needier. She was all soft skin and gorgeous limbs and everything he'd ever wanted. He spread her thighs.

Oh Christ, how he wanted her. Needed to be one with her, buried inside her so deep he wouldn't know where he ended and she began. To feel her, tight and wet and sleek around him.

In his world, in the twenty-first century, a girl he loved begging for him to take her virginity wouldn't be an issue. He'd need a condom, of course...

But there were no condoms here. So he wouldn't come inside. He'd pull out. It was the fourteenth century, and he had to play by the rules.

"Anna..." He kissed her. "Are you sure?"

She circled with her pelvis, teasing his cock, and he sucked in air from a sudden onrush of pleasure.

"I am," she whispered. "I havena been so sure in my life."

Goddamn it. Goddamn it to hell. He couldn't resist that.

"It might hurt, sweetheart..." he said. "I'm not an expert, of course. But it might hurt the first time."

"I ken. I dinna think anything will hurt with ye..."

He groaned as her words echoed within him in a sweet ache. He looked deep into her eyes. He would be a dead man by now if it wasn't for her. He would be back in the twenty-first century if he hadn't grabbed his sister's leg and traveled in time. And he wouldn't be with her. This princess, this seductress, this warrior. This Highland woman he was ready to die for.

They may not have a tomorrow. All they had was now.

And as the storm raged and beat against the house like the Middle Ages had raged and beat against him for the past three years, as thunder roared and heavy rain drummed against the roof above their heads, he looked at her and he knew.

He loved her. And he'd love her his whole life.

And nothing would ever give him greater happiness than making love to the woman he loved.

Still looking into her eyes, he felt her with his hand. She was wet and slick, her arousal dripping from her. He didn't know what to do to make it less painful; he only knew he wanted to give her pleasure. All the pleasure in the world.

Rubbing her clit and seeing her arch her torso into him and gasp, he positioned his cock against her entrance. She was hot and velvety, and just touching her there spilled a liquid jolt of pleasure through him. His heart raced. This was about to happen. He pressed, and she was tight. There was a barrier he couldn't pass through. He gently started to dig in, stretching her, watching her, continuing to rub her clit. She gasped, digging her nails into his back, her legs wrapping around his hips and pressing him into her.

The pleasure of her flesh against his was so intense, he was barely holding off from plunging into her balls deep. "Does it hurt?" he asked, breathless.

"Nae," she whispered on an exhale, her eyes liquid and black. "It fills me, I want more of this...more of ye...inside me."

He swallowed hard, holding on to the last bits of his restraint, trying not to do exactly what she'd asked him to.

"Okay," he said, swallowing, and twisted himself gently into her, massaging her slick clit.

"Ahhh...." she gasped, arching into him. "Oh, David..."

She was opening to him, her thighs falling farther apart. He pressed in as gently as he could, more and more, and then the pressure, the barrier that held him off, was gone and he was inside of her.

She gasped again, the sound half pained, half ecstatic. He froze, almost unable to believe the unbearable softness and tightness he was surrounded with. Her.

They were one. He breathed deeply to stop himself from withdrawing and plunging in again.

"Does it hurt?" he asked.

"A wee bit," she said and drew him closer with her hands, "Just a wee bit... 'Tis a sweet pain..." Her eyes glistened. "Like the first time stepping onto a warm pebble beach... Yer feet are warm and some pebbles are sharp, and others are smooth... And there's that sea at the end of it and 'tis where ye belong."

"Okay, sweetheart," he said. "The hard part is over. You tell me any moment you want me to stop. Any time it's too much. All right?"

Her eyes melted, glowing with that warmth and love that made him want to be a better man. Made him want to stop time and let her warmth wash over him. Wash all his suffering away.

He kissed her and moved inside her, removing his finger from her clit as his hand was pinned between his body and hers. He moved slowly but angled himself so that he was also stimulating her clit. She let out a long, porn-star-like moan into his mouth. Liquid pleasure, better than any alcohol, spilled through his veins as he moved.

She was so smooth and hot and tight and so wet he slid easily in and out. She was wriggling under him, thrusting her hips into his with his rhythm, searching for her own pleasure against his cock. It was slow at first as he let her get used to him. And he was letting himself get used to this...to his first time...learning how to move to give her the most pleasure.

And how not to come inside her like he'd feared most of all... like he couldn't allow to happen.

They sped up, both hungry, both breathless. Both unable to stop or think or breathe.

This tightness, this sweet pleasure was building in him, and he knew it was building in her. He saw the signs. He knew how to make a woman come without penetrating her; he'd done it for years.

Now it was even better.

She was sweaty and flushed; her eyes were half-closed and never leaving him. Her lips were red and full, and she was biting her lower lip, licking it. She was gasping and yelling and digging her nails into his back.

And he missed it.

She was coming. Her flesh was milking him, tightening around him in a perfect, gorgeous rhythm... She was screaming his name...

He should have pulled out.

His own orgasm slammed into him in a fiery flow.

And he was coming inside of her, all tense and helpless. And as the intense pleasure of the orgasm was dying out, he collapsed on top of her, their breaths coming and going in the same rhythm.

He stretched in the bed and took Anna into his arms. As he kissed her forehead and held her, warm and his—truly his now— he couldn't fall asleep. He listened to the storm raging outside. And he wondered what would happen once it was over.

And how he could ever return to his miserable existence after the glory, the fullness of the life he'd known with her.

Even if it would be in the twenty-first century.

CHAPTER 22

Anna stirred and woke up, enveloped in a hot, hard male body. The storm still battered the house, though she didn't hear thunder anymore. The fire had died, but they weren't cold at all.

It was still dark inside the house, but strips of dull light had appeared between the shutter slats and along the stone windowsills. So it must be morning. Nine days until John the Baptist.

Nine days of freedom.

She kissed David's hard chest, and he stirred and pulled her closer. She closed her eyes, inhaling his scent. He still smelled like river, but also like horse and like leather and steel. Like a warrior.

The warrior from the future who had made her a woman. They had made love three more times during the night, and even though she hadn't felt it then, she was sore now.

God forgive her, she was a maiden no more. She had sinned, and why oh why did the sin taste so good? She'd given her most precious commodity, her virginity, to a man who would never be her husband. Her chest ached and tightened from guilt. So she'd need to think of ways to fake it. She would need the help of her maidservant. She could be trusted. Anna had heard that blood could be collected from the kitchen, from a chicken or other slaughtered animal, then carried secretly in a small vial hidden in jewelry. And she could lie still and cry in pain as her future husband took her...

God, she hated herself for thinking of such lies... But if that was the price to pay to bring her father Stirling Castle, she'd do it. She'd burn in hell for it, but at least she'd have a life worth living.

Only two days until she'd need to meet Philip for the secret introduction meeting. God, what were they all thinking? Did they still believe she was alive and would return? She needed to hurry, even though she didn't want to. With the thunder having passed, the storm would likely cease today, as well. Though part of her hoped it wouldn't.

"What are you thinking about?" came David's hoarse voice, and she looked up at him. His sleepy face was handsome and so dear her heart ached.

If only he could belong to her like her heart belonged to him...

"This," she said and stroked his face. "This heaven here. Part of me wishes I could have ye here forever. We'd work the land on this farm. Raise children. Lie here every night, lawful husband and wife, loving each other, sharing every day until the day we die."

Aching sorrow crossed his handsome features, and she realized her mistake. "I'm sorry," she said, looking down. "Yer future dream doesna have ye staying in this age, does it?"

His chest froze under her cheek, and she looked up. His Adam's apple bobbed as he stared into the dark thatched slope of the roof. "No, it doesn't."

Hearing him say it out loud hurt, and she stopped breathing, hoping he would say something else. He was silent for a while. Then when he looked at her again, his eyes softened. He tightened his arms around her. "But it doesn't mean I don't want you in my future. I know you're the one Sìneag intended for me. The woman I am destined for."

Her very being felt light and warm, as though a ray of sunshine beamed from the sky right through her. "David...I... dinna think I'll ever love anyone like I love ye. Even though we were born centuries apart, for the first time in my life I feel like I belong. With ye, I dinna feel like an outcast nae more."

His eyes glistened. "So do I, sweetheart," he said, his voice croaking. "This farm, with the storm outside and the world shut out... It's like home."

He leaned down and kissed her. The kiss was tender and slow, tantalizing lashes of tongue and lips, and so much gentleness, she could dissolve in it like butter. He brought her up, and she felt him already hard. She climbed on top of him, feeling the silky, hot hardness of him press into her inner thigh.

"I want you to ride me..." he whispered, his eyes hot and dark on her.

"I'm a wee bit sore, David."

"Ride my face then..."

She froze as a rush of heat sizzled her cheeks. "What can ye mean?"

He pressed at her arse with his hands, indicating he wanted her to move closer to his face. "I mean, come sit on my face," he said. "You'll love it. I promise."

Just him saying this brought a throbbing heat down into the apex of her thighs and her inner muscles clenched. She bit her lip, her breathing accelerating, her pulse thumping in her temples. She moved over him and higher until she was sitting on his chest. He looked at her sex, right in front of his face, and blew air on it, and she clenched again.

"Come here," he growled and caressed her inner thighs with his hands, gently pulling her towards him.

With her cheeks blazing hot, she obeyed, and gasped as his mouth connected with her aching sex. He kissed her there. Once. Twice.

"Does it hurt?" he asked, looking up at her.

She'd already forgotten all about the dull ache and looked down at him. "Nae... Got nae pain, David... Just yer mouth... Ahhh..." She arched her spine as he pulled her back to his mouth and moved his tongue over her. "Ahhh."

Aye, he was teasing her there, right there, in the center of all that was good and pleasant and blissful. Gentle sucks and flicks of his tongue and rubbing against it, and she was heading straight for that cliff, as if riding a horse that had lost its mind, that couldn't be stopped. And then she flew over, into the sheer bliss, clenching, quivering, aching, and soaring.

When her shaking stopped, she moved back and collapsed on top of him, chest to chest, stomach to stomach, legs to legs. He was still rock-hard and hot, pressed against her stomach. He brushed a strand of her hair off her face. "You're delicious. I could never have enough of you."

She put her chin on his chest and looked at him. "Nor could I have enough of ye."

Then she crawled down. None of her climaxes were good enough if they weren't with him inside of her, connected to her in the most intimate way.

She was wet, and he was still hard, and she wanted him inside. She straddled his pelvis. He frowned darkly as she took his erection in her hand and directed it into her entrance.

"Anna, you are sore... Oh God... Are you sure?" She sat right on him, and it slid well as she was still full of her arousal, stretching her tight internal muscles so deliciously, the little ache that she felt was like butter on a honey cake. She gasped and sat even lower on him, feeling him stretch her to the very core, to the deepest depths of her.

He tensed and went rigid, his fists clenching on top of her hips. "Oh God, you're so fucking hot and tight and delicious," he groaned out. "Christ..."

She put her hands on his chest. His handsome face was soft and hard at the same time, his eyes half-closed and dark on her, his jaw tight, the muscles over his cheekbones taut. She suddenly felt she had power. Her whole life, she'd been powerless. As a bastard and as a woman, she'd always been at the mercy of the men in her life: her uncle Aulay, her father, and her would-be husband. She didn't have a choice about her future like men had over theirs.

But not now.

Now, she had all the power.

All control. She could ride him hard and bring him his release quickly or bring him sweet torture with slow gliding and teasing. She began moving up and down on his cock, feeling the delicious friction of his hard erection against her sensitive tissue. He was gasping, without turning his eyes away from her. As she accelerated the rhythm, chasing that pleasure, she felt her breasts bounce, her thighs burning. His eyes were on her chest, and he bit his lower lip, and the long, stiff groan of a wolf escaped his throat.

She loved it. She loved that he wanted her so, that she was the one deciding what would happen, even if it was just for now. She was throbbing, both with the ache of her first time and pleasure of him teasing her in the places she wanted the most. And then she wanted it harder. She wanted to feel the edge. She wanted everything.

Her climax slammed against her as his did him. With a jerk, he pulled out of her, leaving her quivering and gasping.

He scooped her into his arms right away and pressed his face into her shoulder.

"I'm in love with you, Anna," he whispered.

"And I am with ye, David," she echoed.

And as she lay and breathed in his arms, she knew... He knew, too...

Love wasn't enough.

Her world was not his world. And it never would be.

And she realized she still didn't understand why. "When ye're in the future," she asked, and he looked up at her, "what will ye do? Why do ye want to go back there so much when ye have yer clan and yer sister here...?"

And me.

But she didn't say that out loud.

He sighed and lay on his back and rubbed his forehead. "I just... If I managed to show everyone that even with dyslexia I can be as good as my professor parents and my sister, who has a PhD, I thought I'd prove that I was worth something, too."

"What is...dysle—xia...?"

"It just means I have a harder time than most people reading and writing."

She chuckled. "Ye are lucky to be able to read and write at all. And what is a pee aitch..."

"PhD? It's the highest university degree."

"Oh, yer sister is clever. So are ye, David. And yer parents are dead, aye?"

"Yes."

"And yer sister...that PhD...she's nae that nae more, aye? She's the wife of a laird..."

He sighed. "Yes."

"So...I guess I just wonder if ye're chasing the dream of a lad who isna ye nae more?"

He was silent for a long time, blinking, staring into the darkness. "It's like you're reading my fucking soul, Anna. Christ...I wondered that, too. But I guess that boy is still inside me. I just don't feel like I'm worthy here." He looked at her, all hard edges and tight muscles. "In your world, there are three types of people. Those who fight, those who work, and those who pray. Those who fight"—he looked at his sword by the bed—"they have the power. Your chiefs, your knights, your overlords. Wars rule your world. I wasn't raised like that. I'm competitive, and I like to win, but I wasn't raised believing I had to kill people to prove my place in life. I was raised believing I had to be smart and get a good education to be worth something. With dyslexia, learning was difficult. Being the same as everyone else was difficult. But my strong body, my football skills gave me a place at college...a chance to be worthy. When I got my acceptance letter...that dream was finally within my reach. I could finally be proud of myself and know my dad and my mom would have been proud of me, too. I was looking forward to that life—graduating, getting a good job. Maybe starting my own business. Buying a nice house. A car. Having a family one day. I'd provide for them. Give them the security and love and comfort I didn't have."

Anna frowned. Some of what he'd said she didn't understand. "What is a job?" she asked. "And a car? And a business? And why are they important?"

"Cars are like carriages, but horses don't need to pull them. They use gas, which is a natural resource, like oil. People drive them using a steering wheel instead of reins."

Her mind raced, trying to imagine a cart that drove itself. "Sounds like witchcraft..."

He chuckled and told her more about his time. It worked differently in his age than in hers. There were no feudal lands, and everyone could own land if they had means to buy it. While in the medieval world, land was money, in his world, skill, brains, and hard work were also money.

In his world, she wouldn't need to marry anyone to ensure her future. She wouldn't need to guard her virginity as a commodity to be traded by her father for a castle. In his world, women could get a job or run their own business. In her world, widowhood could give a woman freedom and wealth, but she didn't want to wait until her husband died to be free.

She looked around. "I understand that a house like this probably isna comfortable to live in compared to the houses in yer future. But is the car and the house and the job worth leaving behind the woman who loves ye?"

He closed his eyes and ran both hands through his hair. He sighed and looked at her. "Not if you put it like that, Anna. Part of me is singing with happiness from being with you. Part of me is shitting myself. Not because of the house and the car. No. But other stuff. A man can't be drowned just for trying to talk to faeries in my time. People don't have to carry swords to defend themselves. Women can earn their own money instead of depending on their husband or father to provide for them.

"I'm still an outsider, Anna, and I always will be. And I'll never live my life to the fullest here. I want to prove myself, be proud of myself. And I can't do it here, even though I love you." He gently stroked her naked arm, sending sweet tingles all over her. "I've been trying to get home forever, but I could only use the rock once I found the love of my life. Now I've found you. I think this means I can go home. But the thought of leaving you makes me want to tear my chest open and cut my heart out."

The pain in his voice stole her breath and felt like a thousand claymores cutting her into ribbons. "Aye, we love each other," she said. "But it doesna mean anything. I am still the daughter of a king. And in this world, I must marry Sir Philip."

He blew a long breath out, then hid his face in her stomach, tickling her skin with his hair.

Anna swallowed, blinking to stop her tears. "And I want ye to be happy, and so..." It killed her to say it out loud. "I want ye to go. I want ye to have yer freedom."

He looked up at her, his eyes bright, a grin on his face. "Then come with me! I heard another Highland woman went to the future with the man she fell in love with...and my friend Raghnall Mackenzie chose to leave this time for Bryanna, a woman from the future. It's possible. Let's go together, as soon as the storm ends. Come with me to the future. You won't have to marry anyone, and I'll help you adjust, and we'll be together. You'll be free."

She stilled, unable to move. The words were seductive...going to the future with the love of her life, being free of her duty to her father and never having to face the consequences of her lost virginity...

She imagined those cars that moved without horses. The houses of glass and stone that anyone, not just nobles, could own. The world where women could decide their own futures and be free. Where a person's birth did not define their worth.

She liked it. And she knew it was true because David had given her more freedom of choice than anyone in her life. Made her feel loved and valued and respected.

But that was only a dream. A wish that would never come true.

"I thank ye for the offer, David," she whispered. "But I have a duty to my father. I need to keep Scotland safe and help bring the war with England to its end by marrying Philip Mowbray."

His face wrinkled with pain. "Duty to your father?" He chuckled bitterly. "The father you've only spent a couple of days with in your life? The father who only calls for you when he needs you for political reasons?"

Every word was like a lash against her wound, hitting right where it hurt. He was saying out loud the exact words and doubts she'd thought to herself.

"You need to put yourself first, Anna," he said. "You need to understand you are worth everything with or without his approval. Or anyone else's."

She sat up and shifted away from him. For the first time in a long time, she didn't want to touch him or listen to him. Tears burned her eyes. "Ye dinna understand, David. Indeed, because as ye said, ye're an outsider. Truth is, nae matter how much I dream, love is never an option for a woman like me. Nae love for myself and nae love for someone else. 'Tis nae something a bastart like me has a right to."

CHAPTER 23

Despite her harsh words, Anna didn't think she'd ever been so glad for a storm to continue. The wind and rain kept ravaging the countryside, the drumming of raindrops like music. Thunder and lightning returned. Even the short walk to the stables to take care of the horses was an ordeal.

They had made love again at night, passionate and hard, as though their bodies spoke—as though their bodies said they were sorry for their words and that they wanted to spend every moment clinging to each other, entwined, entangled forever.

They shared the MacDowell uisge and cooked. The remnants of the oats in the sacks in the corner were all moldy, but the mushrooms were edible and there were still somewhat dry but usable parsnips, wild carrots, and wild garlic in the root cellar. Together, they made a soup.

"Anna, are you all right?" David asked as she chopped wild carrots into tiny bits.

She cleared her throat and smiled at him. "I just worry what's happening in Stirling. I'm supposed to meet Philip tomorrow. But we can't leave during a storm like this. It would kill us out there." What if Sir Philip was angry because she hadn't arrived? What if they were fighting because of her, killing each other?

"Look," David said, throwing cut parsnips into the boiling cauldron. "I wish it was different, our situation. And I know you do, too. We'll never have this again. Tomorrow, hopefully, we'll be able to leave. For now, let's just…"

"Aye," she said and grinned. "Let's pretend like 'tis just ye and I, and there's nae Philip, nae Father, and nae time travel."

Day after day, Anna did her best to forget about the things she couldn't change and enjoy her time with David. He told her about his life in the modern times—about the game he played, about running water and glass windows and light and warmth easily available in homes. There was no need to have castles because no one would come and try to take your home away. At least not in the country where he lived—United States, he called it. Trade and information seemed to be the biggest powers there.

People didn't need to get married to form alliances; they could marry for love. It was an odd concept for her…one that she liked.

The good girl, the noble lady in her felt guilty for having sinned before marriage, and she knew God would punish her for that somehow. She would accept the punishment. It was worth it. She'd always remember these days of happiness, feel them like the beads of a rosary in her hands.

The rain battering the walls was like a shield around them, keeping the outside world at bay. At one point, she broke down. They were lying in bed after making love, sated and lazy and warm and heavy. Her head lay on his biceps as if it were a pillow, her hand and his intertwined.

"Dream with me, David," she said as she kissed his hand. "What would our life be like together if ye did stay? What if ye could be happy here, with me? What if ye could accept this time for yer own? Just for a moment, please?"

He sighed. "It's easy to imagine, sweetheart. I'd be the luckiest guy in Scotland. Being with a girl like you… We'd have a small estate somewhere, I think. A house like this or maybe a small castle to protect you. But in a better condition and near a loch."

"Aye." She giggled.

"I'd make love to you every night, go riding with you..."

"Swimming?" she asked, surprising herself. "Swimming doesna terrify me so much nae more."

"Yeah." He chuckled. "I'd love to go swimming with you. I'd teach you football, maybe we'd play together...teach our kids..."

He'd told her "kids" was not only used for baby goats in his time but for children, as well.

"Ye'd want to have bairns?"

He chuckled and kissed her hand. "Not right away, maybe. But yeah. I've always wanted children at some point in my life."

"What about what ye said about achieving things...house...car...success?"

He was silent for a few moments. "I've always been interested in business. That's what you guys call trade."

"Aye," she said. "My clan is powerful and rich because of trade."

"Yeah," David said. "That's what I want to do with my life in the twenty-first century. Start my own business. So I guess I'd want to find a way to do the same here."

He asked her about the details of trade—the prices for wool, how long it took for ships to arrive, the politics. Bruges, a staple town in Flanders, was an important port in Europe that bought Scottish wool for a good price, and it was very much valued.

"But that's raw material," he said. "If you guys already offered manufactured products from fleece, like yarn or even clothes, they would be more expensive."

"Ye sound like my uncle Aulay." She giggled.

They kept talking, painting the future they would never have. And when he fell asleep, she cried silently on his shoulder because he would return to his time after her wedding.

Three days before John the Baptist's Eve, they woke up to

blazing sunlight that shone through the slits around the windows and door, and the chirping of the birds.

No wind. No rain.

When Anna opened the door, blinding white reflections jumped off the water in the muddy puddles. A thin fog had formed from the sun evaporating thick layers of water. The air was humid and heavy. Anna felt heavy, too, like the very world was pressing on them, making it hard to breathe.

But she knew it wasn't truly the weather weighing her down, but the knowledge that her time with David would soon be over.

CHAPTER 24

"We're too late," Anna said, sitting on her horse by David's side.

As David watched arrows fly from the walls of Stirling Castle down onto the Bruce's army, screams and the roar of angry Scots came from the distance. The army couldn't get into the castle, but they were trying. Siege stairs had been lifted. Warriors climbed and fell, dead or wounded. Bruce's warriors sent flaming arrows at the walls, and thin strands of smoke rose into the air. David knew they needed to ride into the Bruce's camp, stop the unnecessary bloodshed. But it would be dangerous to cross the open ground with a battle going on.

"We're not late, your wedding is tomorrow," he said as he turned to look at Anna, and his breath caught.

Her back was straight and proud as she sat on the horse she had decided to call Ayr, her face pale and her hair dark and thick and waving in the wind. The goddess of the hunt, of the battle. The princess stolen and put into the depths of darkness.

He'd brought her here, to her wedding, to the end of her freedom.

The end of his happiness.

Something rustled and a twig snapped behind him, and he

turned sharply to look over his shoulder, peering into the shadows among the pine trees.

"What is it?" She looked back, her hand moving to the dirk tucked into her girdle. "The MacDowells again?"

His hand lay on his claymore. He listened and watched. Trees rustled and bushes swayed. Birds chirped, undisturbed by the uproar of a battle by the castle. Wind brought the scents of woodsmoke and death from down below.

A squirrel darted between the trees and climbed up a trunk, watching him. Did the squirrels of this time take special pleasure in tormenting him? Or was he just too jumpy after all he'd been through?

"No," he said. "Not this time."

After the storm, David and Anna's journey had been slow as they'd passed through debris, fallen trees, and overflowing rivers and brooks. Two times, they'd had a close encounter with the MacDowells, and both times they'd had to change their route, delaying their arrival even more.

"We should make haste," Anna said as she looked at Stirling again. "They're hurling stones from the castle now."

Her voice was quiet, and she didn't move. David stared at her, hoping to catch her glance. Hoping to talk to her one last time. Hoping for a goodbye...or, on the contrary, hoping—and afraid— she'd change her mind and would run away with him to the future.

But she didn't look at him.

"Many lives have been lost because we werena fast enough," Anna said and pointed her finger at the army. "See that banner? 'Tis my father. We must go there."

David was about to lose her forever. Cut out a part of his soul. He would rather eat dirt than deliver Anna to Philip. But he had to.

She'd said she could not come with him to the future because of her dedication to Scotland and to her father. But did he still want to return to the twenty-first century? Yes, he did. The scholarship, he reminded himself. That chance to prove himself...

But to whom? To his aunt and uncle who'd never truly cared about him? To his dead mother and father? To his sister who already loved and approved of him?

To his old friends who'd probably forgotten his name by now?

He was in love with a Highland princess from the Middle Ages.

But, like she had said, love wasn't everything.

There was another snap and a rustle behind them. David turned and ducked as an arrow flew past him.

Behind them, dozens of MacDowell and English horses emerged from the shadows. Dugald MacDowell looked astonished as he recognized David next to Anna. They were about fifty feet away.

"Anna!" he yelled, spurring Daisy. "Go!"

She dug her heels into Ayr's sides, and together they flew across the empty field.

SHOCK WASHED OVER ANNA LIKE A WAVE OF COLD SEAWATER. The shadows in the woods behind them were like death coming out of the darkness in the oubliette.

Like the day Dugald MacDowell had ambushed their clan, taken her prisoner, and diminished her to someone insignificant. Someone to forget.

Nae, never again.

She spurred Ayr with the kicks that must have hurt the poor horse. Ayr neighed and launched forward. Anna leaned lower and gripped with her thighs. Running for her life. "Hya!" she cried. "Hya!"

Her dagger was tucked into her girdle, and she wouldn't hesitate to use it if she had to. She'd kill anyone before she'd let them take her again.

"Hya!" cried David, who rode by her side just a little behind her. "Hya!"

"Get them!" she heard Dugald's voice. "Faster, ye bastarts!"

Arrows flew around them, spiking the ground. If only her father noticed them galloping through the field. If only he could send help. How stupid would it be if Anna was caught so close to him? And she wouldn't let them have David. Never.

"Father!" she called.

"King Robert!" roared David through the thunder of hooves.

There were three hundred yards between them and Bruce's camp when she saw anti-cavalry troops run towards them, their pikes swaying in the air. Dozens of them, then hundreds. Horsemen mounted and galloped to their aid.

And then she saw the MacDonalds.

Uncle Aulay, impossible to miss, held his claymore high in the air as he galloped roaring the MacDonald war cry, "Clann Domnhnaill! Clann Domnhnaill!"

Right by his side, Colum, like a dark warrior on his black horse, galloped with a bow in his hands, shooting arrows at the enemy. Behind them, first dozens, then hundreds of warriors— Scottish knights, MacDonald men, and those of other Highland clans—galloped at the enemy with a battle roar. Bruce's banner moved towards her quickly.

From her right and behind her, hoofbeats drummed louder and louder. Her hands and feet going numb with fear, she turned.

Dugald.

Just like that first damned day, he was upon her. She took out her dirk. She wouldn't make just a scratch this time. "'Tis over, lass," he growled, reaching for the reins. "Dinna fight this or ye will be hurt."

She slashed at his arm. Her dirk opened the sleeve of his tunic right above the gauntlet, splashing crimson on her. Dugald yelled in pain but didn't stop, and the taste of the blood of her enemy made her stomach churn.

But it gave her more determination and more fight.

"Ye bastart!" she cried and stabbed again, plunging her dirk deep into his lower arm.

He cried out and slowed down, disappearing from her vision.

The Bruce's anti-cavalry troops planted themselves in a long, protective line, the pikes protruding like the needles of a giant hedgehog. There was a gap between the pikers, and she and David flew through it, galloping into the midst of her father's warriors. She couldn't believe they'd made it. She turned to watch what was going on behind her, but the battle was quick.

There were too few of MacDowells and English on the field to fight Bruce's army. A hundred of the enemy against hundreds, maybe even a thousand of Bruce's warriors. Aulay and Colum were at the front of the fight, but soon most of the enemy was racing back towards the protection of the forest.

She looked at David, who dismounted, panting hard, and approached to help her down. "Are ye all right?" she asked as she gave him her hand, making a quick scan of his body.

"I'm fine," he said. "Are you?"

A set of stairs was brought to her horse, and holding David's hand she descended to the ground like a proper noble lady should. It was odd, and she didn't care for it. She wasn't a proper lady, never had been. She'd always been somewhere between a bastard and a noble, she realized. Running away from the former and never quite making it to the latter.

With the enemy gone, hundreds of pairs of eyes were watching her in a circle. Bearded and shaggy-haired Highlanders, clean-shaven knights in polished armor. Warriors in *léintean-croich* and chain mail coifs.

The crowd parted. Bruce's banner, a red lion on a golden background, flapped in the air as a man approached.

The face she'd seen in her dreams for the past seven years.

The high cheekbones, the strong nose, the eyes hard and dark... The face features like her own.

He looked older now. Silver streaked his ear-length hair. A scar that she hadn't seen before ran diagonally across the left side of his face. Wrinkles cracked his weathered skin.

And yet, he was prouder and more magnificent than she'd remembered him. Broad-shouldered and straight-backed, with chain mail covering his clearly powerful body. He held a broadsword in his hands before sheathing it.

He stood and looked her over briefly as though she were a piece of property he needed to make sure was whole. He asked someone to blow a war horn and moments later a loud, sad call sounded through the air, resonating in her like the ache of an old wound. The stones stopped and the arrows didn't fly anymore.

"Ye grew up," he said.

He didn't make a move towards her. Didn't come to give her a fatherly kiss or hug. She gave him the courtesy that etiquette required of a subject to her king.

"Aye, Yer Grace," she said.

She should say something more. "Well met," perhaps. Or "God bless ye." Or "Are ye well?" But the words were stuck in her throat like stones. This was what she'd sacrificed so much for. For him. For his affection. To have a father and be a family. To be important to him. For a glint of approval in his eyes.

She'd sacrificed her future. David had offered to take her with him to the twenty-first century. She could have chosen David. She could have abandoned this man who stood like a statue staring at her without a sign that she was more to him than a virgin he could trade for a castle. And she wasn't even a virgin anymore.

Her feet were cold, her legs weak. She held her hands together like a noble lady. They were still wet and red with Dugald's blood.

Bruce's eyes were now on David. "Who are ye? Ye look familiar."

David nodded to him. "I am David, brother of Lady Rogene of clan Mackenzie. We met in Eilean Donan when ye helped to fight clan Ross."

Bruce's frown relaxed in recognition. "Oh, aye. I remember ye. Ye fought bravely. Ye and Lady Rogene have that odd accent..."

"He helped us save Anna from Carlisle," said Colum, who stepped from the crowd and laid his hand on David's shoulder. "I'm thankful to ye that ye brought her here whole and safe. We had to draw the attackers away that night. Then we looked for ye at the cave the next day, but ye were gone."

"She had to save me," David said hoarsely, his eyes dark as he looked at Anna as though there was no one else in the world. "She would have brought herself here safely. You've got a real treasure of a daughter, Your Grace," he said. "She would have stopped at nothing to come to you."

A glimmer of gratitude and affection flashed through Bruce's eyes as he studied her. "Such high praise," her father said. "I am glad ye're here. It means the wedding can take place tomorrow as planned."

Anna's stomach dropped. David's face darkened, and a grimace crossed it. Bruce's confirmation of the wedding was the final blow to any hope of them being together. She fought tears burning her eyes.

"Why did it take ye so long to get here?" Aulay asked.

As David answered Aulay's question, telling him about how the English and MacDowells had hunted them, and how he'd fought Goiridh, and how Anna had rescued him from the villagers of Kennifar, and of the storm that had kept them in the croft, she kept watching him, drowning in his eyes, lulled by his voice, marveling at the very presence of him.

"Oh, aye, the storm," Aulay said. "It wrecked several docked ships and kept us all huddled in our tents for days."

Done with Aulay's questions for the moment, David stood watching her, still and solemn and as wounded as she.

Aulay came to her and, disregarding etiquette, engulfed her in a warm bear hug. She hugged him back, and it was on his chest that the tears that she'd fought broke through. He looked down at her. "Lass, what is the matter? Ye're here now. Ye're safe. I'm sorry we couldna come and recover ye. I canna forgive myself for allowing Dugald to take ye in the first place. We thought ye were dead. We brought Laoghaire here to offer her in yer place, but yer groom refused her."

She stood back. "Do ye think he will still accept me?"

Bruce came to stand next to her and put a gentle hand on her shoulder. She almost died of the touch.

"He will," the king said. "He wants only ye."

Her eyes locked with David's, and her chest tightened at the incredible pain and sadness in his eyes. Because, just as Philip wanted only her, she wanted David and no one else.

CHAPTER 25

"Wʜᴀᴛ ᴀʀᴇ ʏᴇ ᴅᴏɪɴɢ?" said a female voice behind Anna's back, and she turned sharply, releasing the four bent fingers of her hand.

In the semidarkness, the flames of three tallow candles jumped and flickered and so did Laoghaire's shadow on the canvas wall of the camp pavilion. Laoghaire was breathtaking, a proper noble lady. Her dress was of a rich, ultramarine blue, with roses embroidered with golden threads. The long, angel sleeves were embroidered with golden patterns of leaves and florets. On her head, she wore a jeweled circlet over a crocheted wool net that held her hair. Her cheeks were pink, and her lips were full, and her big, long-lashed eyes were sharp and attentive on Anna.

"Nothing," Anna said. "I'm just tired."

The hot bath she had taken still stood in the middle of the pavilion. Robert the Bruce was supposed to stay in this large tent, but he'd given it to the women and their lady's maids instead. Anna appreciated the gesture, but she'd take sleeping on the ground in David's arms anytime.

Laoghaire slowly walked to Anna and looked her over. "Ye were whispering and bending yer fingers. Were ye counting something?"

Anna stood up from the chair she was sitting on and took a blanket from the single bed. The floor was laid with rugs and soft under her bare feet. She felt clean, her skin and her hair were breathing and singing. As she'd bathed, she'd craved David's presence in the tub with her. Had he been given a chance to wash up? Unlikely.

How soon would he leave? They hadn't had a chance to talk. Surely, he'd stay the night... But would he stay until the wedding ceremony tomorrow?

Before bathing, she'd checked her undertunic and herself for blood from her courses, but there was none. She'd last had them before she was kidnapped, and they were due sometime around now.

When Laoghaire came in, she'd been counting days.

She didn't know if she should be worried. She'd never been very regular and never bothered to remember or write down when her courses were due. Over the past moon, she'd gone through an ordeal—been hungry and thirsty for days, been kidnapped and held prisoner. Her courses may be postponed because of the shock.

On the other hand, she had been lying with a man for the past ten days...

If she was pregnant... The thought brought a rush of icy cold through her. But also a flutter of joy.

David's child... Part of him within her, hers forever. A life growing inside her...

"I was just counting how many days I was away," she said and turned away, blood rushing to her cheeks.

Laoghaire sat down on the chair Anna had vacated, facing her. She reached out to the table and poured two cups of wine and offered one to Anna. Wine was imported from France and very expensive, but not to her uncle Aulay. "It's been three days since I arrived from Islay to take yer place as Sir Philip's bride. And three days since he rejected me."

Anna took the cup of wine. Laoghaire glared at her, then drank the wine without blinking.

"I am sorry to hear he rejected ye," Anna said.

"Well, it seems a bastart is more acceptable than a perfectly legitimate and well-bred woman. With a big dowry. With manners. With the blood of warriors in her veins."

The words stung, but Anna had been hurt so much worse. She sat down and drank two sips of red wine, and the flavors of black currants and herbs she'd never known played richly on her tongue. The alcohol mingled with her blood, bringing warmth and making her head spin.

"Believe me," Anna said. "Ye dinna want to trade places with me. Ye can have Sir Philip."

She loved David. She was a fallen woman possibly pregnant with his child. And she wondered if sleeping without him would bring the nightmares of the oubliette back.

An expression of concern clouded Laoghaire's beautiful face. "What happened to ye, cousin?"

Anna chuckled uncomfortably and drank more. "Ye ken what happened to me."

"Nae everything. Ye were perfectly excited when ye departed from Islay. And now ye seem like ye're going to an execution, nae to a wedding. I would think a bride that had been kidnapped and kept prisoner would be more relieved to be in safety. To meet her future husband. So what happened?"

Anna cleared her throat. "After being trapped in the oubliette for what felt like eternity, I was chased by the MacDowells and then stuck in a storm for a sennight. I'm just tired."

"Aye, the storm raged for days here, as well," Laoghaire said slowly. "How did ye survive that?"

"On an abandoned farm. Thankfully, there was a house where David and I could shelter."

Laoghaire sat back and bit her lip. "David, aye?"

Feeling like she'd said too much, Anna shrugged one shoulder. "Aye. He was protecting me the whole time."

"A handsome man," said Laoghaire, pouring more wine for Anna. "Isna he?"

He was the most handsome and attractive man Anna had ever laid her eyes on. But she knew where Laoghaire was leading with this, so she said, "I didna notice."

Laoghaire let out a long sigh and leaned back in the chair, looking at the dark ceiling where shadows from the candles played and danced. "Plenty of time locked in a house alone with a man who isna yer husband…"

Laoghaire always knew how to hit right where it hurt. There was nothing as damaging to Anna's reputation as Laoghaire's suspicions, even if Laoghaire didn't know anything. Just a shadow of doubt in Anna would be enough to make Philip back away from the deal.

"Laoghaire," Anna said. "Do not assume anything."

"I dinna, cousin. Just tell me I'm wrong and I'll believe ye."

Problem was, she was exactly right. About everything.

"Ye are wrong, Laoghaire," Anna said firmly.

Laoghaire took a sip of wine. "If ye say so, I believe ye. Yer father, the king, is betting much on yer virginity. And I am sure, as he is, ye wouldna do anything to compromise that. Wouldna it be treason?"

Anna stood up and marched through the pavilion. She ached for a different world. A world where, like David had said, virginity was not an important condition, where she wouldn't be a negotiation piece in powerful men's games. Instead, she lived in a world where her reputation could be ruined by gossip. And her father didn't even talk to her. He didn't spend time with her like she had hoped. He had brought her to the bridge in front of the Stirling Castle gate and held his hand on her back while Sir Philip Mowbray stared at her from the top of the wall.

And once Sir Philip had seen her with his own eyes, he'd nodded and yelled that the wedding would be tomorrow and disappeared.

Then her father was off doing his important things.

She was just a way for him to get the castle. And she was giving her life and her happiness for that? And if she was pregnant, her child's life?

Tomorrow was the wedding. Tomorrow she'd lose David forever. Tomorrow, her only chance at happiness would be lost.

Anna lay down on the bed, pulled the blankets over herself, and turned with her back to Laoghaire. "Dinna ye fash, cousin. Tomorrow I will give Stirling to my father."

The mattress dipped as Laoghaire sat on the bed and laid her hand on Anna's shoulder. "I dinna fash. I am glad ye are alive. We were all very worried for a while."

Anna froze, as though in the presence of a deer she didn't want to spook. Laoghaire's affection was rare, even though Anna knew Laoghaire cared for her more than she'd shown.

Then Laoghaire stood and called for her maidservant. Under the rustling of clothes and the quiet murmuring between the two women, Anna struggled to fall asleep. She felt cold and empty at her back, where David had faithfully kept her warm. Darkness was creeping at her from all corners, and even the presence of two other women didn't keep it away.

She should get used to it. Even her new husband wouldn't be able to give her the safety and warmth that she needed...because he wasn't David.

CHAPTER 26

THE CAMP WAS QUIET, sleeping, but in David's head voices screamed and laughed despite two whole horns of uisge that he'd drunk with Colum with a sole purpose.

To forget. To forget that he'd brought the love of his life to marry another man. That she may be in trouble because he'd taken her virginity.

That he could still change it all and convince her to choose him. Run away with her.

But something must have been wrong with the uisge because it didn't make him forget any of those things.

In fact, he remembered them more forcefully than ever before.

And so, in darkness disturbed only by the smudges of camp-fires, he made his way between tents and men sleeping outside on the ground and dark outlines of sentinels by the fires.

Finally he reached the ladies' pavilion, its dark-red cloth black in the night. He may have stumbled and almost fell a few times... He wasn't sure. He wasn't even sure why he'd come to the pavilion. But it was like a flame, and he was a goddamn moth about to burn himself. The uisge only made him want to be with her more. It didn't dull anything.

When he touched the red canvas, the tent was quiet. He could smell something feminine around it, something flowery and clean. Even in his drunken mind, he knew barging into a women's pavilion at night was a bad idea.

And, really, he should get back to his bedroll next to Colum by the fire.

But he lingered. The cloth of the pavilion was rough and dusty under his fingers... He hadn't realized he was touching it.

"Anna!" Her name came out before he realized he was saying it. "Anna!" he whisper-yelled louder.

There was a rustle behind the cloth wall, and he waited, holding his breath. He looked around. Somewhere in the absolute blackness of the sky, distant fires flickered, and he knew they were the sentinels on top of Stirling Castle. From the small tent nearby, a man's snore reached its thundering climax and stopped abruptly, then resumed a few moments later.

The entrance to the pavilion shifted, and a dark figure came out. He couldn't see the face, but he knew it was her; he'd have known her out of a billion people. The way her shoulders angled, the proud, graceful bend of her neck.

"It's me," he whispered loudly.

"David?" She hurried a few steps from around the corner of the pavilion. A weak glow fell on her now from the nearest campfire, and he could see her face. And suddenly he didn't need any light to see. The very air brightened around him and vibrated. She furrowed her pretty arched brows, and he ached to reach out and kiss that crease in her skin away. She was holding a blanket around her shoulders.

"I wish I was that blanket," he said and only then realized he'd spoken out loud.

She blinked her big, dark, tilted eyes and hastily looked around. "Is everything all right?"

"Yeah...well...no. Did I wake you?"

"Nae, I couldna sleep. What's wrong?"

"You're marrying another man. That's what's wrong."

She didn't say anything for a few beats, just looked at him, breathing. And if he was right, she swayed just an inch towards him.

"Ye kent this all along," she said slowly. "We both ken we have nae future. We never did and we never will."

She was right. But it still pierced his heart like a bullet. He wished it wasn't true.

"I still want you."

There was a camp of warriors around them, men who'd kill him on sight for looking at the king's daughter the wrong way. And yet, he reached out and cupped her face. The moment his skin touched hers, a flash of tingles shot through him.

Her eyelids lowered over her darkening eyes, her lips parting. She felt that, too.

In one movement, he took her into his arms and kissed her. God, her mouth... The taste of her, the succulent taste of her that was all softness and sweetness, and yet the feel of her body was strong in his arms.

She clung to him, her arms wrapped tight around his waist, her fingertips digging into his back, and he wanted more of her. He wanted her legs pressing around his hips, her heat around him, her sleek, tight depths...

She gave out a groan as he deepened the kiss...

And then he felt a push and she was gone from his embrace.

"What are ye doing?" she whispered angrily, panting.

Her blanket had fallen on the ground and lay in a heap around her feet. She leaned down and picked it up and wrapped it around herself.

Her absence was like a black hole. He took a step forward, unable to stand the distance between them. "Anna..."

She took a step back away from him. "Ye're drunk, are ye nae?"

He hung his head and felt strands of his hair fall around his face. He dragged his fingers through his hair, looking straight at her.

"What does that have to do with anything? I still want you and love you. It fucking shreds my heart to pieces that you're going to marry someone else."

She shook her head and took another step back. "If ye really loved me, ye wouldna have dragged me out here and put my reputation in danger in front of the whole camp. Anyone can see us."

"Let them."

"Ye're nae thinking clearly. Mayhap in yer world a man and a woman can be together with nae consequences. In mine, women marry out of duty and to secure our future. And if ye canna understand that..."

He took a step towards her, and she took another back. "Anna, please..."

"Please what, David? What?"

Yeah...please what? Was he ready to ask her to marry him? To go to the King of Scots and ask for her hand? To abandon his dreams, his search for a way out of this reality?

Even with his mind foggy and moving at the speed of a snail, he couldn't imagine that.

"Nothing. You're right. I put you in danger. I couldn't imagine being apart from you... It's the first night that I don't have you in my arms and...I can't imagine how to deal with it."

"Well, ye'll have to. Ye'll have yer whole life to sleep without me. In a warm, comfy bed in a house with the miracle of light with no fire and warm waterfalls running at yer will."

She turned to go inside, but he couldn't leave it like this.

He caught her by the elbow and gently turned her to him. "Part of my heart is going to die if you become someone else's wife."

Anna's throat moved, and her eyes watered in the darkness. "Ye think mine wouldna?"

As she whirled around and turned her back to him to walk away, he looked up. He thought he saw a shadow move quickly to hide behind the corner of the pavilion. But it was so dark, and he was so drunk, he wasn't sure if the shadow was simply the cast by the flames of the nearest campfire.

Anna disappeared into the pavilion, and he stood like a statue, unable to take another step away from her. He sat down at the entrance and waited to make sure he didn't see any danger. But the alcohol in his system finally did its job, and his mind gave in to sleep.

CHAPTER 27

DAVID'S HAND clenched around the handle of his claymore. It was good he stood in the crowd next to Colum and Aulay MacDonald, who knew this wasn't a gesture of aggression. He didn't need to peer around the backs and shoulders of the warriors and noblemen in front of him, as he was taller than almost everyone else—except for Colum and Aulay.

He watched Anna's figure, her back straight in her rich wedding attire. She stood at the front of the congregation at the right side of the church in Stirling village. Sir Philip Mowbray—a tall, handsome, and perfectly respectable man in his early forties, with intelligent blue eyes, a full head of hair, and a short beard—stood in front of the second half of the crowd at the left of the church. Behind him were the warriors, knights, and noblemen of Stirling.

In front of all of them, a priest was reading a blessing for John the Baptist. The scent of incense was thick and nauseating. He was hungover from yesterday.

The church was rather big, much bigger than the one in Dornie. Long, glassless, gothic windows lined the walls. A large wooden cross hung on the wall behind the altar, which sat under a tall, pointed arch. It was semidark, even during the day, with candles doing their best to light up the space.

Before, he'd drunk to forget he was in the Middle Ages.

Last night, he'd drunk because the thought of Anna in another man's arms was a stake piercing his heart with every breath.

She was his.

His.

And yet, he and Anna both knew she wasn't and would never be his. Seven of Sìneag's previous matches had resulted in a happy ending.

But this time, she was wrong. So wrong.

As the priest kept mumbling monotonically in Latin, David craved another uisge. He wondered why he hadn't left Stirling yesterday. He'd brought Anna here, to safety. He was free to go. And yet, he was torturing himself by remaining to watch the wedding. To watch her marry another man.

Finally the Mass was over, and the groom and the bride were brought to stand before the priest. As David watched the two of them, Philip—handsome and noble, wearing a brocaded tunic with a jeweled girdle on his hip, a shirt with puffed sleeves, and knitted tights, along with a floor-length mantle with petal-shaped scallops over his shoulders. And Anna—small and thin and looking like a proper princess in her rich robe of brocaded silk shot through with gold and silver threads. The panel down the front of her robe had metallic spangles. It made her skin look like porcelain and her hair like ebony. David felt the nausea rise to his throat. She was where she was supposed to be. This was her destiny.

And his was to be back to the twenty-first century.

Philip was ogling Anna with the eyes of a man who appreciated a woman. Possessive and admiring. He knew he'd scored high. Who wouldn't? But the translucent complexion and the delicate figure were an illusion. She knew how to fight and how to ride a horse better than he did. And she knew how to swim and how to hunt and cook on a campfire.

She was everything.

And this man would suffocate her. Trap her inside a castle, keep her doing what she'd never enjoyed: being a proper lady.

Philip leaned down and murmured to Anna, something sweet and intimate, David could tell, and she smiled broadly with a nod.

If there was a hell on earth, David was in it.

Then the priest started talking, and David resisted an urge to rush to the altar, push Philip away, and stand there, being blessed and married instead.

He remembered his sister's wedding roughly three years ago. It hadn't been in a church but in front of one, like most weddings here. This one was inside, probably, because they'd just heard Mass for John the Baptist and might as well just stay here and get the marriage done.

Rogene's wedding had been full of tension because Angus was about to marry Euphemia of Ross, and Rogene had stopped it. And still, clan Mackenzie stood by her and Angus no matter what. Raghnall, Angus's younger brother, who'd become David's friend and whom David missed. Catrìona, who about month later got married by the same church to James, a police detective from the twenty-first century.

Homesickness enveloped him like a heavy blanket. But he wasn't missing the twenty-first century. He was missing Eilean Donan. His clan. The people who would always have his back.

Had he been an idiot to keep struggling to find a way through time all these years? Should he accept that this was his life and that this was where he belonged?

If he found a stone right now, would he be able to force himself to go through it, to leave everyone he loved behind?

Sir Philip leaned to Anna and whispered to her, "I hope to be a good husband to ye. I will be nothing but kind to ye and treat ye with the respect ye deserve, Lady Anna. Ye dinna need to worry."

She found herself smiling back because that was what a bride did to a groom who said nice things.

"I thank ye, Lord," she said to him.

What he said was what any lass wanted to hear on the day of her wedding to a man she'd never met before.

But as the priest mumbled the words of blessing and said things about God and marriage, she found herself looking back at the crowd in the church. About one hundred people—fifty from the Bruce and MacDonald side and roughly the same from the side of Sir Philip. Laoghaire stood next to Uncle Aulay, her eyes hard and unforgiving. Colum was solemn and thoughtful, focused more on Robert the Bruce standing in front of him than on the wedding.

Her father...he was at her wedding. As a lass of twelve, she'd never even hoped for that. And look at her, she had achieved all she'd ever wanted. Her father being at her wedding. Him acknowledging her. A good man, an important man marrying her. Her wedding meaning something beyond just the ties of two clans and noble homes—this wedding would save lives and bring her country closer to the independence for which thousands of people had fought.

And yet, her eyes kept being drawn to David. The priest's mumbling quieted, and all she could hear was her heart beating quickly. David, so handsome, with his sharp angles and his eyes as dark as a midnight forest, glaring.

His were the only eyes she'd ever want to hold her in their dark depths. His was the only body she'd ever want next to hers at night. His was the only scent she wanted to fall asleep to.

But it wouldn't be David's.

It would be this man's. And as noble and kind and handsome as he seemed, he wasn't the one she loved.

She would be imprisoning herself for the rest of her life, putting herself, and maybe her child, into that oubliette. As a woman, and as a bastard, she was a pawn in the game of great men. Her father appreciated her doing his bidding, but he wouldn't give her the love she needed because no one could. She'd spent her whole life trying to please others so that she could secure her future. She'd stopped being her true self long ago, that day when the sea had almost taken her and brought her father back to her.

And now she would be a wife to someone who wanted her to be a noble lady, like her father did. And yet, the only time she felt truly free was with David. He understood her. He knew women were more than just proper noble ladies who made clothes and ran a household and raised children.

"Lady Anna?" asked a voice.

She shuddered and looked up. The priest was looking at her with a cocked eyebrow and lips pursed as though he'd swallowed a spoonful of vinegar. Sir Philip was frowning at her.

"Aye?" she asked.

"Do ye take Philip Mowbray as yer husband?" the priest insisted.

She looked at Sir Philip, whose frown deepened with every moment that passed. She looked at her father, whose jaw protruded under his short-cropped beard. And she looked at David, who was breathing fast and looked ready to jump into action at her command.

This was it. Just like back in the wave, one simple decision would define her life. To yield to the force of others or to take her destiny into her own hands. Was it not what her father did, too, as well as William Wallace? Fight against a much stronger force for the right to live their own lives?

And so would she. She hadn't done it before, but she would now.

"Nae."

Silence lay over the church like a blanket. No one breathed

or moved. The fat in the tallow candles crackled softly. And only one face bore relief...and love.

David's.

Sir Philip stared at her in astonishment, blinking. "Lady Anna..." he said. "If I gave ye any indication I wilna be a worthy husband to ye—"

"Sir Philip, I assure ye, it isna anything ye did."

A shape moved in her side vision. "Then why?" her father demanded, approaching her and Philip in a couple of wide strides.

"If I dinna give my permission, I canna be wed," she said. "Ye canna force me."

"Do ye realize the shame ye're bringing to me, to yer clan? The grievance to Sir Philip? The consequences to this war?"

"I am sorry to inconvenience anyone," Anna said, "but I am sure there are other arrangements that can be made. And I wilna do something I dinna want to. Ye, Father, ye took the throne of Scotland and ye refused to yield to England. Ye're still fighting for yer right to make yer own decisions. Well, 'tis what I want, too. Ye abandoned my mother—had ye nae done that, I wouldna have been a bastart. Ye never came to see me or wanted to ken me, until ye needed me for yer politics. And I canna pretend nae more that ye want anything else from me than what my marriage brings. Ye're forcing me into a life I dinna want. How is it different than what the English are doing?"

He was silent, guilt coming through his rough, handsome face. "Anna, I assure ye, had it nae been for the war, I'd have been by yer side..."

"But 'tis nae why she's refusing Sir Philip," said Laoghaire, coming closer to the altar.

Everyone turned their heads to her, and she was beautiful with her proud, stern features. Her hair was done in smooth locks that fell over her shoulders. Her dress was lilac and gold.

"What is the reason, child?" said the Bruce.

"Laoghaire!" her uncle Aulay came forward from the crowd. "Dinna say anything ye will regret."

"The reason why Anna canna marry Sir Philip is because she is nae a virgin. And she may be with another man's child."

A gasp and a growl ran through the crowd. Philip's face reddened. Bruce's nostrils flared. Mortification and anger hit Anna simultaneously, cold and heat, stillness and the need to move. Laoghaire had just embarrassed the king and completely destroyed Anna's worth to him and to Sir Philip.

But at the same time, Anna had reclaimed her worth in her own eyes.

"Who?" boomed Sir Philip.

"The man who spent the last two sennights with her," said Laoghaire and looked at David. "'Tis nae a malicious rumor. I saw them in each other's arms last night."

A hundred pairs of eyes shot to him. But David didn't look embarrassed or afraid. His eyes never left Anna's and there were questions in them.

Was she really with child?

And if so, how could he leave her now and return to his time?

"I will kill ye!" the Bruce roared and unsheathed his sword, launching into the crowd. "Ye dishonored my daughter!"

"If anyone will kill him, 'tis me!" roared Sir Philip, unsheathing his sword, as well. "The deal is off, Bruce! Men! Everyone! To battle!"

Anna's legs weakened as a hundred men drew a hundred swords and a fight began.

CHAPTER 28

As David drew his claymore and blocked the first enemy's thrust, he didn't feel the usual clash of his sword against another. He didn't hear the yells and roars of warriors around him, the war cry "Clann Domnhnaill!" echoing off the walls of the church.

All he heard was Laoghaire's voice saying, "She may be with child." All he saw was Anna's fear. Not surprise. Not outrage at a lie.

Fear that she'd been discovered. Fear of the truth that had been revealed.

As he lifted his sword to stop another blow, he wondered what he would do now. He was in love with Anna, and now she might be pregnant with his baby. Those had been his greatest fears for the past three years, the reason he'd remained a virgin. And they'd both come true. How could he leave now?

No, he couldn't leave. He wasn't a man who would do that.

His arms and legs were as heavy as lead. The dirt-packed floor of the church sucked him in and held him and didn't want to let him go.

He was really stuck here now. Bound and forced to stay.

Unless...unless Anna would want to go with him, now that she wasn't marrying Philip. A wild joy, a burning expanded his chest and made bubbles of excitement suffuse his very core. She'd said no to Philip. She'd said *no*.

Was she saying yes to him?

The thought was a blast of energy in his chest. He thrust his sword deep between the man's ribs and he fell with a grunt of pain.

Ignoring the stab of guilt, he looked over the heads of the fighting men, searching for Anna. She was behind the altar, shielding Laoghaire and fighting a man with her dagger. He saw Robert the Bruce come to her rescue, grab the man by the collar from behind, drag him away from her to the nearest wall, and slam his face against the rocks.

A little assured now that Anna had the protection of her father, he started making his way to her, moving around the fighting men, ducking the blades that flashed around him. But he didn't make it.

The swoosh of a mace and a flash of something dark next to his face made him duck. When he regained his balance and held his claymore with both hands, he saw it was one of Mowbray's knights in proper, shining metal armor—the visor of his helm was up, though, and sharp eyes were glaring at David out of a fierce face.

He had never fought someone with a mace. But he'd seen the wounds left by it: heads smashed with brains spilled on the ground, limbs crushed despite protective armor, looking like minced meat mixed with bone. The mace was what they called a morning star—a round head with what looked like two or three dozen spikes planted all around it.

David gulped.

The knight roared, swinging the mace back and bringing it down on him. David brought his sword forward and blocked the handle of the mace. The impact was like a whole football team crashing into him.

It was so much stronger than any sword, the vibration went through him. But he held his ground. He now had Anna and maybe a baby to think of. He could still take her to the future. He had to fight for that, for her, and for him.

For love.

The knight brought the mace back and hit David with it again and again, and David barely brought his sword up to parry.

He was retreating. Step back after step back, he was losing the swing area he would need to properly wield his sword.

The knight, getting angry and impatient, swung the mace aiming for David's stomach, protected only by a *leine croich*, and he jumped back. His foot caught on something—a dead body, he realized—and he fell on his back.

The knight lifted the mace high above his head, ready for the final deadly blow. But as he did that, he revealed the space between his chain mail and cuisse, the upper armor on his thigh. Before the man could bring the mace down on David, he hauled himself up and thrust his claymore into the unprotected slit.

Blood burst at him in a fountain of gore; he'd no doubt cut the femoral artery. The man grunted and let the mace drop to the floor then staggered back and fell, the pool of blood soaking into the dirt-packed floor like water.

David stood up, breathing hard, looking for the next attacker. Something was thumping hard in his chest...his heart. He was still alive.

The fight was still in full swing. The forces were equal, and he saw Colum and Aulay MacDonald and Iàcob fighting. Bruce was swinging his sword, too, as fierce and as brutal as any other warrior.

Dead and wounded lay on the floor, and the air in the church was thick with the iron tang of blood and sweat and excrement as men lost their bowels dying.

And then he saw Philip. And across the battle scene, Philip saw him.

The man was furious, his eyebrows drawn together, his nose a straight line.

And David knew this would be it. Philip strode towards him with his great sword drawn, candle flames bouncing off the long, broad blade. He was not in armor; he was a groom dressed to get married to the daughter of the King of Scotland.

And David had robbed him of his beautiful, future wife. Of being related to Robert the Bruce.

"Aaaargh!" Philip roared as he charged at David. The grunt carried across the church, louder than the sounds of the battle around them.

He hammered his sword into David's. David staggered from the impact and pushed across and down to bring Philip's blade to the ground. When Philip freed his sword, he came at David again and again from left and right and left and right. The strength of his blows was like the force of that storm that had stopped Anna and him.

David's hands were slick with the knight's blood, and it was hard to hold the handle.

"Ye bastart!" yelled Philip as he lifted his sword for another blow. "Ye are a man of nae honor." A slash across. He got too close, and a cut on his cheekbone stung David. "Ye took the virginity of an innocent lass destined for another man!" Philip swung his sword from the other side, aiming for David's kidney, but David parried it. "Ye ken nae laws of chivalry, ye whore's son! And ye will pay for dishonoring a lass!"

With the next step back, David felt a hard, rough wall pressing against his back. He was cornered. He couldn't swing properly to defend himself.

Philip brought his sword back for the final thrust that would finish David. "Rot in the swamps of Bannockburn, ye bastart..."

As the blade came at David in a metallic arc of death, the memory came.

The swamps of Bannockburn.

Bannockburn...

That was what Rogene had told him and what he had struggled to remember. He hadn't made the connection that Bannockburn was near Stirling.

But now he knew. Bannockburn would be where Bruce would have the most important battle of the war.

And it was here, by Stirling.

Because the deal had to be about the battle, not about the girl.

He brought up his sword to block Philip's, but he didn't have enough swing. Philip was pressing David's own sword into his neck, and only the sheer force of muscle allowed David to hold him off.

"Stop!" David grunted. "Stop!"

Philip's face was a mask of fury, his eyes dark under his eyebrows. His bared teeth were white against his bloodstained face and beard.

David's own blade was ripping into the flesh of his neck.

"You're right, man," David croaked. "I was wrong to sleep with your betrothed, and I don't blame you for wanting revenge. But I love her! It's not just about lust. And I know you're a good man who doesn't want more people to die."

Philip's face lost some of its anger, and the pressure against David's neck subsided. "Once ye're dead, I will stop this."

David grunted, "I have a proposal."

Philip frowned. "Ye have nae right or place for proposals."

"Just listen to me, please. You're a man of honor. Let's make another deal."

Philip narrowed his eyes and David continued. "Give him one year. If Stirling isn't rescued by the English, you will give it to the Scots freely. You would avoid unnecessary bloodshed. It also means if England wins the war, you're still in their good graces. Your people have already suffered a lot. You will live in peace for a year and the Bruce will back off. Isn't it what you wanted with the wedding in the first place?"

Philip blinked several times, thinking hard. He squinted his eyes at David. "How—?"

"This will give you back your power."

Philip cursed under his breath and released the sword.

"Stop the fight!" he yelled, and as his voice carried across the church, men were lowering their weapons. "Bruce! Where are ye? I need a word."

As Bruce made his way to Philip, he looked sideways at David. "This doesna mean ye are forgiven. I imagine 'tis nae a good thing to have the King of Scotland as an enemy whose daughter ye dishonored."

David swallowed hard. As he watched Philip and Bruce talk, he caught many angry eyes on him. Aulay came to talk to Bruce and Philip, too, but Colum was by Anna's side and was glaring at him.

Finally, Bruce and Mowbray shook hands. Mowbray looked around at his troops and Bruce's warriors.

"Be witness, everyone. Robert the Bruce and I just entered a chivalric agreement. He will retreat from Stirling, but if within a year, by John the Baptist in the year 1314, we are nae rescued by King Edward II, I will freely give Stirling to Robert the Bruce's command with nae fight."

As Philip and his men looked through the wounded and the dead and started leaving the church, David's body flooded with relief. Anna was unharmed. She hadn't married another man. And further bloodshed had been prevented.

But his relief died when he met the furious gaze of the King of Scotland.

CHAPTER 29

ANNA SHOOK as she stared at the dead bodies littering the floor of the church. Dim daylight was thrown on the blood, the gashes, and the severed limbs from the narrow windows high above. Candlelight cast a sickly yellow light on the dented armor and bloodied swords. The air in the room was suffocating, the stench sickening.

"Anna, I am sorry..." Laoghaire whispered into her ear.

Her cousin's hand clenched tightly to Anna's. Laoghaire's eyes were wet and desperate, her chin trembling.

"I have been so foolish... All this death...all this carnage...and for what? I should have never said anything."

Anna squeezed her cousin's hand. "It's all right, Laoghaire. 'Tis not yer fault. 'Tis all my doing. Ye didna say anything that wasna true."

And now, she didn't have to marry Philip.

But this was what she had caused.

"Go hide over there," she said to Laoghaire, pointing at a small alcove behind the altar.

As her cousin did that, Anna realized the guilt was mixed with the strange elation in her chest, like she was full of warm air.

She was free. She had freed herself, but at a cost. The cost of men's lives. The cost of whatever punishment her father would bring upon her.

Because he was furious. He was looming over David, yelling at him. And yet, David kept throwing glances at her, like he couldn't wait to talk to her.

But why was her father so angry with David, when David had found the perfect solution to the situation? She should be worried about her father's wrath, which would surely turn against her soon. But strangely, she didn't care.

She didn't want Bruce's approval anymore. Whatever he needed her for, she'd always be a bastard daughter to him, and he'd always have more important things to do than have a relationship with her. What did she expect, anyway? Invitations to feasts and hawk hunts? Staying for a visit with him and his wife? Some sort of gesture of his affection?

No. She'd outgrown that, anyway.

Much more important was David, and her own approval of herself. That she stood up for herself and respected her own actions.

However, Bruce could still harm David.

"Is this true, ye bastart?" he bellowed at David. "Did ye dishonor her?" He turned to Anna. "And are ye really with child?"

Silence fell on the church, and Anna slowly descended the low staircase from the altar and made her way through the carnage, carefully stepping around the dead bodies. David held her in his gaze, making her all tingly and warm as she walked.

What could she say? If she said yes, Bruce would want them to marry. And David would do the right thing, stay with her. And so, she'd be his jailor. She'd be Dugald MacDowell, imprisoning David forever in the oubliette of their marriage.

But she wasn't that person. She never wanted him to be captive. She loved him; she wanted him to be happy and to be free.

Even if it wouldn't be with her, in the time where she belonged.

She stood before Bruce and looked into his eyes, straightening her back as much as she could. She felt clammy from the sweat and the sprays of blood on her face and neck.

She opened her mouth to deny it, but David interrupted her. "Yes, Your Grace," he said. "It's all true. I dishonored her. She may be with my child."

Bruce's lips tightened in a thin line, and he growled and shook his head. "Ye son of a whore. Ye dishonored the daughter of a king. And nae just that. Look around ye. Ye dared to undo all the progress I had achieved through years of blood and the deaths of hundreds of men. Through so much sacrifice."

Anna's heart lurched. "Father, please, 'tis nae his fault…"

But Bruce raised his sword towards David. The blood on the blade glistened as he pressed the edge against David's chest. David swallowed sharply, his Adam's apple bobbing. "Dugald MacDowell slit my two brothers' throats," the Bruce growled low. "The English quartered and killed my brother Neil in Kildrummy Castle and took my wife and daughter prisoner. They're still captives with the English. Countless clans lost their men. Daughters, sisters, and mothers lost their fathers, brothers, and sons. And I had a chance to win a bloodless victory, and ye have undone that."

Anna's limbs cooled as she started realizing the depths of her father's fury. "Father, please punish me… David didna—"

"Yer Grace—" said Aulay.

"Please, Yer Grace…" said Colum.

Bruce only pressed the edge of the sword harder against David's chest. "As a father I wilna tolerate ye dishonoring my daughter. Every Scotsman kens a man who does this will be killed."

To Anna's horror, David paled and nodded. "I will accept my fate, Your Grace."

"Nae, Father." Anna came to him and laid both her hands on

the Bruce's arm holding the sword and tugging it down. It was like tugging a tree branch. "Please, dinna kill him. He didna rape me. It was of my own accord that it happened..."

Her uncle Aulay stepped next to David. He was sprayed with blood, too, the side of his hair caked with gore, but Anna didn't think it was his wound. Probably the blood of the enemy. "Yer Grace," Aulay said, spreading his arms in a placating gesture. "May I remind ye, David is a Mackenzie, yer loyal clan that, like us, didna leave ye in peril and hid ye and gave ye men when ye were vulnerable and needed support the most."

Bruce's jaw protruded in anger. He looked between Aulay, David, and Anna as he thought it over, then spat loudly onto the ground and lowered his sword. "Aye. God's arse, ye're right. Ye're Angus's brother-in-law. I canna do that to him. I wilna kill ye. But ye must marry Anna. And ye'll be in debt to Bruce. So if I call on ye one day, whatever I need from ye, ye'll do it."

David, still pale, nodded solemnly. "I will, Your Grace."

But to Anna, this still meant she was imprisoning David and keeping him captive. "But, Father, I wilna do it."

The looks of horror on everyone's faces made her feel small, and she straightened her shoulders and raised her chin. Colum leaned to her. "Cousin, dinna ye anger the king nae more than needed. I dinna think ye can negotiate any more good fortune for yerself or David."

Bruce was staring at her like she were a demon. Colum was right, she realized. She did need to agree, even though she'd be making a choice between David's life and his freedom. Even though she knew this would be the death of his dreams and the end of his goal to return to his time. She felt her heart sink knowing she was the reason for that.

"Aye," Anna said. "I was wrong, Father. I will marry David. If he would have me."

"Good," Bruce said and wiped his sword with the side of his rich tunic, then put it back into the sheath. "'Tis decided, then."

With her heart beating hard, Anna looked at David. Were

they really engaged now? Guilt was a tombstone in her chest as she met his gaze. He didn't look like he hated her, though she knew he was probably hiding it. She wished that their engagement could be a happy one. A celebration of love, rather than an escape from death. Nevertheless, here they were. A bride and a groom. Standing two steps away from each other. Close, and yet impossibly far apart. Only one night ago they had slept wrapped around each other, and he had touched her everywhere, known her body intimately.

And yet now, they couldn't touch. If only she could take his hand into hers and smell his scent and talk to him...

"Anna." It was her father now who looked straight at her. "May I have a word with ye?"

Anna nodded and the two of them walked outside into the fresh air and sunlight. The thatched roofs of Stirling village were so bright in the sunlight, her eyes hurt after the long semidarkness of the church. The dead men, both Bruce's and Mowbray's, had been lain on the ground to bury later. Bruce led her around a corner, away from the morbid sight.

When he stopped in front of her, his eyes looked concerned. "Were ye treated badly in Carlisle?"

"Aye, Father," Anna said. "I wilna try to defend Dugald MacDowell. He is my enemy, too. He kept me in an oubliette, Father, and wanted to leave me there to die."

Bruce cursed under his breath. A solemn, angry expression crossed his face as he looked away from her and into the distance. "I am sorry, daughter," he said. "This shouldna have happened."

"He said it was revenge on ye because ye ransacked Galloway and took the castle away from him. He said something about taking me from ye and destroying yer chance for a peaceful deal for Stirling."

Bruce sighed out. "Goddamn that man. He will never stop, will he?"

Then she remembered something. "Ye must be careful,

Father. England has sent a treasure ship with much armor, swords, and gold to Ireland. He boasted about it to me, never imagining I would be rescued."

"Aye, Ireland has always been a base from which England attacks Scotland." Then he paled as, seemingly, some sort of realization relaxed his features. "Daughter, ye may have told me one of the most important pieces of news of the century. They must be planning the next invasion of the Highlands... Oh Christ the Lord, I must ask my advisors. The Bishop of Moray has connections—I must send a messenger to him. And Aulay has friendly connections in Ireland with his trading network. He will learn what he can, too."

Anna felt a tinge of pride as he said all that. She was useful.

Bruce squeezed her shoulder. "I am proud of ye, Anna. I wish I could have marrit yer mother because I loved her. I would have loved to have ye as my legitimate daughter. I was coming through for ye, doing right by ye. This marriage with Philip would have been good. Aye, I wanted this because it would be helpful to this war, but ye would have needed a good husband eventually. And Philip is a good man, despite him being on the enemy's side. He's honorable and a kind man who would be a good husband and give ye a good life."

Butterflies soared in Anna's heart at his words. His dark eyes watered as he cupped her face. "Circumstances didna allow me to be by yer side. But I am proud of the young woman that ye grew up to be, even if I wasna part of yer life. I hope to correct the error. There's an island that used to belong to the MacDougalls, a longtime enemy the Cambels helped me destroy. I will give it to ye as yer dowry. Ye may live there with David. And I want ye to be in my court whenever ye wish."

Anna's chest fluttered. She felt like she was soaring. Tears prickled her eyes. "Oh, Father..." she whispered. And for the first time in her life, her father wrapped his arms around her, and she wept tears of forgiveness and love into his blood-caked tunic.

But would he think the same of her once David disappeared and she, like her mother, gave birth to a bastard?

CHAPTER 30

THREE DAYS LATER...

"Row!" came Aulay's booming voice through the waves crashing against the birlinn. "Row!"

The MacDonald laird stood at the steep bow of *Tagradh*, his eyes moving between the sail, the horizon, the coast, and the rowing men. His silvery hair danced in the breeze, and David was glad this powerful man was busy with navigation. Aulay hadn't talked to David in the past three days, and his attitude was icy.

David clenched the gunwale, the wood smooth and wet under his fingers. Twenty-six men, thirteen on each side, worked the long oars, and the boat slid through River Clyde into the Firth of Clyde like a hot knife through butter. Cold droplets splattered David's face from the oars and the waves.

The birlinn looked like a Viking ship. It had a long, low body with a single mast and a square sail with a red armored hand fisting a cross.

At the end of that long ship—close enough, but impossibly far—was the love of his life. Hugged by Laoghaire, Anna kept her hand to her mouth and another hand to her stomach. She probably had seasickness, perhaps even combined with morning sickness. He hadn't had a chance to talk to her; she'd been kept away from him in the women's pavilion in Bruce's camp, and later when they'd traveled down the River Clyde to board the ships, she'd been in a carriage together with Laoghaire and their maidservants.

He ached to talk to her, to ask her how she felt and if she really wanted to marry him. He didn't want to force her into anything, but he also wanted to take care of her and, if she was pregnant, the baby. He wanted her to know he was there.

In the middle of the boat, down in the opening in the hull were sacks and crates and boxes as well as weapons and armor that the MacDonalds were bringing home to Islay. A few horses were there, too, including Daisy.

The Scottish coast passed by quickly—the rugged hills and cliffs, brown and reddish rocks, green moss, occasional bushes and low trees. His stomach dropped with awe every time he looked at the rough, rugged country, often barren and unyielding to humans, but so beautiful it was hard to believe it was real. Part of him knew it wouldn't be the worst thing in the world to live here, to see this wonder of nature every day, to be part of it. What were skyscrapers and brownstones compared to this?

Colum came to stand by David's side and leaned over *Tagradh*'s gunwale with his elbows. "I have to say, man, ye disappointed me. Ye were supposed to take yer payment in gold, nae in pleasure."

David sighed. "Yeah. Well. It was never just about pleasure. I am in love with her."

Colum shook his head and squeezed David's shoulder. "Love is nothing before duty."

"If you had found us back in that cave by Carlisle, nothing would have happened. We waited for you. With sunrise, the English camped near the cave. We managed to escape, though we had to go on foot because they got Daisy. And why was the clan not in Ayr?"

"From what I heard, the MacDowells chased them away and they had to move higher up the loch."

Colum retrieved his horn flask of uisge, opened the cork, and handed it to David. The sharp scent of alcohol tickled his nostrils, and a part of him rejoiced and wanted to take it and make himself feel light and careless again. Happy.

But he didn't truly want it anymore. The void he'd been trying to fill with alcohol was not there. There was something else instead, something he didn't understand yet himself.

Colum clapped David on the shoulder. "Ye'll be part of the clan when ye marry. After my uncle and I give ye a good thrashing for dishonoring Anna."

"Fair enough, man," David said. "If you want to hit me, I won't mind. I deserve it."

Colum gave a long sigh. "Ye make it verra difficult to nae like ye. Despite what ye did, I ken ye're a good man. Ye helped us save her. Without ye, she may have died there. So I'll be happy to have ye as my brother and clansman. But ye must promise ye will never break Anna's heart."

David nodded. The sky was gray and cloudy, but David was warm. "Thanks. I don't ever want to break her heart."

"Good." Colum took a large sip of uisge. "And people will be wary of ye at first. But they're still wary of me, too. I understand what 'tis like to make an impossible choice and then work yer whole life to atone for it. So it will be the two of us in the clan. Two outcasts. Two men who were wrong but want to make it right."

David frowned. "What happened to you? What did you do?"

Colum took another large gulp of uisge, his eyes darkening as he watched the coast passing by. "The English kidnapped me. At the Battle of Methven in 1306, when Bruce lost everything and had to run. I was hit on the head with a shield and blacked out. When I woke up, I found myself tied up and being carried somewhere in a cart with two dozen more of Bruce's most important knights and warriors. My head hurt so much I thought a blacksmith was hitting it with a hammer. I kept emptying the insides of my stomach, and everything was fuzzy, but I kent I was with the enemy. After a long journey, we arrived at Berwick Castle."

He was silent for a while, watching the passing land, his jaw working under the short beard.

"Chivalric law guides us to treat war hostages well, allow them a chance of being ransomed..."

"Yeah..." David said, his heart sinking. He didn't like where this was going.

"But Edward I, who was the king back then, was so furious at Bruce that he abandoned the chivalric law."

David's heart sank.

"He ordered all the hostages to be drawn, quartered, and beheaded without a trial. I was among them. I watched my sword brothers, the knights and warriors I'd fought beside, being killed in the worst possible manner." His voice shook, down to a whisper. "There were nae burials. Nae honoring the lives of those men. And I was next."

David swallowed a hard knot watching the man.

"But 'twas Philip Mowbray who saved me."

David frowned. "Philip?"

"Aye. I had protected his fifteen-year-old nephew, barely a pup, at Methven. The lad should have never been there, at the battle. Sir Philip told me he'd owe me a life. And then, just before Edward gave the order to execute me, Philip had begged him not to."

David fingered the wood. Philip Mowbray must have had a strong code of ethics. Perhaps he would have been a good husband to Anna, as much as it killed David to admit it.

"I wasna afraid to die," Colum continued. "I was ready. I'd done my duty. I would be glad to die for my king and for my clan. But then, when I was spared...I was asked to join the English side. And when I refused..." His voice broke. "They did something. Nae to me…to someone else. Something I could never reveal…something I could only put an end to by switching to their side. So, betraying my clan and my king, I said aye."

"Look, man, you were put in an impossible situation. How did you get back?"

"My uncle Aulay and my clan came for me a year later. They fought the English to get inside the castle, only to see that I wasna a prisoner nae more. That I was wearing English clothes and carrying an English sword."

"Oh…no."

"My uncle gave me a choice. The clan would take me back if I wanted to go. Or if I'd truly sworn my allegiance to the English, they would leave me alone and return home. I was still a MacDonald and a Highlander. So I left with my clan. Even though everyone kent I had switched sides."

David felt for him. Trapped in the Middle Ages, David had had to adapt and act like a medieval Scotsman, even if it meant killing enemies to protect others and to survive. Something he never would have considered acceptable in his own time. Colum had to do the same thing with the English. Only, Colum had escaped that life when his clan rescued him. David, on the other hand, was still imprisoned. And always would be. "Damn. That's why Marcas and others are still wary of you."

"Aye. Now I have sworn an oath to dedicate the rest of my life to serving my king and my clan. I'll do whatever it takes to restore my honor. I will die for my king if I must."

Sadness weighed on David. Colum's determination was admirable. He had his future carved out for him; he knew what he was doing, and he had a goal.

David's future was forever lost. The future he'd wanted his whole life. College. A good job. A career. To distinguish himself. To start a business. To prove that his dyslexia would not weigh him down.

He'd never have that now. Even though he loved Anna, was that enough?

The shores of the loch were receding into the distance, the birlinn entering the open sea. Aulay called for Colum, and he left.

David saw Anna making her way through the boat, holding on to the boxes and the mast and then coming to stand by his side. A warm wave of tingles shot through him at her presence. He hadn't really talked to her since the day before the wedding, and he'd missed spending his days and nights with her. Her hair was floating in the wind, her dark eyes shiny and deep as she looked at him. Her cheeks had gained color, her hair was shiny and her full lips red. He ached to kiss them, to drink her taste again, to nip at her lower lip.

"Are you allowed to talk to me now?" he asked.

She looked back at Laoghaire and then forward at Aulay. Both were staring at her with frowns. "I think 'tis safe that I wilna strip my clothes and cling to yer neck when there are fifty people around." She chuckled.

"Are you all right?" he asked.

"Aye, just a wee bit nauseated."

He ached to take her into his arms but settled for covering her hand that lay on the wooden side with his. Hers was cold and small and silky. "You know I won't leave you now. I won't let you down, Anna. You don't need to worry."

Anna squeezed his hand back and was silent for a while as she watched the water moving under the birlinn. "David, ye shouldn't stay."

He blinked. Something cold and heavy weighed at his stomach. "What?"

"Look...David, I am nauseous because of the ship, nae because I'm with child. I got my courses earlier today, I just didna tell anyone."

Cold shock hit him. She got her period... So there'd be no baby? Loss, sharp and sad and heavy, wrestled in his gut. "Are you sure it's your period? Not pregnancy bleeding?"

She smiled sadly. Her thumb fingered the indent in the boat.

"I am sure. Ye dinna need to worry. 'Twas nae pregnancy. Only a few days late. All the events of the past weeks must have been hard on my body. So, there's nae reason for ye to stay. Ye may leave. There's a rock on Islay, I'll bring ye to it."

His windpipe tightened, and sadness prickled at the backs of his eyes. He didn't know he would feel so disappointed, so at a loss. He realized then how much he actually liked the idea of having a little family with Anna, even if it would be here, in medieval Scotland. He must have grown up. He was ready to live the life of a man, not a boy.

He turned to her and took both her hands in his. "I still want you to come with me. Let's get married here, or in the future, and go through the rock together. Please, Anna. Come with me."

The skin where he was touching her hands was charged with soft electricity. He was flying now, floating in the air holding her hands. Her eyes were big and glossy as she watched him. The almond shape made him think of a cheetah, breathtakingly beautiful and yet wild and knowing her own will. She swallowed and bit her lip, shaking her head.

"Nae. I canna."

Rejection hit him like a train. Pain radiated through his heart. "Why not? You can be free there, with me. We don't even have to marry. But no one will ever force you to do anything you don't want. You can learn a skill...maybe become a swim instructor...or a teacher of Gaelic...or...whatever you want. There are so many ways to make a living and have a good life. As long as we're together."

She pulled her hands from his, leaving an emptiness around his fingers. "I am needed here. Just as ye want to make a life for yerself in the future, I want to be useful here."

The very air hurt as he took his next breath. "How?"

"I want to help lepers. They're outcasts...a wee bit like me. They are nae well cared for, and I want to change that. They're just people suffering from a disease, even if 'tis sent by God. Someone should help them and make their lives easier. Besides, I may still be useful to the king and contribute to Scotland. And I dinna think I can do much in yer future. As wonderful as it sounds there."

"What about me? You'd contribute to me, to your and my happiness."

She shook her head. "I release ye from needing to marry me. I dinna want to be yer jailor and dinna want ye to be trapped with me. I will survive without ye—my clan and my father wilna let me down."

She gave him a final, sad nod, her back straight, her shoulders proud as a queen's, then turned and made her way back to Laoghaire. As David watched her back, his heart felt like it was breaking into a million pieces. Hurt spread from his chest into his whole body. A dark abyss was expanding under his feet.

She wanted him gone. There was a rock on Islay. She'd released him from an obligation, and he was finally free.

But, for the first time, he realized the true cost of that freedom.

CHAPTER 31

THEY ARRIVED at Islay on the evening of the same day. The sun was low in the sky, sinking behind a bank of clouds, but it was the end of June and full darkness would not come for some time yet.

On one side of Lagavulin Bay, Dunyvaig Castle loomed over the cliff. The tower of the main keep was tall and menacing, the men-at-arms standing atop it a threat to unwelcome guests. Inside the bay, Aulay maneuvered the ship masterfully among anchored birlinns, trade galleys, and fishing boats until they reached the port. A village was spread over the ground behind the port, clearly busy, with hurrying people looking like ants in the distance.

They docked, and as David's feet hit the firm ground, he knew this was it...the end of his search for a way home. But he wasn't ready to say goodbye. He wasn't ready to lose Anna forever. He wasn't ready to never see Rogene again, even though he had been pursuing the time traveling rock for three years.

Anna came to stand next to him, turning to Aulay. "Uncle, is it all right if I take a walk with David? Show him the place where I grew up?"

Aulay scratched his beard and looked at Colum. "I wouldna want ye to be alone with him, Anna."

"He will be my husband, and he saved my life. How much harm can be done?"

David frowned at her. Why didn't she tell everyone the engagement was off? And that there was no baby?

Colum nodded. "Uncle, 'tis all right. I trust him."

Aulay sighed deeply. "I suppose. Aye. But dinna go too far. If ye're nae back by the sunset, I will cut off yer ballsack and feed it to ye, aye?"

David nodded. "You have my word."

"Come, David," she said in a low voice as she passed him. "I'll take ye there. Ye wilna need to stay here a day longer."

He watched in bewilderment as she walked away through the busy streets of the village. He followed her, pushing through people who smelled of fish and pigsties and woodsmoke. His ears rang with the sounds of feet slurping through the muddy ground, people talking, chickens and geese squawking, and sheep bleating.

Once they passed through the village, she led him across green and rusty grass, over hard, rocky terrain. Anna's cloak wavered in the wind a few steps in front of him, her hair a dark, floating mane. He finally caught up with her. "Anna, are you sure you want me to go?"

"'Tis what ye want, aye, David?" she said without looking at him. "I want to give ye what ye want. I love ye too much to entrap ye and make ye miserable."

She loved him... And he loved her even more for this, for setting him free, for making the choice for his freedom.

"I love you, too," he said, trying to stop her, but she kept marching.

"Aye...well. Love isna everything. We both ken that."

After about ten minutes, they began climbing a large hill with ruins and boulders at its top. With every step, David felt like he was heading to an execution, to that bridge over the river in

Kennifar. Only it wouldn't be his life that he'd lose. It would be his heart. His happiness.

It would be part of his soul.

Then they stood over the rock that sat at the base of a crumbled rock and mortar wall. There they were, the carvings. The handprint.

Once again, he felt the strange energy of the stone—some sort of buzz in the air and in his gut. It would open this time, he knew. It would. Because he had found the one person who was his destiny, just as Sìneag had wanted.

Anna stood before the stone, straight and solemn, her hands clasped by her stomach. She looked at him, small but majestic. "Ye are free, David Wakeley," she said, her voice firm and soft. He'd told her his real name during their time at the farm. Hearing it now, on her lips, was so intimate. "I hope ye will be happy there."

He thought she wavered towards him, like a grass touched by the wind. But she remained where she was.

If she didn't want to take that step, he would. He needed one last reminder of what they both would never have. Something to take with him and hold on to forever. Grasping her forearms, he took a large step forward, pinning her to the one piece of a crumbled wall that was still straight.

"A kiss goodbye, then," he growled into her mouth and covered her lips with his.

He kissed her for the hundreds of years that would separate them. For the dozens of lifetimes that would pass before he would be born, never knowing that his love was back in time. He kissed her for the one lifetime that they would never share.

He kissed her so that she'd remember him as he would never forget her.

His blood boiled as it always did when her lips touched his, when her tongue lashed against his, when he felt her small, soft breasts against his chest and her curves against his hardness. She was gentle and soft where he was strong and hard. And her scent...a feminine mix of flowers and sunshine and sea. He needed to engrave it forever in his senses.

When he pulled back, she was breathing hard, her eyes dark and wet and shiny under her long eyelashes.

Without another word, she twisted out of his embrace and was gone. Emptiness seared at him as he watched her walk down the hill. With every step she took, a void spread in his soul, as bottomless as a black hole.

He thought about calling out to her. Begging her for another minute by his side. Dropping onto his knees and pleading for her to come to the future with him.

But he didn't. He locked his knees and clenched his fists, restraining himself from making a single move. When she disappeared from his sight, he forced himself to turn to the rock.

The sudden scent of lavender and freshly cut grass brushed against his senses. He knew what it meant. Sìneag was here somewhere, and the tunnel through time was open.

The old David would have been angry at her for keeping him here. But he wasn't that man anymore.

The carvings glowed, just like that fateful time when Rogene had gone through the stone and David had come along for the ride.

Sìneag appeared from thin air next to the rock. Like the previous time, she wore a green hooded cloak, her red hair spilling over her shoulders in waves. She gave him a bright smile. "Ye found the woman ye're destined for. As I kent ye would."

"Yeah," he said sadly. "Like you knew I would. I should be angry at you. You trapped me here for so long. But I'm not. I'd do it all over again for her."

Sìneag sighed deeply and bit her lower lip.

"Why are ye nae moving?" Sìneag asked. "Ye ken if ye touch the stone, ye will travel through time."

The pull of the stone's magic was strong. Finally, his way back home was within reach.

He inhaled sharply. "I know."

Love isna everything, he remembered Anna's words. She could have come with him, but, like him, she was choosing something other than love.

"Are ye unsure if ye want to leave?" Sìneag asked.

"Through that rock is everything I had thought was important to me most of my life. Playing football. Earning a degree. How proud I'd be at the graduation ceremony. Getting an important job, making lots of money. I'm just trying to decide if it's all worth it."

Sìneag nodded and sat down on the remnant of a wall. "Worth is an interesting thing... Time is worthless to me, a wee thing to play around with. But for ye humans, time is everything."

David swallowed hard as he watched her porcelain features, eyes gleaming with something between mischief and empathy.

"Ye will get old," Sìneag continued. "And, sorry to say, ye'll die one day. And that day, how would ye look back at yer life? With yer bonnie house and yer shiny car... Would they fill yer soul, and would they be worth it, spending the most precious thing ye have...time?"

He could find someone else, he wanted to say. But even if he found a woman he might want to marry, he'd never love her as desperately and fully as he loved Anna.

Anna was not just a piece of his heart.

She was his very soul.

"Life here," he said as he looked back down the hill where Anna had disappeared, "with Anna would be colorful and warm. There would be hardships, yes, but also happiness and joy and so much love."

Sìneag sat quietly, watching him with a knowing look.

"All my life," he continued thoughtfully, "I had this void in me. I felt I was not good enough because of my dyslexia... thought I was dumb. But all I needed to do was accept myself as I was." Anna, with her heart of a lioness, had stood up for herself, having more courage than some armies.

"But for three years, I've been making it here. I learned sword fighting. I traveled through Scotland. I survived medieval battles. And, most importantly, I always did the right thing by my sister and her clan.

"So I don't need to return to my own time to find proof of my value. If my parents looked down at me from heaven, I think they'd be proud of me."

Sìneag's eyes were wet, and she wiped away a tear and looked at it, puzzled. "Oh... See, ye made me cry. If it makes a difference, I am proud of ye, too, David."

He grinned and looked back at the Islay landscape below. "She pushed me away to free me. But I can only be free when I'm with her. And the home I've always looked for is here"—as though an oven had been lit inside his chest, heat spread through him—"inside me. But it will only be complete with Anna."

He turned to Sìneag.

He didn't need to fight against this land, against the feudal laws and wars he couldn't change. It was his—good, bad, and ugly. His to love and cherish, his to live and breathe, like Anna.

Love pulsed through him, pure and hot. He leaned down and kissed Sìneag on the cheek, feeling her cold tears on his face. She touched her skin and blushed.

"I won't need the passage, Sìneag. I'm in the place and time where I belong. I just need to tell the person I belong with, as well."

He turned around and walked down the hill. Halfway down, a figure appeared from behind a boulder, and he stopped breathing.

Anna.

Her eyes were round, her hands shaking.

With the heat in his chest pulsing, he scooped her into his arms and whirled her around. Her feminine scent was in his nostrils, her weight light in his arms. He put her on the ground to kiss her.

But he caught empty air instead of her lips.

She bent over to her side and vomited.

Astonished, David watched her retch. A moment later, he came to his senses and held her hair back as she emptied her stomach.

"Are you all right, sweetheart?" he asked.

Breathing heavily, she straightened and wiped her mouth with the back of her sleeve. Her cheeks were flushed, and her forehead misted with sweat. "I'm all right... I heard everything. Are ye really staying?"

"I'm not going anywhere," he said, cupping her heated face. "I'm staying because all I've been looking for is you."

Her sweet face spread in a happy smile that tightened his chest. But she bent over and retched once more, heaving.

When she was done, she put her hands on her knees, breathing heavily. David studied her. "You vomited because I whirled you?" Realization flashed in his head like a light bulb. "Wait...are you still pregnant?"

She sighed and smiled shyly. "I think I am."

"Christ!" David pulled her into his arms and kissed the top of her head. He wanted to shield her from everything. Be her and their baby's protector. Be her home and her world, just like she was his. "You just made me the happiest man in the world."

She giggled into his chest and sagged against him.

"I found my home with you, Anna. I built a life for myself in this time that is richer than any life I could have imagined in modern times. This is where I belong. There's just one thing to clarify. Without your father insisting and your uncle threatening to cut off my balls, this is me, asking you, the girl I love. Will you marry me?"

She looked up at him, joy sparkling in her dark eyes. "Aye, David. What a happy woman I am. Marrying my protector from the future, the love of my life."

EPILOGUE

One week later...

"Do ye, David, take Anna to be yer wedded wife, to
have and to hold from this day forward, for better or for worse,
for richer or for poorer, for fairer or for fouler, in sickness and in
health, to love and to cherish, till death you depart, according to
God's holy ordinance?" asked the priest.

David held Anna's hands in his, standing before the priest by
the entrance of the church in Dunyvaig village. The day had
been a bit cool for July, with north winds blowing strongly, but
the sun shone brightly in the cloudless sky. Anna's hair flared in
the wind, her dark eyes glistening with joy, her lips spread in that
smile he could never get tired of.

This was it. The moment he'd remember for the rest of his
life.

"Yes," he said. "I take you, Anna, and thereunto I plight thee
my troth."

The words of the vow went through his bones and settled in
his marrow. She beamed and brightened, as beautiful as the land-

scape around her, the one and only for him, the lost part of his soul he'd been lucky enough to find.

"I now pronounce ye husband and wife," said the priest.

David took a step to Anna, pulling her into his embrace and sealing his lips with hers. The crowd around them cheered, five hundred or so people. He'd stolen kisses throughout the week, pulling her behind a corner of the kitchen or into a dark alcove of the castle. But with this kiss, he claimed her in front of clan MacDonald and clan Mackenzie and the whole world.

His *wife*... His wife who tasted like a dive into a secret waterfall at night. Who smelled like the Highlands. Who felt like home.

When he pulled back from the kiss, she was breathless and flushed and bright-eyed. The crowd roared and cheered again, and Anna and he turned to face them. He locked eyes with his sister, who held little toddler Paul on her hip. Teary-eyed, she gave him a bright smile through the crowd. Angus stood by her side, a one-year-old girl in a carrying bag on his back. Catrìona and James were there, too, and Catrìona was round with their first child. Laomann and Mairead stood by their side as well as Iòna and other Mackenzie clansmen and women.

His family.

One week was short notice, but Aulay had been kind enough to send men with a few birlinns to Eilean Donan and pick up the important guests.

David and Anna were hugged and congratulated and blessed. Then the feast began. It was set in the great hall and outside, since the weather was good. The cooks made several bonfires in the bailey and roasted boars and let salmon stew boil. The whole week, the ale house had been brewing ale for the occasion, and now the servants carried pitchers and set them on the long tables arranged with benches outside.

A small platform had been constructed in the middle, where a band of musicians played lute, flute, and drums, and a singer sang a beautiful Gaelic ballad. It reminded him of Raghnall, and

David wished that he could be here as well, but he knew Raghnall was happy in the future with Bryanna. David wished Dùghlas could be here, too, as well as the Cambels, who hadn't been able to make it on time.

The bailey was full of laughter, talk, and music. Rogene and Angus with their kids and Catrìona and James with Seoc, their adoptive son, came to David and Anna. Rogene gave David a big hug, and he scooped her into his arms and held her for as long as he could without tearing up. She pulled back and cupped his face, tears welling in her eyes. "I'm so glad to see you. Congratulations, you two! Many, many happy years to you and as much happiness as comes your way!"

"If we're half as happy as you and Angus," David said, "we will be very happy, indeed."

"Congratulations, man!" Angus engulfed him in a bone-crushing bear hug and clapped him on his back, then retreated. "'Tis a fine union with a fine woman and a good clan. I am proud of ye. I wish ye both much health, wealth, and happiness."

Little Paul, who was now two years old, held up his little palm. "High-fai, Uncle Dafee!"

David grinned. "What? Who taught you to do a high five?"

Paul giggled. "Uncle James. High-fai!"

David sank to a crouch before his nephew and high-fived the little hand. The boy giggled proudly and held his hand up again. "High-fai!"

Laughter came from all around them as David kept high-fiving his nephew. Soon, the little boy got bored and ran to chase after a butterfly.

"I'll keep an eye on him," said James. "Paul, friend, watch out, police are coming! Wueee!" Paul squealed and sped up down the bailey in his uneven toddler run as James chased him, making the sounds of a police siren and drawing curious and confused stares from all the guests.

Rogene beamed and looked at Anna. "I'm so glad you're my sister-in-law. I know you're a special woman if David chose you."

"Aye, 'tis me who's lucky, Lady Rogene," Anna said, making David's heart warm and tighten. "I can only thank a certain faerie who brought us together."

David, Rogene, Angus, and Catrìona all chuckled and exchanged meaningful looks. Rogene took David by the elbow. "Excuse me, everyone, I'd like a word with my brother, if that's all right? I haven't seen him for two years."

As they walked away from the group and sat at an empty table, Rogene looked him over carefully, her gaze worried and motherly. She hadn't aged much, just gathered more stature and confidence. She was the wife of a clan chief, sort of a queen of a small kingdom, and she acted accordingly. She was dressed in a clearly expensive brocaded dress with a belt embroidered in silver and gold threads. Her dark hair was done in a tasteful braid under a pleated linen torque with a chin band. David knew how respected and loved she was in the clan alongside Angus.

She took his hand in hers. "Why didn't you write me? You promised."

"I'm sorry. I should have. I was angry and upset with myself. And you know how hard it is for me to write."

"I know. Still. I wish you'd made an effort."

"I will, Rory. Aulay is allowing me to take part in the trade business, and I have some ideas to gain higher profits. I already talked to him about them, and he likes them."

She chuckled and looked at him with admiration. "So you are really okay with staying here?" she asked as she laid her hand on his. "You've been so desperate to return. Your scholarship...your future..."

He looked at Anna across the green grass of the bailey, and as she caught his gaze, warmth spread through him. "I'll be okay anywhere she is." Anna gave him an intimate, secret smile. David leaned over to Rogene. "And she's pregnant."

Rogene widened her eyes. "She is? Congratulations! But you just got marri— Oh, you didn't."

He sighed. "Yeah. I did. I deflowered a princess and stole her virtue. A goddamn Tristan."

"With a happy ending... Wait... Oh my God, that's why they forced you to marry her?"

"There's a bit more to it. You remember the Battle of Bannockburn?"

"Of course I remember the Battle of Bannockburn. June 24, 1314. The most important battle of the wars of independence. It will bring Robert the Bruce a decisive victory over England. Why?"

"Well...until about ten days ago, it was not supposed to happen. Anna was going to marry Philip of Mowbray and, in exchange, he had promised to give Stirling to Bruce without a fight."

"I don't remember anything like that from history."

David briefly told her what had happened with Anna, their adventures on the road, and the events in Stirling when they returned.

Rogene pursed her lips. "History is a funny thing. Sometimes we have no idea what really happened."

"Yeah."

She squeezed his shoulder. "I'm so proud of you. And so glad you're staying here, with me. Promise I'll get to see you more often."

He took her hand in both of his. "Promise." And in his heart, it was not just a promise but a vow. "I am so glad I am staying, too, to see you. That was what I regretted most through my travels, that I didn't get to see you. Didn't get to tell you how actually great it is that we're on this adventure together. That I got to experience all this thanks to you. You are my family. Always have been. Always will be."

Rogene cupped his face with both her hands. "I love you, brother."

"I love you, too, Rory."

He pulled her into a big hug and held her. This was what this adventure had taught him, too. Not to postpone things that needed to be said or done. And not being afraid to tell people he was close to how he felt. Especially in the Middle Ages, where death came more easily and the next opportunity might never arrive.

"How's your life?" he asked.

She smiled. "It's good. Really. We're happy. Sometimes Angus drives me nuts with his Scottish stubbornness... But we always know what's most important—love and family. And you know what's funny?"

"What?"

She chuckled. "Well... People started thinking of me a little bit like a seeress."

David chuckled. "Really?"

"Yes. A couple things I warned about came true. You know, stuff I know from historical research. And now all kinds of people are asking for an audience with me to predict their futures."

David chuckled but then got serious. "You need to be careful about that. There are people who might kill you for being a witch."

She sighed. "I know. That's why I never meet with those people and never say anything when people ask me. Besides putting my own life in danger, revealing the course of history could alter it in unexpected and potentially harmful ways. The Battle of Bannockburn, for example. Historically, Bruce will win. But there will be many deaths, of course. And it all might change if people fiddle with history."

Paul ran to Rogene with a squeal and collapsed on top of her knees, followed by James, still making police car sounds, who came to a roaring stop. He was panting with exaggerated heaves of his chest.

"Mr. Paul Mackenzie," James said. "I'm afraid you're too good of a driver, and I acknowledge my defeat. The police cease all investigation."

"Good." David took two cups of ale standing next to a jar in the middle of the table and stood up, handing one to James. "I think the police deserve a fresh, cold drink."

James chuckled and gladly accepted the cup. Rogene took one, too.

"To another goddamn modern-day person trapped back in time for love," toasted James. "May you live a long and happy life with Anna. And I bet you won't be the last. The cheeky little faerie is at work again, mark my word."

They chuckled and drank. Then David returned to Anna and didn't step away from her again.

The celebration got louder and merrier, and by the evening, it seemed, the whole island was there, eating, drinking, dancing, laughing.

Throughout the festivities, Aulay sat somewhat away from the others, with a goblet of uisge, watching dancing couples with sad eyes.

Anna sighed. "He never got over his wife's death," she told David.

A pretty noblewoman in her late twenties came to sit by his side. She was clearly flirtatious, a smile on her lips, her eyes seeking his. But Aulay was polite and courteous and nothing more. After a while, the woman gave up and walked away. Aulay threw the contents of his goblet down his throat and called a servant for more.

The music changed, with minstrels telling stories of King Arthur, of Celtic heroes of the past, of chivalrous knights and noble ladies, and, by David's special request, of Tristan and Isolde.

And through all that, David didn't let go of Anna's hand. He felt like his bones were replaced with warm, tingly goo when he was next to her. He kept whispering to her how beautiful she was and how happy she made him.

It was dark outside, and the feast returned to the great hall. David and Anna sat by the fireplace, and she sagged sleepily against him. Aulay and Colum sat nearby, and David and the two MacDonald men talked about the wool trade.

Someone hurried through the bailey, and as the man drew closer, making his way through the crowd, David saw that he was dressed in traveling clothes.

"Laird..." the man called, and Aulay raised his hand. The man rushed to him and started to say something quietly into his ear, but Aulay stopped him and looked at David.

"Ye're part of the clan now." He turned to the messenger. "Talk, man."

Anna raised her head and looked at them sleepily. "What's going on?"

The messenger cleared his throat. "The English treasure ship carrying armor and weapons never made it through the Irish Sea. It never arrived in Ireland."

Anna's face brightened. "Which means it was probably run aground or sunk by the storm."

"Aye," said Aulay. "Ye did good, Anna, delivering that news to the Bruce. I will send word to him. It may have sunk. But it might also be on one of the islands or even the Irish shore. I am sure he'd want us to find it before the English. Finding that ship could mean fewer lives lost in English attacks. It could even be a deciding factor in the war, having that armor on our men instead of theirs, being able to feed the Bruce's warriors."

Colum added, "We must spend every moment searching the sea until it's found."

"Right. Do you want me to come with you?" asked David.

"I canna take a new husband away from my favorite niece. Later. I want ye to go to Eilean Geal and make yer new home with yer bride. But I wanted ye to be aware of what is happening in the clan. Once we get the ship, we may need ye."

David felt proud he was now part of the clan's business and accepted by Aulay and Colum. "Of course. Count on me."

As David and Anna walked to their bedchamber, Anna looked over her shoulder at Aulay. "Every unwed woman in the clan wants to either bed my uncle or marry him. But he doesna see any of that."

David looked at him thoughtfully. He was tall and powerfully built. He supposed the clan chief was even handsome, in that rugged Highlander way. But his eyes looked like they had seen too much pain and sorrow. "If he's not ready, he won't fall in love."

"Ye were nae ready and ye did. He's still young. Any woman would be lucky to have him."

David shook his head. "Do not say that out loud! Sìneag might hear you!"

Anna giggled and they kept walking.

Later, when they were falling asleep, and David held her tightly in his arms, he marveled at the magnificent life that was about to begin here, one he would have missed if he had gone through the rock. "I love you, Anna," he said. "You gave me everything I have ever needed."

"And I love you, my time traveler. You have been my protector from the moment I met you."

As her lashes drifted shut, he whispered, "I always will be, my fierce Highland princess."

～

THANK YOU FOR READING HIGHLANDER'S PROTECTOR. Find out what happens next when Aulay, Anna's uncle, and the chief of clan, meets Jennifer, his soulmate from the future, in HIGHLANDER'S CLAIM.

SHE MUST RETURN TO THE TWENTY-FIRST CENTURY. HE'S holding her captive. Could her love be the treasure he longs to claim?

. . .

READ **HIGHLANDER'S CLAIM** NOW >
"I just loved it. Such a lovely hymn to parenthood."

SIGN-UP FOR MARIAH STONE'S NEWSLETTER:
http://mariahstone.com/signup

READY FOR YOUR PIRATE?

Other mysterious matchmakers help modern-day people find their soulmates; also during pirate times. If you haven't read James and Samantha's story yet, be sure to pick up PIRATE'S TREASURE.

A pirate desperate to lead an honest life. An executive who falls through time. One last chance to right the wrongs of the past.

READ **PIRATES TREASURE** NOW >
"A swash-bucking, adventurous, and heartwarmingly unique MUST-READ"

. . .

Or stay in the Highlands and keep reading for an excerpt from HIGHLANDER'S CLAIM.

~

Irish Sea near Isle of Achleith, Scotland, July 2022

Dr. Jennifer Foster spread her right arm into the space beyond the charter boat. As seawater sprinkled all over her face and her bright, salad-green and lemon-yellow dress with purple flowers, she squealed.

Her girlfriends, sitting by her side at the end of the boat, squealed with her. They all held plastic champagne glasses.

"Shh," said Natalie drunkenly, "your champagne is sticking out."

Natalie made a movement to shove the dark-green neck of the bottle back into Amanda's purse, but her hand slipped, and she giggled. So did Jenny, Kyla, and Amanda.

"I don't think MacGrumpy over there will tell MacBoss," said Amanda, then drank the rest of her champagne from the glass in one gulp and took the bottle back out from her purse. "Not for the tip we're going to give him."

While Amanda poured more bubbly into her glass, the boat jumped on the waves, and she poured half of her serving onto the deck. Jenny raised her glass.

"Here's to us," Jenny toasted. "Four strong, independent women in their prime! We have our careers, our money, and can eat our cake, too!"

"Yeah!" echoed her girlfriends, clinking their four glasses together.

Amanda added over the edge of her glass, "And to the sexy Scottish guys I've been banging for a week... And Jenny has not!"

Jenny flashed a glare at her best friend but said nothing. She threw back the drink and the bubbles tickled her throat. "I also did not get divorced recently."

"Not recently," said Kyla as she tucked her shining, dark hair behind her ear. "You did three years ago, and you still haven't slept with anybody."

Jenny scoffed. "Pfff. Like it's a bad thing."

"Excuse me!" cried Amanda as she struggled to keep her blond hair out of her eyes. "Sweetie, I love you, but you sound a little judgmental."

Natalie looked between them. She was sporting gorgeous designer sunglasses and a bright-red sundress that was striking against her dark skin. After a week away from her two kids, with more hours to sleep and time to breathe, she looked fresh and full of energy. "Girls, don't fight. I know what'll help!" She took the bottle of champagne from Amanda's hand. "This!"

As she poured more champagne, emptying the bottle, Jenny glanced at her and at Kyla. "I always wanted what Kyla and Natalie have. Kids. Family. And yet, I'm thirty-nine, and..."

She trailed off, unable to say the words. The brilliant blue sky —so rare for Scotland—and the sapphire seawater hurt her eyes. Tightness in her throat didn't let any words out.

What she wanted to say was, she was thirty-nine and her time was running out. She had had three unsuccessful IVF rounds with a sperm donor in the past two years. The IVF failed to implant because of her endometriosis, no doubt, an incredibly painful condition she had lived with her whole life. Her periods had been agony. She had learned to manage it and live with it, but the worst thing was that her chance of getting pregnant and carrying her own child in a natural way was very small.

Her last chance to have her own baby was in fourteen days. The fertility clinic was booked a year in advance, and that was the only time slot they had for her to start the hormone treatment to extract her last viable eggs and freeze them.

She couldn't even think about sleeping with anyone...

"*And*," Amanda continued for her after a long pause, "you're one of the most sought-after private pediatric doctors in New York City, together with me, your partner. You and I have a thriving practice, help a lot of kids get well, and…excuse me for bragging, but we're not exactly hurting for money."

"Amanda!" said Natalie.

"Oh, come on," said Kyla. "It's not like they're using the kids. They deserve their success. It's you and I who are stuck at home wiping snotty noses and chasing after preschoolers."

Jenny smiled. "I want to chase after preschoolers," she said to Natalie and Kyla.

Her life felt incomplete without a child of her own. Something big and sweet was missing, and that emptiness was like a giant hole in her soul that sucked and ached.

"But you don't want to give up your clinic, do you?" asked Natalie. "Amanda and you have been building it for ten years."

Jenny gave out an uncomfortable laugh. Suddenly, it was all becoming too serious and too much to the point. Through the roar of the boat's engine and the noise of the waves crashing against its sides, the voice of her ex-husband was trying to break through in her mind. *Deep down, deep, deep down, men want to take care of women and women want to be taken care of. If only you worked less and spent more time with me…if only we'd started a family earlier…*

And he had started on a family—only, without Jenny. He had a two-year-old daughter now and his new wife was a stay-at-home mom. Exactly how he wanted his relationship to be.

And Jenny…Jenny had zero little girls, only a handful of eggs left, one empty apartment, and a terrifying, sinking feeling in the pit of her stomach that she was too late. That she'd never have her own baby to hold and to adore, to inhale that dear, sweet baby smell.

That Tom had been right. That it was all her fault. All of it. Had she given in and let him take charge and sold her part of the clinic to Amanda, she could have spent more time with him. He wouldn't have cheated on her. They'd still be together. Had she started trying to get pregnant at thirty-two, like he'd suggested, she'd have her own little girl or boy to love and to spoil. A little girl or boy with Jenny's naturally pale red hair and Tom's green eyes.

"And I admire you so much," said Kyla. "You and Amanda achieved what I have dreamed of but didn't dare. And yet the four of us went to the same medical school."

Jenny sighed. "I'm the one envious of what you have," she said. "All of you have kids. Even if your marriage didn't work out, Amanda, you still have a son. And you, Natalie and Kyla, you have happy families. It's most likely too late for me."

"Don't say that," Kyla said. "Women get pregnant in their late thirties and early forties all the time. Cameron Diaz had a baby at forty-seven. Naomi Campbell gave birth at fifty."

The boat jumped over a wave and Jenny's chin rattled. "Yes, but—"

Amanda linked her arm through Jenny's. "Here's what we'll do." She pointed at the sea. "The moment we step on that Irish coast, we go to a pub. And this time, you will come."

"I came to the pubs in Scotland."

"Yeah, right. I mean, this time, you will flirt with hot Irish men, and you'll have lots of sex with them—yes, *multiple* them—and if you get knocked up...well...oops."

The ladies giggled. "Amanda, don't be silly," said Natalie. "She won't get knocked up by an Irish guy."

"Because she should get knocked up by one of those Highlanders back in Scotland..." said Kyla over the glass of champagne.

They all laughed. It seemed Jenny was the only one who didn't feel the humor.

"Oh yeah," Amanda said. "As someone who's tried the local cuisine multiple times...and tasted multiple dishes, if you get my meaning...I can highly recommend it."

"We can even extend our holiday!" cried Natalie, raising her glass. "Yes, we have one week left, but we can just return to Scotland for a few more days..."

"Actually, we can't," said Jenny. "I have an appointment in two weeks to start the hormone treatment for egg extraction."

The smiles on the girls' faces fell. "Really? Has it come to that?" Kyla asked.

"Yeah. I only have ten more eggs left, and this is my last chance to have my own baby. And I'd still need to use a surrogate."

They were all silent, looking at her with pity.

"Come on," Jenny forced out with a smile. "Cheer up. Enough about me. We are celebrating Amanda's divorce. Even if it's not in warm and sunny Hawaii."

"That's the spirit!" cheered Natalie.

Amanda rolled her eyes. "I picked Scotland and Ireland because I wanted 'real men' who will take charge and call me 'lass' and make me forget everything. And let me tell you, Highlanders do exactly that."

Jenny giggled. "Oh yeah? I'll stick with Hawaii, where men are gentler and take care of you."

"Oh, believe me, Scottish men can take care of you very well." Amanda winked.

The roar of the ferry motor huffed and puffed. The boat jerked to a halt. Then started again. Then the roar turned to a weak droning and the boat stopped. As they rocked gently on the waves and the vibration of the motor that she had felt for the past hour died down, Jenny had the disorienting feeling of the floor moving under her feet.

There was nothing but open sea all around them, except for a small island with a lighthouse that rose above the water about five hundred feet away. The island was rocky, with an oval top, like a giant head sticking out of the sea. It must be about three hundred feet high and five hundred feet long. Typical for Scottish landscapes, green and yellow moss covered the steep slopes.

"What's going on?" muttered Amanda.

The motor started again, and the boat moved but then died. Then again. This repeated six or seven more times before the captain's door opened and the boatswain stepped onto the deck. He was a man in his sixties, with a balding head of gray hair and a short, gray beard over a sullen, deeply wrinkled face.

"Tough luck, lasses," he grumbled. "Captain says the motor may have died. We will have to dock at Achleith and wait for a coast guard rescue boat from Islay. I doubt ye make it to Ireland today. While the captain waits, I will take ye to Achleith so that ye dinna fall overboard from yer drinking. There's an ancient ruin with an interesting rock that people on Islay believe is a home of the faeries."

"Sounds good," Jenny said and then looked at her girlfriends. "Does that sound like a celebration to you?"

"Sure," said Natalie and stretched her arms out. "I'll take any adventure before I have to go back to my happy, boring reality."

"If we go back to Islay," said Amanda, "Jenny's having sex with some Highlanders."

Jenny giggled and shook her head.

The boatswain went back into the captain's cabin and with more whirs and low droning and stopping of the motor, he directed the boat towards the island.

When they finally stopped close to the island, Jenny realized there weren't even any trees or bushes. Just green moss and cliffs and the lighthouse. The boatswain helped them into the dinghy and rowed them to the gravelly beach.

Once they stood on the firm ground, Jenny regretted her choice of flip-flops and the thin, floaty satin dress with patterns of bright, spring-green leaves and—a tribute to Scotland—violet flowers. Even in July the wind was cool, and it flapped her skirt around, leaving her short legs covered in goose bumps. She could feel every pebble and rock through the soles of her flip-flops. The four of them took selfies all together with the boat anchored several dozen feet away and the island looming over them like a giant cork head. She realized she'd forgotten her purse, which held her phone, back on the boat and felt strangely naked without it.

"Well," Amanda said as she took another bottle of champagne out of her bottomless designer purse, "the mood is kind of a bummer. It's an adventure, girls! Come on, let's keep the party going."

Jenny woo-hooed, and, despite the odd looks from her girlfriends, they were good sports and echoed her as Amanda popped the cork and poured champagne into four plastic glasses.

"To celebration!" cried Jenny as the four of them brought their glasses together high up in the air and drank.

Giggling, they made their way up the steep slope. The damn flip-flops slipped, and her feet threatened to slide out of them.

The top of the island was round and covered with moss and grass. The old lighthouse stood on the north side. Its white paint was chipped, and cracks ran between the brown bricks. Based on the broken glass of the lantern panes, it was probably not even functioning.

It was all so breathtakingly beautiful, the piece of land she stood on tiny compared to the vast sky and the endless sea. And her best friends were right by her side.

"I'm so thankful for you, girls," she said. "And am so glad we're on this adventure together."

With her head spinning, Jenny hugged Amanda and Natalie by their waists. Amanda hooked her arm around Kyla's shoulders and the four of them stood and breathed and looked at the sea around them. Seagulls squawked and wheeled over their heads.

"To many more adventures!" Natalie raised her glass.

"Hear! Hear!" the three of them echoed.

"Even if no one comes and we die here!" announced Amanda. "We'd die together."

They laughed.

"Look, there's that faerie rock that MacGrumpy talked about," said Jenny, looking in the direction of the lighthouse.

When they turned to the rock, a strong wind blew in their faces, bringing the scents of sea and grass and lavender—which was strange as she hadn't seen any lavender on the island.

It was a large, flat boulder sunken into the ground. Around it, Jenny could see other stones protruding from the earth, probably the remnants of some sort of an ancient tower. The rock itself had carvings that Jenny thought could be a river or something...it was hard to concentrate. What she found most interesting was the handprint.

"Oh, look!" said Jenny. "Someone is giving us a high five through that rock!"

They giggled. Jenny stepped closer to the rock and sank to her knees. Amanda followed her and gave a high five to the hand. Natalie giggled and did the same.

"I could almost feel someone high-fiving me back," she said. "Thanks, man."

"Or woman," said Kyla and high-fived the hand, too.

"Oh look, let's go to the other side of the island," Amanda said. "Maybe there's more stony body parts we can high-five."

The girls walked away, but Jenny still wanted to give her own high five. When she put her hand over the rock, the carvings started to glow, and she stopped.

"Cool..." she mumbled, narrowing her eyes to try to see better. "What is that?" She looked over her shoulder. "Hey, girls! Come back! Am I super drunk, or is the rock glowing?"

"It's you, hon!" cried Amanda without turning back. "You're glowing! Because you're beautiful!"

Jenny shook her head with a smile. The scent of lavender and grass became stronger. She looked around. A seagull sat ten feet away from her, watching her glass of champagne with a ferocious curiosity.

"Hey there, little guy. Are you seeing this glowing, too?" she asked. "Maybe you should have the rest of my champagne. Clearly, I had waaay too much."

A shadow fell on Jenny. "Ah, finally, girls, look..." She raised her head.

A redhead in a hooded green cloak stood over her. She

smelled strongly of lavender and grass. Where had this woman come from on a deserted island? Hmm...strange.

"You smell nice," Jenny said. "Natural. I like it."

The woman beamed. "Oh, thank ye. No one has ever said that to me. How kind of ye."

"Do you see the glowing, or is it just me?" Jenny asked, pointing at the rock.

The woman giggled. "Oh, I see it, lass. 'Tis me who makes it glow."

Jenny swayed. "Really? How?"

"My name is Sìneag. I help people to go through the river of time and find the person they're destined for."

Jenny blinked. "Really? How?"

"Doesna matter how. What matters is why. There's a person for ye through that stone."

Jenny shook her head. She was *so* drunk. She put her glass down on the grass, and it fell and spilled its contents. "Um... At the expense of repeating myself...again... Really? And how?"

Sìneag bit her lip to stop a smile and sank to her knees next to Jenny. She was so pretty. A delicate, strawberry-shaped face, green eyes with long eyelashes, porcelain-white skin. And those cute freckles on her nose and cheeks. "You're beautiful," Jenny said. "Something about you is so...different. Are you from another time, too? Maybe you're a princess?"

Sìneag chuckled. "I'm nae a princess. I'm a faerie. And the man ye're destined for is the chief of clan MacDonald of Islay, Aulay. A true Highland laird with a big heart."

"And a big kilt..." Jenny giggled. "Sorry. Bad joke. So, he'd love me, you say? And yet, my husband said no man will love me until I stop being so selfish. And when he said selfish, he really meant independent. So, you're saying Aulay would love me even if I worked a lot and didn't give him babies?"

Sìneag smiled, but her eyes were sad. "He'd love ye if ye were old and wrinkled and dinna have a hair on yer head, Jenny. A

Highlander's love is forever. All ye need to do is place yer hand into the handprint."

Jenny raised her eyebrows and studied the handprint. How drunk was she that she was letting herself believe all this? "So, you're saying if I give a high five to this medieval hand, I'll time travel?"

Sìneag nodded. "Aye."

"What about my girlfriends? Do they have a hot Highlander waiting for them? Well... two of them are taken, but Amanda..."

Sìneag shrugged and said nothing. Jenny looked back over her shoulder. The three figures of her girlfriends were at the other edge of the island, a hundred or so feet away.

"Let's go time travel, girls!" Jenny cried.

When none of them reacted, she turned back to Sìneag.

There was no one.

The seagull was still there, giving her an unblinking stink eye. Wind ruffled its feathers gently.

"Did you see where she went?" Jenny asked.

When the seagull didn't reply, she shrugged, looked at the glowing rock, and high-fived the hand.

Only, instead of solid, cold rock, her palm went through empty air and fell forward and down into darkness. She screamed and flapped her arms and legs, trying to hold on to something, but there was nothing but wet, cold, damp air. And then she sank into oblivion.

Keep reading HIGHLANDER'S CLAIM.

GET A FREE MARIAH STONE
BOOK!

Join Mariah's mailing list to be the first to know of new releases, free books, special prices, and other author giveaways.

freehistoricalromancebooks.com

ENJOY THE BOOK? YOU CAN MAKE A DIFFERENCE!

Please, leave your honest review for the book.
As much as I'd love to, I don't have financial capacity like New York publishers to run ads in the newspaper or put posters in subway.

But I have something much, much more powerful!

Committed and loyal readers

If you enjoyed the book, I'd be so grateful if you could spend five minutes leaving a review on the book's Amazon page.

Thank you very much!

SCOTTISH SLANG

aye – yes

   bairn - baby

   bastart - bastard

   bonnie - pretty, beautiful.

   canna- can not

   couldna – couldn't

   didna- didn't ("Ah didna do that!")

   dinna- don't ("Dinna do that!")

   doesna – doesn't

   fash - fuss, worry ("Dinna fash yerself.")

   feck - fuck

   hasna – has not

   havna - have not

   hadna – had not

   innit? - Isn't it?

   isna- Is not

   ken - to know

   kent - knew

   lad - boy

   lass - girl

   marrit – married

nae – no or not

shite - faeces

the morn - tomorrow

the morn's morn - tomorrow morning

uisge-beatha (uisge for short) – Scottish Gaelic for water or life / aquavitae, the distilled drink, predecessor of whiskey

verra – very

wasna - was not

wee - small

wilna - will not

wouldna - would not

ye - you

yer – your (also yerself)

ABOUT MARIAH STONE

Mariah Stone is a bestselling author of time travel romance novels, including her popular Called by a Highlander series and her hot Viking, Pirate, and Regency novels. With nearly one million books sold, Mariah writes about strong modern-day women falling in love with their soulmates across time. Her books are available worldwide in multiple languages in e-book, print, and audio.

Subscribe to Mariah's newsletter for a free time travel book today at mariahstone.com!

facebook.com/mariahstoneauthor

instagram.com/mariahstoneauthor

bookbub.com/authors/mariah-stone

pinterest.com/mariahstoneauthor

amazon.com/Mariah-Stone/e/B07JVW28PJ